Highlights To Heaven

<u>BOOK YOUR PLACE ON OUR WEBSITE</u>
AND MAKE THE
<u>READING CONNECTION!</u>

We've created a customized website just for our very special readers, where you can get the inside scoop on everything that's going on with Zebra, Pinnacle and Kensington books.

When you come online, you'll have the exciting opportunity to:

- View covers of upcoming books
- Read sample chapters
- Learn about our future publishing schedule (listed by publication month *and author*)
- Find out when your favorite authors will be visiting a city near you
- Search for and order backlist books from our online catalog
- Check out author bios and background information
- Send e-mail to your favorite authors
- Meet the Kensington staff online
- Join us in weekly chats with authors, readers and other guests
- Get writing guidelines
- AND MUCH MORE!

Visit our website at
http://www.kensingtonbooks.com

Highlights To Heaven

Nancy J. Cohen

KENSINGTON BOOKS
KENSINGTON PUBLISHING CORP.
http://www.kensingtonbooks.com

KENSINGTON BOOKS are published by

Kensington Publishing Corp.
850 Third Avenue
New York, NY 10022

First Hardcover Printing: December 2003
First Paperback Printing: November 2004
10 9 8 7 6 5 4 3 2 1

Printed in the United States of America

To my critique group:
Sharon Hartley, Lisa Manuel, Charlene Newberg,
Zelda Piskosz, and Cynthia Thomason.
Your friendship and support throughout the years have sustained me and provided inspiration and encouragement during the various stages of my writing career. I couldn't have done it without you. Okay, you know I really like those great snacks y'all serve. But it's the company that counts.

ACKNOWLEDGMENTS

To all the staff at "Who Does Your Hair . . ." salon, Plantation, Florida: Sharon, Juan, Roxanne, Wanda, Stacey, Karyn, and Lauren. Many thanks for sharing your knowledge and generously giving your time to answer my research questions.

Also, to Margot O'Kane, department head and instructor; Christine Sepielli, instructor; and Ruth Sarrubbo, secretary, at the Cosmetology Department, Sheridan Technical Center, Hollywood, Florida. Thanks for the tour and for sharing your curriculum.

Chapter One

"What do you mean, there's a dead body at Goat's place?" Marla Shore asked Detective Dalton Vail. He stood on her front stoop, his expression as somber as his charcoal suit. Cool March air penetrated the toasty warmth of her South Florida town house while she waited for his reply.

"We received an anonymous tip," he said, his tall form blocking the doorway. "Have you seen your neighbor recently?"

She craned her neck to glance down the street. "I haven't talked to Goat since last week. You know, I've been worried about him. He promised to water Moss's impatiens next door, but the flowers are wilting. Moss tried to reach him, but Goat hasn't answered his door or his phone."

"Isn't that his van parked in the driveway?"

"Uh-huh." No one could miss the vehicle emblazoned with THE GAY GROOMER. Marla recalled the first time she'd seen it. Only a schlemiel like her would assume he must be a caterer for gay couples. She'd learned Goat handled pets, not gay bridegrooms, when a neighbor introduced them.

"I figured he must have gone away for the weekend," she added, "and maybe a friend picked him up. Today is Tuesday; he should have been back by now unless he's on vacation." Her body chilled beneath the flannel lining of her sweat suit. "I'll never forgive myself if he's lying there hurt, or worse. Believe me, I've been trying not to interfere for a change."

Vail patted her arm. "It's likely this is just a crank call, so don't beat yourself up about it. I decided to swing by and take a look rather than assign it to another detective."

"Did you knock on Goat's door?"

He grunted affirmatively. "No one answered. I thought I'd check with you before I do anything else." His gray eyes brightened as he regarded her.

Hey, pal, what turns you on more, the notion of a stiff body or a live one? You liked mine all right two nights ago.

"When did you get the message?" she asked, probing for more information. She'd helped him solve cases before.

"This morning. I had voice mail on my office machine."

She glanced at her Rado watch. "You must have gone to work awfully early. It's only eight o'clock."

"I got in at seven. I was hoping you hadn't left for the salon yet."

"I didn't schedule any clients until later so I could catch up on paperwork. Let's go next door. Moss told me Goat gave him a spare key to use in case of an emergency. Wait here while I let Spooks in."

Striding past the kitchen, she opened a rear door where her poodle had been scratching at the glass. When he bounded inside, she spared a moment to stroke his cream-colored coat. "Sorry we missed our morning walk, precious. I'll take you out tonight."

The dog dashed into the living room to sniff Vail's ankles. "He smells your golden retriever," she remarked upon joining them. "Hurry up, before Spooks seduces you into petting him."

"Sorry, that privilege is reserved for you."

Vail's sexy grin mitigated her anxiety, but not for long. "Come on. I'm really worried about Goat."

She led the way to Moss's adjacent town house, then rapped on his door with a brass anchor that served as his door knocker.

"Ahoy, mates," Moss greeted them in a hearty voice as he swung open the door. A naval cap topped his head of white hair.

"We want to check on Goat," Marla explained. "You still haven't seen him around, right?"

Moss's leathery face crinkled with concern. "Haven't seen the man in days, and his van hasn't moved. Doggoned if I know where he's been hiding." His blue gaze switched to Vail. "Morning, Lieutenant. What brings you here so early?"

A crafty look stole over the detective's angular features. "Marla is worried about your neighbor. You notice anything unusual over the weekend?"

"No sirree."

"Do you have a key to Goat's house?"

"Sure do. Wait here while I get it." A few moments later, he handed over the item. "I'd go with you, but I'm on my way to meet my golf buddies for breakfast. Emma is home if you need anything else."

"I'll let you know what we learn," Marla reassured him before she and Vail turned toward Goat's single-story town house.

"I'll go first," Vail announced. "You stay outside while I look around."

"No way. If Goat is hurt, he'll need me."

He gave her a bemused glance. "You may have worked as Miriam's nursing aide last month, but that doesn't mean you're Florence Nightingale."

Miriam loved it when I took care of her, and I did a damn fine job as an undercover investigator. "We found her granddaughter's murderer, didn't we?"

"Only after you nearly got yourself killed. Give me the key, and don't move from this spot."

She noticed he didn't draw his gun after pushing the door open. Ignoring his advice, she trailed after his rangy figure.

"Goat? Are you here?" she called in a tremulous voice from the foyer. A loud squawk in response made her shriek.

Vail whirled around, his eyes flashing. "I thought I told you to wait outside."

"I'm the concerned neighbor checking on a friend, remember?" Her nose wrinkled. "Dear Lord, what is that stench?" Clapping a hand over her mouth, she glanced at the kitchen to their left, but the odor didn't appear to be coming from there. No dirty dishes in the sink; countertops relatively clean. From the top of the refrigerator, a Siamese cat glared down at her. Its haunches raised as it hissed ominously.

"Ugamaka, ugamaka, chugga, chugga, ush!"

screeched a loud voice that sounded startlingly like Goat's.

Her lips parted as she scanned the combined living and dining room furnished in Early Garage Sale. A brightly colored parrot in a cage stared back.

"Oh, so you're the one making all the noise," she commented, wondering if the stink came from its confines. A gust of wind rattled an open glass door leading to the backyard. "We should let in more fresh air," she suggested to Vail, who stood peering into the master bedroom.

"Don't touch anything," he said in a flat tone.

"What's the matter?" Within seconds, she'd moved beside him. One glance into the bedroom showed her what was rotting. A man's body sprawled across the queen-size platform bed.

She pressed a hand to her throat. "Is it Goat?" she croaked.

"You tell me."

She forced herself to take a closer look. The victim lay on his back. Purposefully avoiding the telltale blotch on his shirt at the level of his chest, she swung her gaze upward and noted his broad nose, wide forehead, and deep-set eyes that stared vacantly into space.

"Thank God, it's not him." Bile rose in her throat, and she swallowed with difficulty. "Goat has stringy hair like straw," she said, focusing on the one thing she knew best. "This man's level is deeper, with bronze highlights. Hey, that pattern looks familiar."

"How so?"

"Cutter Corrigan applies a similar design when

he does highlights. It's distinctive to his style. He used to be my teacher in beauty school," she explained, "and now he runs a salon on Las Olas. Maybe this guy is one of his clients."

"I see." Vail pulled out his notebook, ever handy in a pocket, and scribbled some notes. "You ever notice the victim talking to Goat or visiting his house?"

She shook her head.

"Did Goat tell you anything about himself, his job or his background, where he came from?"

"Nothing." Moisture stung her eyes. She hadn't taken the time to get acquainted with her neighbor by more than a polite hello during her daily walks. She'd been put off by his weird mannerisms. Maybe if she'd known him better, he would have confided in her. "You don't think Goat is responsible for this, do you?"

Vail yanked his cell phone from his belt. "Honey, I'm damn well going to find out. You can leave now. I'm calling in my team. Don't put your hands on anything."

"Goat couldn't have done it. He's a gentle soul who cares about his animals," she said, twisting a strand of chestnut hair behind her ear.

"Do you see extra feed and a full water bottle in that birdcage? And it's a miracle the cat hasn't knocked it over for a meal. My guess is, Goat did the deed and left in a hurry. He didn't have time to think about his pets."

He completed a quick search of the rest of Goat's house before flicking open his cell phone. While he was occupied, Marla glanced in the bathroom. No bodies met her anxious gaze, just the usual male toiletries and a hairbrush that needed a good cleaning. Prowling across the living room, she sidestepped a fat gray cat whose sly expression was fixed on the parrot.

The second bedroom had been made up into a study, with a worn leather armchair, wooden desk, sleep-sofa, and tables with lamps. Another cat snarled as she crossed the threshold. It appeared to be guarding an iguana in a fish tank, or else it was figuring out how to reach the creature. She wouldn't like to be the target of its malevolent glare.

Keeping in mind Vail's warning not to touch anything, she scanned the room for clues. Her jaw dropped as she glanced at the desk. Goat had been reading a biography about Martha Matilda Harper. Could it be mere coincidence that this woman was one of her idols? Marla had written a paper about her for a college history class. At a time when women were struggling for their rights, Harper had opened the first public hair salon in Rochester, New York. By the early 1900s, she'd created the first business franchise system in the country. What interest might Goat possibly have had in her?

"Marla, I thought I told you to leave!" Vail's voice thundered as he approached.

"I'm on my way out!" She turned to face him. "What will happen to Goat's pets if he doesn't turn up?"

"I'll see that they're put into shelters. You go home now and take care of Spooks."

"How will you find Goat? I think you should interview Cutter Corrigan. He may know something about the victim's identity."

"Let me deal with it." Vail's mouth tightened as he steered her toward the front door.

"You're excluding me again!" she cried.

"You'll contaminate the crime scene if you stay, and you don't really want to be here while the team is working."

"How was . . . the man killed?"

"That's for the medical examiner to determine."

Sensing Vail knew more than he cared to reveal, Marla told herself to be patient. Eventually she'd worm the details out of him. "Look," she called as they passed the kitchen. "That's a sound machine on the counter." She delayed her departure to peer at the markings. "This is where the whale cries come from and some of the other animal noises I've heard. And I always thought Goat kept a menagerie inside." Perhaps her neighbor wasn't as weird as he appeared to be on the surface. Curiosity made her wish she could look around more, but Vail ushered her outside. Besides, the odor was enough to make her gag.

Facing the street, she drew in a deep breath of fresh air while considering her next move. Goat must have gone somewhere, and it was always possible he was cowering in the backyard. Even if he didn't commit the murder, he might be afraid of talking to the police. If she could find him first, she'd convince him to tell his story to the authorities.

Around the side, she trod over brittle grass badly in need of a watering. Orange blossoms lent a honeyed fragrance to the air. It was a welcome contrast to the tainted atmosphere inside the house. As she drew open the gate to Goat's fenced backyard, her glance zeroed in on a scrawny goat tethered to a pole. The poor thing bleated at her presence. Had he been tied up the entire time Goat was missing?

Rushing forward, she intended to loosen his harness when she tripped over something spongy. She recovered her balance and glanced at the object. For a moment, she didn't understand what she was seeing. It was pink, with darker patches, except for the head, where its snout pushed through a mass of tangled black fur.

Her stomach lurched, and she let out a scream that brought Vail running.

"Bless my bones," she gasped between sharp intakes of air, "I think it was a dog."

"This creature has been skinned," Vail noted, jotting in his notebook. "Had you seen this animal before?"

She raised her hands. "I haven't seen any of Goat's pets. You know I never went inside his place, although he'd invited me. I was too nervous, hearing all the strange noises. My mistake. I should have given him a chance. Uh-oh, what's that?" Needing a closer look, she headed toward the fence where an empty aquarium lay on the ground. "I'll bet it's Junior's container. Either he's loose in the neighborhood, or Goat took his snake with him."

"That's just dandy, but I'm more interested in the dead dog. It brings to mind something we've been noticing lately in the area. Another department is investigating, but I'll give them a heads-up in case this is related."

She shielded her eyes against the morning sunlight. "What's that about?"

"A possible operation involving pet-fur products, but it's just conjecture at this point. I can't say more."

Marla backed away. "Goat couldn't have done this horrible thing. He rescued Spooks after my house got broken into, and he took good care of my poodle. Goat loves animals. For God's sake, he's a pet groomer." She bit her lip, unable to picture Goat harming anyone. But how well did she really know her neighbor? Holy highlights, she didn't even know his last name.

Engine noises drew their attention. "My techs are here," Vail said. "Do you want me to escort you home?"

"Yes . . . no. I can manage. It's all so awful."

He accompanied her to the front lawn, issued orders to his technicians, then turned his focus back to her. His gaze softened as he thrust a hand through his peppery hair. "I'll stop by your place later to make sure you're okay."

She must look as green as she felt. "I'll be at the salon until six; then I have to run errands. Call me first to see if I'm home."

"You need to hire a manager. Wearing too many hats stretches you too thin."

"You just want more of my attention for yourself."

A smile quirked his lips. "It's tough to maintain a client list while managing your own salon. Not to mention sleuthing on the side."

"You seem to appreciate my playing sleuth," she said, her spirits lifting. "That's why you came to me. You want my help."

"That's not all I need. Assuming I have some free time in the next week, when can we get together again?"

She flushed, aware of what he meant. *At least you're finally admitting why you really knocked on my door earlier.* "I'm not sure."

"Friday?"

"I have to go to services with my mother. It's my father's *yarzheit.* Anniversary of his death," she added in explanation. "How about Saturday night?"

"I'll see what I can arrange for Brianna. She thinks because she's turning thirteen soon, I'll ease the rules. She's been nagging me to let her stay home alone for one night, but I won't go for it. Teenagers require discipline, or they get too wild."

"Can't have that, can we?" She gave him a quick kiss, her mood returning to earth with a solid thunk. "Go to work. I'll see you later."

His voice deepened. "Be careful. You don't seem to go anywhere without trouble finding you."

"It's just my way of keeping you close to me, Lieutenant," she teased. "But never fear; I know you'll be busy this morning, so I'll behave myself."

"I'll believe that when hell freezes over," he muttered as she walked away.

She didn't get too far toward her house. A crowd of neighbors accosted her on the sidewalk.

"What's happening, Marla? Why are all those police cars here?" asked one of her neighbors, Lyn. Lyn was married, with two school-age children. She lived in one of the larger two-story town houses. The architectural variety of Green Hills was one reason why Marla had been attracted to this affluent community in upscale Palm Haven, Florida.

"A man was found dead in Goat's house. Goat is missing. Have any of you heard from him?" She scanned the faces of her fellow residents, which represented a mixture of ages and cultural backgrounds.

"I think he was here on Friday," commented Hector, a handsome Hispanic with a slight accent.

"He must have been at work during the day, because I didn't notice his van parked there until later that evening."

Marla met his warm brown gaze. "Did you see him come home?"

He stroked his mustache. "Not quite, senorita. Goat's vehicle was gone when I left in the morning. He still wasn't home by six when I returned."

"So how did you know he'd come back?" she persisted, curbing her impatience.

"I went outside after dinner, and the van was parked in his driveway along with a small, dark car."

"I remember!" Lyn inserted. "My kids were playing ball, and I warned them to stay away from that junk heap."

Marla's pulse accelerated. "What kind of car?"

"Who knows?" Lyn said, shuffling a hand through her ash-blond hair. She glanced at her house, as though she expected her kids to charge out the front door into the street. "You could ask Craig later tonight. He studies car magazines and can tell you all about the different models."

"I think it was a Corolla," Hector offered.

Marla shifted feet. "What time was this?"

"Just past eight o'clock."

"Did you see the Corolla leave?"

Regret stamped his features. "Nope. I don't think it was much later though, because I heard a commotion outside."

"You heard voices?"

"Doors slamming and tires screeching." Hector gestured to Lyn. They were the closest neighbors to Goat, having houses on either side of his place. "When did you go inside with your kids?"

"We didn't stay out too long. Shanna and John had to finish their homework, then go to bed."

"I heard something else, like a motorcycle," Hector added, scratching his jaw.

So, it appeared Goat had a visitor after he came home from work, around eight o'clock on Friday. Something happened shortly thereafter. By the next morning, the Corolla was gone, along with Goat.

"I'll tell Detective Vail your news when I talk to him later," Marla said, not wishing to disturb him now. The medical examiner would determine the exact time of death, but she wondered if it had occurred Friday evening. Who had driven the Corolla? If it belonged to the dead man, had Goat stolen the vehicle to make his escape? Or was another party involved?

There could have been someone else in the Corolla, she figured on her way home. Perhaps several passengers. They had no way of telling if Goat had more than one visitor, unless Vail found evidence inside his house.

This isn't your business, she reminded herself as she quickly showered and changed clothes. But when she drew up her agenda for the next day, visiting Cutter Corrigan's salon took top priority on her list.

Chapter
Two

By the time Marla pulled into a metered parking space in a lot behind Las Olas Boulevard in downtown Fort Lauderdale, it was ten-thirty. Anxious to reach Cutter Corrigan before the detective contacted him, she hurried onto the boutique-lined avenue, and walked past La Bonne Crêpe, one of her favorite restaurants. Heavenly Hair Salon should be somewhere along the next block. Passing Seldom Seen Gallery, with its intriguing window display, she remembered that she still needed to buy a birthday gift for Brianna.

Not today. Time is running short.

Having never been inside Cutter's salon, she didn't anticipate the marvel that met her eyes. Instead of rows of chairs facing wall-high mirrors on two sides of the room as in her salon, this place was a paragon of modern design and creativity. Directly facing her was a wave-shaped reception desk staffed by an attractive young woman with spiked black hair. Her silver metallic blouse shimmered like the curtains defining each station. Each chair came with its own mirror and utility cart and a sense of privacy. Curved furnishings and a blue and silver mosaic floor added to the modern appeal, but they didn't compare to the neon-blue-ringed platform with a glass enclosure in the center of the room. Cutter Corrigan worked his magic on a client in full view of everyone as though he were a platform artist onstage at a beauty show.

He spotted Marla and waved.

"Can I help you?" the receptionist said with a bright smile.

Marla focused on her perfectly made-up face. The young woman wore wire-rimmed eyeglasses and had relatively plain features, yet she had made herself look striking with cosmetics and style. *It just goes to prove, anyone can be beautiful.*

She smiled in return. "I'd like to see Cutter. I'm the owner of Cut 'N Dye Salon in West Broward. He used to be my teacher in beauty school," she said, handing over a business card. "Is he nearly finished?"

The girl glanced over her shoulder. "It'll just be a few more minutes. Can I get you a cup of coffee?"

"No thanks." While she waited, Marla ruminated on the staff members she needed to replace in her salon. Another stylist, a shampoo assistant, and a decent receptionist were high on her list. The last one was the most difficult to find. She sought an attractive, friendly person well versed in computers who could run the Elite Salon Management software program Marla had recently installed. It wasn't easy finding a motivated individual with the skills she required.

"Marla Shore!" Cutter said as he descended upon her. His medium-frame form embraced her in a bear hug. "How are you, dear?"

Stepping away, she grinned at him. "I'm doing great, thanks. This place is wonderful. How long have you been here?"

His pale blue eyes regarded her with pride. "It's been almost seven years. I heard you have your own place, too."

She nodded. "I opened my salon eight years ago. You must have stayed on at the beauty school after I graduated, then?"

"For a while, but after so many years working as a stylist in other people's salons and then as a teacher, it was time to move on."

"Tell me about it! I never liked working for anyone else."

"A lot of stylists feel that way, but they're not ready for the responsibility that comes with running a business." He waved an arm. "As our reputation grows, I'm pulled away from the chair more every day. I have a business manager as well as an artistic director. But in order to run a successful salon, you have to do more than what the three of us do combined. How's your staff turnover?"

She cleared her throat. "Pretty high."

"Do you have booth rentals?"

"Yes, although I'd like to get away from them. I want more control."

"Then get involved with your political associations." He jabbed a finger in the air for emphasis. "If you join the state board, you'll have a chance to influence decisions about our industry. Did you know I'm supporting a measure to prohibit booth rentals in Florida?"

"I had no idea."

"I've been instrumental in forming a political action committee for the Professional Beauty Federation. Our aim is to raise awareness about the Cosmetologists' Tax Fairness Act, similar to the one in the restaurant industry. If you want to make a difference, you need to participate in your professional organizations."

Marla swallowed, feeling as though she were back in class. "I belong to TSA."

He nodded sagely. "The Salon Association focuses on business. It's good for networking and exchanging ideas. When we first opened, we had a high turnover. After talking to several people at TSA, I realized the ambience in my salon didn't offer anything special."

"But this place is fantastic."

"The decor is exceptional, no?" He tapped her arm. "But I'm not talking about the physical setup. If you want to keep personnel, you have to offer them an environment they won't want to leave. Continuing education is one of our main thrusts. You have to keep yourself fresh and provide a comfort level so new stylists aren't afraid to ask questions. They want more than money and medical benefits. Every two months, we have a meeting where we conduct training sessions and practice new trends. The entire staff is responsible for our success, not just any one of us. That's why you shouldn't hire just anyone off the street. You need people with enthusiasm and passion to join your team, and you must provide opportunities for them to grow."

"Having a good location helps, too," Marla muttered, noting the jewelry adorning most of his yuppie clientele. Las Olas was a tourist mecca, and the winter season saw pedestrians crowding the sidewalks. His salon was located in a perfect locale to attract walk-ins as well as regulars. He offered good advice, though. She had to try harder to fill her vacancies.

"Come, I'll give you a tour."

His hair had grown thinner, although its light wheat color didn't run counter to his fifty-something years. He had covered his gray in a natural manner that Marla admired. As her former mentor pointed out the accoutrements at each station, she observed his effeminate gestures with growing interest.

"We have fourteen styling stations, six shampoo chairs, four nail-care consoles, three rooms for facials, waxing, and massage, plus a color lab," Cutter boasted with a slight nasal twang.

"What's over there?" Marla indicated a couple of booths where customers hunched in front of computers.

"Those are Internet stations. Clients can surf the Web while they wait for their timers to ring. They also like to play with our digital imaging services. It shows how they might look with different cuts, styles, and colors."

You're a little too high-tech for me, pal. Providing quality customer service was her priority. A good scalp massage with a shampoo went a long way toward making your client feel relaxed, not to mention promoting healthy hair. That was more important than all this machinery, in her opinion.

"I'm impressed," she murmured instead. "Tell me, are you still doing your signature highlights? I remember you tried to teach us in class, but no one could get it right. It's the blend of different levels you use, plus the technique."

He beamed widely. "Naturally, you must have the requisite talent. So much of what we do is pure artistry."

Baloney. You just didn't want to give away your secret. "I think I met one of your customers. I recognized your distinctive highlights pattern. It's such a great look, Cutter, that I was hoping to learn the technique. Maybe now that I'm more experienced, I could grasp the principles. Are you willing to teach me?"

"You'll have to come to one of my seminars, dear." His voice had lost some of its warmth. "I work for Regis in my spare time. We do a lot of their photo shoots here."

"I see. Do you have a mailing list so I can be notified when you're doing one of the workshops?"

"I'll be sure to let you know." Grasping her by the elbow, he steered her toward the reception area. "How do you like the West Broward location? I've been thinking about opening another salon out there."

"You want to expand?"

"Why not? We've gained quite a reputation." He lifted his narrow nose in the air.

"Sounds like you're busy enough already."

"Having a business plan is what makes it happen. If you take in good money, you can do what you want. You should make in a day what you pay out per month in rent, for example."

I wish. "What's your average tab?"

"Between sixty and seventy dollars."

"You bring in the right clientele."

"You can do the same, if you nurture your creative side. You'll burn out if you neglect that part." His gaze shone with fervor. "Do you travel to any of the shows, participate in community outreach, involve yourself in any professional organizations besides TSA?"

She squared her shoulders. "I have enough to do sticking close to home. Managing my salon and working behind the chair keeps me fully occupied. How can I fit in anything more?"

Playing detective lately has been a time drain. So is this discussion. I came here for a reason. How could she turn their conversation to the corpse in Goat's town house?

"You're ambitious." He perused her face. "I could tell when you were in my class. I knew that either you'd go back to school and finish your college education, or you would seek alternatives beyond the confines of a salon. Tell me truthfully, have you never thought about teaching, entering competitions, becoming a platform designer? There's so much more to do than stand behind a chair all day!"

"I love fixing hair. That's what I do best. Customer satisfaction is my goal." She fought for the right words to describe her philosophy. "If you promote healthy hair with quality products and attention to details like scalp massage, customers will know you care. And if you're a good listener and make each person feel special, they'll leave the salon feeling better about themselves. Beauty is more than style and products. They'll return because they anticipate a pleasurable event."

He pursed his lips. "You can get carried away with idealism and lose sight of the business aspects. Maintaining balance is crucial to success."

"I don't think you can ever get carried away by caring too much. Martha Matilda Harper is the perfect example." She noticed his mouth tightened imperceptibly. "Coming from the serving class, she understood what quality service meant. She attracted customers into her community's first public hair salon by giving them a clean, luxurious experience. Do you know that Jacqueline Kennedy and Lady Bird Johnson used her for a hairdresser? She was an astute businesswoman, so it's possible to have the best of both worlds."

Harper, she recalled, had had floor-length hair that advertised her healthful treatments. Marla glanced at herself in a mirror. Her chestnut hair had a glossy sheen as it curved inward toward her chin. She wore a cream-colored top, tan slacks, and a caramel blazer. Which one did she look like, a businesswoman or a talented artist? Both, or neither?

Maybe Cutter was right, and she'd been neglecting important aspects of her business. That could account for her high turnover rate and the fact that her rival, Carolyn Sutton, had been siphoning off customers.

"Why do your beautiful brown eyes turn away from me?" Cutter demanded. "I read people well, and my perception tells me you are not fulfilled, regardless of what you claim. What really brought you in to see me today? Did you want help from your old teacher?"

She met his keen gaze. "I told you. I want to learn your highlights technique." A deep breath fortified her. "This person I saw, he was a gentleman with a broad nose and wide forehead. Might have been in his forties. He had bronze highlights with your pattern."

Cutter's skin paled. "You saw . . . When was this?"

"It was over the weekend."

"Where?"

Standing in the middle of the salon, Marla shifted her purse to her other shoulder. "He was with a friend of mine," she hedged.

"Who?"

She wondered why he suddenly seemed unable to speak except in monosyllables. "His name is Goat."

He stared at her, his jaw dropping open. "Where did you see them? I must know!"

"Goat is my neighbor," she said, without directly answering his question. Did Cutter know his client was dead? "What was . . . is your customer's name, the man with those highlights?"

A mask closed over his face. "I have no idea who you mean. I do bronze highlights on lots of people."

You're lying. I can tell by the way you're sweating. "Do you keep client records? Maybe it will jog your memory. A name might help me remember where I saw the guy last."

His eyes turned glacial. "I have to get back to work. Let me give you some advice, Marla. Stick to salon business. That's your safest bet. If you get too involved in other people's affairs, trouble will find you."

Didn't Vail say the same thing earlier? "Thanks for the tour," she replied as Cutter ushered her out the door. It remained propped open to let in the

cool breeze. Reluctant to leave, Marla hovered on
the sidewalk. He hadn't identified the dead man,
but Cutter definitely knew something, and it involved Goat. She bit her lower lip in concern.

"Hey, doll," called a stylist who leaned against
the wall, smoking a cigarette.

Marla glanced in her direction. She had the typ-
ical chain-smoker's look: dry skin, pinched face, thin
frame—as though she'd rather consume a cigarette
than a meal. Too many people in their business still
smoked. She couldn't understand why, but then,
she didn't comprehend why anyone would inhale
toxic substances into their lungs. At least her salon
was a smoke-free environment; she couldn't abide
contaminated air. It gave her a headache and stuffed
nose. All of her staff members were nonsmokers,
and customers understood they had to go outside
to light up.

She remembered the story told by one of her
mentors who had been a beautician in the seventies. The hairdresser had just sprayed her lady after
a back-comb, shampoo, and set. Then the customer
lit a cigarette. The hair spray had alcohol in it, and
her bangs started smoking.

Marla smiled, pushing the image from her mind
as she approached the young woman. "Hi, I'm
Marla Shore from Cut 'N Dye Salon."

"Call me Jax." The girl threw her stub on the
ground and mashed her platform shoe on it. "I
couldn't help overhearing some of what you said
to Cutter."

"Oh?" Marla raised an eyebrow.

"That man you described, I know who he is."

Marla stepped closer, unable to suppress her eagerness. "He's one of Cutter's clients, isn't he? Do you know his name?"

"The man is Yani Verkovich, but I'll bet he's more than a client. You could tell they were close just by watching them together."

"You mean they were friends outside of business?"

"Intimate friends, if you know what I mean."

Cutter and Yani? She'd always suspected her instructor was gay. Apparently, it was obvious to others. "Why are you telling me this?"

The woman ran stiff fingers through her spiked yellow hair. "Cutter has been acting strange lately. Like, it's getting tough to work with him, man. I've been here for five years, and I've never seen him so hyper."

Marla glanced inside the shop, but Cutter had disappeared into one of the back rooms. "What do you think is bothering him?"

"I was hoping you could tell me." The girl's dark eyes studied her. "He talks on the phone a lot to this Yani dude."

Not anymore. An image of the man's body materialized in her mind. What had he been doing in Goat's house? "Did you ever catch anything they said to each other?"

"I don't normally listen in to other people's conversations, doll. Maybe they were having, like, you know, a lover's spat?"

"So you think Cutter's tension stems from personal problems." Here was a witness corroborating that Cutter knew the dead man. But how did her neighbor enter the picture?

Jax shrugged. "I don't know why else Cutter

would get upset when Yani called. Where did you meet the guy?"

Marla moved aside as a couple of tourists charged past. "As I told Cutter, I met him through my neighbor. Have you ever seen your employer with a fellow named Goat? He's a scrawny sort, likes to wear Hawaiian shirts with a sheepskin vest. Has straw-colored hair and a sparse beard. Imitates animal noises."

"Man, he sounds weird."

"He's different, that's all." A pang of sorrow pierced her heart. She missed Goat's unique presence in the neighborhood. He'd danced to a jingle whenever she saw him, and she realized now that his antics had brightened her days. If she hadn't been so hesitant, she would've gotten to know him better. Shoulda, woulda, coulda. Regrets bind you to the past. They wouldn't help her find Goat now. Presumably Jax had never encountered him.

"Jax, can I have your number in case I need to call you? I'll let you know if I find out anything."

The woman tugged on her tank top. "I don't know. This is still a good place to work, if Cutter would get his act together. I don't want to get in no trouble."

"Here's my card, then. If anything else comes up, please give me a call. I may be able to help."

"Why are you here, anyway, asking about this Yani dude?"

Marla gave a casual smile. "I recognized his highlights pattern and hoped Cutter would teach me his technique."

"Ha! Cutter is a great educator, but there are some secrets he keeps."

No kidding, Marla thought as she strode away.

Glancing at her watch, she noted she just had time to stop at the Palm Haven police station on her way to the salon.

Vail rose from his desk chair when she entered his office. "Marla, I thought you went to work."

She sauntered up to him and kissed him boldly on the mouth. "I just couldn't stay away from you," she answered, pressing her hands to his chest.

His eyes gleamed darkly. "Yeah, right. Why do I get the feeling you have something to say that I won't like?"

He seemed so overwhelmingly tall. Maybe it was her flat-heeled shoes, and the fact that they were standing so close together. An inner warmth stole into her veins as she sniffed his spice cologne.

Tilting her chin, she stroked his clean-shaven jaw. "Now, Dalton, isn't it enough that I can't wait until this weekend?"

She felt his response as their bodies touched, his arms tightening around her. "If you're trying to distract me, you're succeeding too damn well. How am I supposed to do my job?"

"I have information that will help. But, first, did you locate Goat?"

"Hell, no. I just got back to the office twenty minutes ago."

"Find any clues in his place to who killed that guy?"

"I can't discuss the details. You know that."

"You also know you can trust me."

Desire warred with duty in his expression. "This is bad business, honey. I don't want you to get hurt."

"I'm worried about Goat. He might be in trouble."

"That's an understatement."

Her mouth gaped, and she stepped away from his embrace. "You didn't find evidence that he . . . murdered Yani Verkovich, did you?"

"Who did you say?"

"I found out the dead man's identity. Or should I say, his presumed identity. I visited Cutter Corrigan."

"Who?"

Great, she'd reduced him to monosyllables, too. "He's the hairdresser I'd mentioned who used to be my beauty school instructor. Cutter is known for his distinctive highlights design. I stopped in at Heavenly Hair Salon on Las Olas. I didn't tell him his client was dead, only that I'd seen him recently. Cutter got upset and wanted to know where I met the man."

Vail rolled his eyes. "I knew it. You're screwing things up again. Interviewing people before I get to them is not recommended, sweetcakes."

"Another stylist told me Yani's name and confirmed he was Cutter's client," she plowed on, disregarding his remarks.

"In the meantime, you raised a red flag in front of Cutter," Vail said, drawing his brows together. "If he is involved, you may have put yourself in the line of danger. Or, at the very least, he'll be forewarned when *I* see him."

"I got the impression he doesn't know Yani is dead."

"In that case, he may blab about your visit to his friends, one of whom could be the perp. Gossip flies in your business, doesn't it?"

"Well, yes, but—"

"You should've let me handle it."

"You never told me how Yani was killed, assuming you confirm his identification."

He opened his mouth to speak, but just then the phone rang. "Lieutenant Vail here." Listening, his eyes widened. "Brianna, what do you mean, you're bleeding?"

Chapter
Three

"**B**rianna!" Vail yelled as they stormed into his house.

Marla hadn't let him go home alone. She'd accompanied him, nightmarish thoughts crawling through her mind. As he reset the alarm, she noted with relief that his house security hadn't been breached. Their golden retriever, Lucky, barked a loud greeting and slobbered over Marla's knees. The dog's ruckus should have been enough to scare away intruders.

"Honey, where are you?" Marla cried.

"I'm in my room," Vail's daughter called, her voice sounding as nonchalant as though she'd phoned asking if she could go to the mall.

"Why isn't she in school?" Marla asked as they pounded down the hallway, the dog bounding excitedly at their heels.

"Teacher workday. What the hell happened?" he demanded, halting in the doorway to Brianna's bedroom.

Marla peered over his shoulder. Brianna's wide brown eyes regarded them with scorn. She lay on her bed, dark hair in a ponytail, a towel wrapped around her slim body. Another towel, streaked with blood, lay heaped on the rose Berber carpet. Apparently, she'd been reading, because a book rested spine-up on her stomach.

"I cut myself in the shower. I'm sorry if I scared you, but I didn't know what to do. It stopped after a while. I put a couple of Band-Aids on."

Vail's jaw thrust forward as he stomped into the room. "What do you mean, you cut yourself?"

Brianna glanced toward a poster of Brad Pitt on the wall. "I was shaving my legs."

"Shaving? Like with a razor?"

Marla smiled as she grasped the situation. "What else do you use to shave? Your daughter is growing up."

Vail's bushy eyebrows grew so close together, Marla felt an urge to give him a trim. His massive form seemed to swell as he folded his arms across his chest. "You're not allowed to shave yet," he told his daughter in a brusque tone. "You'll be thirteen next week, and that's still too young."

"All my friends shave their legs!"

"Like who?"

"Like . . . like Melissa, and Amy."

"That's not everyone."

"So what? I don't want to be the only one who looks like a dork." Swinging her feet over the edge of her bed, Brianna sat up. "You treat me like a baby. You have to face the fact that I'm getting older."

Her towel slipped, and Marla caught Vail gulping convulsively. "Put some clothes on. You'll get sick if you lie around like that," he ordered.

"That's another thing," Brianna whined, her face screwed into a pout. "I need to go shopping for a few things. Marla, you tell him."

Startled, she stared at the girl. "What do you mean, honey?" When Brianna glared back, silent, Marla's cheeks warmed. "Oh. Yes. Uh, Dalton, perhaps you'd let me go with Brianna one afternoon?"

"I can get her whatever she needs. What's that on your cheek?" he queried his daughter. "Did you scratch yourself there, too?"

Brianna tilted her chin defiantly. "Not quite."

He peered closer. "Don't tell me you were putting on lipstick."

"So what if I was? You act like I'm two years old! You won't let me do anything. Everyone I know hangs out at the mall."

"Yeah—where all the predators are waiting to grab you."

"Get a life, Daddy."

"I will not have you using makeup at your age so you can attract men!"

Feeling a surge of sympathy for the preteen, Marla touched his arm. "Dalton, these are things only a woman understands. There's nothing wrong with—"

"She's my daughter!" he thundered. "Don't tell me what to do. She'll have plenty of time to grow up, as she calls it. I don't believe in rushing things."

"May I speak to you a moment in private?" Taking his arm, Marla directed him into the living room. "You don't have one ounce of understanding for what a teenage girl requires," Marla said in a hushed tone when they were out of range.

"Teenagers require discipline; otherwise they get into trouble. Brie isn't ready, for all she thinks she is. Maturity comes with age."

"Shaving your legs and learning how to apply makeup has nothing to do with maturity. Those are just a matter of grooming."

"That's just the start. Next thing you know, she'll want to go out with boys."

"Holy highlights, you're really uptight. I agree that she is too young to date, but you can't keep her tied down forever," Marla said. "With proper supervision, a little more freedom might help teach her to make the right choices."

"Like you know how to raise a child?" he sneered.

She recoiled as though he'd slapped her. "I didn't come here to listen to your insults; I'm only trying to help. I think it's best if you take me to my car."

"Gladly."

Marla strode down the hallway. "Brianna, if you want to talk later, call me at home." She glanced at the brooding expression on Vail's face. "That is, if you're allowed to use the telephone."

"Thanks, Marla. I will." Brianna, a sullen look on her face, collected her jeans and shirt and headed for the bathroom. "At least I cleaned up the mess I made in there, Daddy. You should reward me."

"Ha! You'll spend the rest of the day on your homework, young lady."

"I'm glad I realized how narrow-minded you are before things got more serious between us," Marla said after a tight-lipped journey to the police station. "I thought you wanted me to become involved in your daughter's life. You let me take her to ballet class, and we were just beginning to really get along. Now you disregard my advice like it has no value." She drew in a deep breath. "You have some serious problems, Dalton, and I feel sorry for your daughter. But until you're willing to listen, don't bother calling me again."

She shut the passenger door gently, resisting her urge to slam it closed. Blinking rapidly, she stalked to her car. *This rotten day has just gotten worse,* she thought, feeling as though a weight had settled in her stomach. What more could go wrong?

"Hey, Marla," called Nicole as she shuffled into the salon. "Where have you been? You missed your twelve o'clock wash-and-blow. I was getting worried. You usually call if you're late." The cinnamon-skinned stylist gave her an anxious glance.

"I offered to do the lady, but she refused and left," said Giorgio apologetically from his station across the room.

"Figures." Marla smiled wanly at the handsome Italian. "I had a busy morning. Found another dead body, had my first big argument with Dalton. What's a missed appointment compared to those?"

Her dejection must have shown, because Giorgio put down the hairbrush he was cleaning and hastened over to her. "What are you talking about?"

Nicole wasn't engaged with a client at that moment, either, so Marla drew them together. "My neighbor Goat is missing," she said in a low voice so the other operators wouldn't hear. "Dalton Vail found a man's body in his house. I recognized the highlights pattern on the victim."

"You were there?" Giorgio's dark eyes widened.

"I live a few doors down from Goat's place. He's the wacky neighbor I told you about who imitates animals. No one had seen him for a few days, and then Vail showed up at my door asking about him."

"And you discovered a dead man in Goat's house?"

She nodded. "I recognized his highlights. Only one master stylist is capable of that particular design. My former beauty school teacher, Cutter Corrigan. He has a salon on Las Olas."

Giorgio's eyes narrowed. "Did you tell the detective?"

"I did more than that. I spoke to Cutter myself. When I went to tell Dalton about our conversation, we were interrupted. His daughter needed attention."

"Whoa, slow down, girlfriend," Nicole said, her warm cocoa eyes radiating sympathy. "Did you learn anything from your former teacher?"

"Cutter revealed very little, but he knows something. Not that Vail appreciated my report."

"What happened between you?" Nicole asked.

Marla told them about Brianna's latest escapade. "Dalton implied I have no experience in child-rearing, so he won't listen to my advice regarding his daughter."

"No!" Giorgio exclaimed.

Her lower lip quivered. "That man is the most obstinate, domineering . . . I don't know why I was ever interested in him. He's way overly protective and refuses to compromise. I can't deal with his hang-ups."

Nicole's glance fell to her right hand. "So why are you still wearing his ring?"

She twisted the gold setting holding a brilliant amethyst stone flanked by tiny diamonds. "It's mine.

Dalton gave it to me as a gift, so why shouldn't I keep it?"

"Uh-huh."

"Besides, I haven't given up on Brianna. That poor girl needs a female role model to guide her."

Nicole's eyebrows rose. "And you're offering for the job? I thought you didn't like children."

"You know how I feel about kids. After Tammy drowned . . . I can't risk facing that kind of pain for one of my own."

"Seems to me getting involved with Brianna will bring the same responsibility and risk. Vail probably fears for his daughter's safety, and rightfully so. Remember, she almost got killed by that nut case in the athletic club last month."

"How could I forget? It doesn't condone his yelling at me. The man's wife has been dead for over two years, and he still won't let another woman into his life in a way that matters."

Nicole planted her hands on her hips. "If you're finished with him, then I'll dye my hair green. You're a sucker when it comes to needy cases, Marla."

"You tell her," pitched in Giorgio with a grin.

"Stow it," Marla muttered. "Your one o'clock perm is here, Nicole."

"We'll continue this later." Nicole blinked. "Oh, yeah. We have two applicants coming in this afternoon to talk to you about the stylist and shampoo assistant openings. They're sisters: Jennifer and Joanne Cater. Jennifer has her cosmetology license and a few years' experience under her belt. Joanne is graduating from Nova University as an accounting major. She needs supplemental income until she gets established."

"Okay." Marla shrugged and turned away. Hopefully, they'd be better candidates than the other prospects she'd interviewed lately.

"Wait," Giorgio called, "you didn't say if you located your neighbor."

She turned her head back in his direction. "No one has seen Goat."

"That's too bad. Maybe—"

"I can't talk now," she said, interrupting Giorgio to greet the client who'd just walked in. "Hi, Abby. How are you?"

The tall brunette grinned. "Great, thanks. And you?"

"I'm fine," she lied, selecting a royal blue cape from a drawer in her rollabout. "Have a seat and put this on while I get your solution. I'll just be a minute."

Marla didn't subscribe to gossiping with staff members when a client sat in her chair. Customers deserved special treatment, and that meant they got her full attention. Part of her pride in her work derived from offering herself as a listener, providing support and encouragement. A warm glow filled her when patrons left feeling better about themselves and their appearance than when they'd walked in.

Giorgio followed her to the storeroom. "Did you hear about Louise Cunningham?" he said from behind her.

"Who?" Marla squeezed a tube of coloring agent into a bowl, then added developer and bleach. Abby was a level eight, so a Framesi level six should lighten her strands with an attractive auburn tint.

"Louise worked at Nina's House of Style. I heard on the news that she was a hit-and-run last night."

"How awful." She pursed her lips. "That name sounds familiar. I think Louise might have been in my class. Did she survive?"

"No. That's why I'm worried about you."

"I don't get the connection."

"Our profession is getting dangerous. Didn't another hairdresser drown last month?"

"Beats me. I never heard anything about it."

He patted her back. "Maybe you should take a vacation, since you tend to attract trouble."

"No way." Grabbing a stiff brush, she mixed the formula with jerky motions.

"I'm right, and you know it. Is it a coincidence that another dead body popped up in your backyard?"

"Sure." Scooping up the bowl in one hand and a pile of foils in the other, Marla spun toward the door.

"No, it's not. Disaster follows you home. You'd better be careful."

She gritted her teeth as he persisted on her trail.

"You said your neighbor was missing," he continued doggedly. "Maybe his customers or suppliers have heard from him. You might suggest to Detective Vail that he get in touch with them."

"Good idea. Thanks."

"Is Goat responsible for killing that man?"

"Why do you care?" she snapped, stopping to glare at him.

Shrugging, he spread his hands. "You've had some close calls, and I don't want to see you get hurt."

"You sound just like Dalton. Why don't you men realize I can take care of myself?" Noting his pained expression, she felt contrite. "Sorry, but I'm tired of warnings. If you'll excuse me, my customer is waiting."

Louise and I might have gone to the same vocational school, she thought to herself later, discarding the used foils after Abby departed. *If so, we both had Cutter Corrigan as our teacher. Who was the other stylist that drowned?*

A sense of urgency compelled her to search the newspaper archives on her home computer that night, but the hairdresser's name didn't ring a bell. Giorgio was scaring her for no reason, she decided. Dozens of hairdressers worked in Palm Haven and other Fort Lauderdale suburbs. Why should she be concerned about a drowning victim who happened to be a stylist? Still, it would make her feel better to check her class roster at the beauty school, if they kept records back that far. She'd pay them a visit when she had some free time.

Her hand hovered over the telephone in her study. Should she call Vail and ask if he'd confirmed Yani Verkovich's identity? If the girl at Cutter's salon had been correct, how did Cutter's client arrive at Goat's place? Moreover, if Yani's relationship to her former teacher had been more intimate, how did he relate to Goat?

She'd never seen a woman in Goat's company. If he was gay, had *he* been in a relationship with Yani? His van proclaimed him as THE GAY GROOMER, which she'd initially assumed referred to his sexual orientation. If it did, could some sort of love triangle with Cutter be involved?

Don't go there, she told herself. *This is Vail's territory. It's up to him to determine motive, means, and op-*

portunity. You don't even know how the victim died.
Damn Dalton for cutting her off! She needed information, and he was her only source.

No, he wasn't. He discussed his cases with Brianna. Hoping the girl would call tonight, Marla had kept the phone line free. When it rang at eight o'clock, she snatched up the receiver.

"Oh, hi, Ma," she greeted her mother.

"Don't sound so excited. You were expecting Dalton?"

"I don't think so. We're not speaking to each other."

"What happened?" Anita demanded, not one to mince words.

Heaving a sigh, Marla gave the same story she'd told Nicole and Giorgio.

"He's just going through a phase," said her mother reassuringly. "Pay him no mind. He'll come around."

"Why are you calling?" Marla asked, changing the subject.

"I didn't hear from you all day. I started on my new blood pressure medication today. I thought you would care about my reaction."

"And?"

"No difference. I'm seeing Dr. Schultz next week. He's in your area, near the salon. If you have a slot free, I'd like to stop in to get a haircut."

"I don't have my appointment book here. You'll have to call in the morning and check with my receptionist."

"Geez, Marla, even your brother is more accommodating!"

"Michael is a stockbroker. He doesn't see clients on a continuous basis all day."

"So? He always has time for me. You're getting entirely too self-centered. Remember, if you do for others, they'll do in return for you. That goes for family as well as friends."

"Thanks, I needed to hear that. I've had a bad day, and this conversation is just making things worse. Is there anything else?"

"Roger and Barry want to go to services with us Friday night."

"Oh no." The words slipped out before she could stop them.

She heard her mother suck in a breath of disapproval. "I don't know what you have against Roger, but he's a delightful man. I have a good time when we're together, and that should make you happy."

"I'm glad you've found someone, but I find it too much of a coincidence that he enjoys all the same things you do."

"You think I'm blind? I know he's trying to impress me."

"And he eats too much. That guy is a *fresser.*"

"No, he's not, and that's a very unkind thing to say. He just enjoys the sensual pleasures in life."

Marla didn't dare ask what else her mother was including in that statement. "Good for you," she murmured, petting Spooks, who had nudged her hand.

"His son is a charming young man, and he likes you. Barry is a good catch, and not someone you should toss off so lightly. Especially if you and Dalton are having a disagreement."

"I'm not interested in anyone else."

"We'll see."

"I have more pressing matters," Marla insisted. "My neighbor Goat is missing. I'm surprised you didn't hear it on the news. Dalton found a dead body in Goat's house. I know someone who can identify him."

"Don't give me that bowl of borscht. You are not involved in another murder!"

"I'm worried about Goat. I want to do what I can to help locate him."

"Heed my advice, *bubula*. Lock your doors and stay inside."

Easier said than done. Extricating herself from the telephone, she decided to take Spooks for a last outing before retiring for the evening. She'd hoped to get some bookkeeping done but was too tired. Or maybe disappointment had set in because neither Brianna nor the detective had called.

Next door, she rapped Moss's brass anchor on his door.

"Ahoy, mate!" Moss responded to her summons. "Any news about Goat?"

She compressed her lips, holding tightly on to Spooks's leash. "Detective Vail found a dead man in Goat's town house."

"A dead man!"

"It wasn't Goat," Marla said quickly, noting the old man's sudden pallor. "The police want him for questioning, but no one knows where he's gone." She paused. "I thought I might check with his customers and associates, if I can locate them."

A gleam entered Moss's eyes. "You know, I've been wondering what to do about his mail. The box may be near to overflowing by now. He left his spare mailbox key with me."

Marla winked. "I could clear his box out for him."

"Yes, you could. Wait here." When Moss returned,

he handed over the key along with a piece of paper. "My latest limerick," he explained, grinning at the poodle, who kept resisting Marla's efforts to curb his friendly advances.

Marla glanced down as she read:

Beware the Ides of March
Make sure your shirts have starch
If you want to succeed,
You'll follow the creed,
Just don't step on anyone's arch

A broad smile lit her face. "Very good. You may be right with your warning; it's the third one I've heard today."

She thought about his poem while walking to the mailbox cluster at the end of their street. *Speaking of March, I have to get Brianna a birthday gift, assuming I'm still invited to her party a week from Saturday. What about her date with Dalton this weekend?* She assumed that was off, a conclusion that left her feeling distinctly bereft.

She opened Goat's mailbox and retrieved his correspondence. Juggling a large manila envelope in one hand together with the dog's leash, and a stack of assorted items in the other, she proceeded along the dimly lit sidewalk. Words scribbled on the front of the large envelope jumped out at her as she let out the line so Spooks could do his business. *Articles on Harperites enclosed.* How strange. Had Goat sent for these? Why was he interested in information on Martha Matilda Harper's followers? According to the return address, the sender was a woman, Jenny Stanislaw, in Mount Dora.

This case got more curious by the moment.

Goat, reading up on a famous icon in hairdressing history, associated with a dead man who might have been connected to Cutter Corrigan, master stylist. Did the past provide some sort of link between the three of them?

She signaled Spooks it was time to move on. They'd only stepped a few paces ahead when something slammed into her shoulder blade with the force of a deranged flamingo.

Chapter
Four

Marla stumbled forward. Pain and numbness coursed from her right shoulder down her arm. Her nerveless fingers lost their grip, and the mail she'd been carrying fell to the ground. Before she could regain her balance, her hair was caught in a vise, and she was yanked upright by its roots. A cry of pain escaped her lips.

Stunned, she became vaguely aware that Spooks's leash was no longer in her left hand. Blood thrummed in her ears, competing with the dog's wild barking.

"Get lost, pooch," a raspy voice said. In her peripheral vision, she saw a man's leg kick viciously at her pet. Spooks, whimpering, ran off, the leash trailing after him. "Now it's your turn," said her assailant, tightening an arm around her throat until she could only gasp for breath.

Through her sweater, she felt the wide girth of his chest and the strength emanating from his sinewy form. Remembering her women's defense training, Marla attempted to stomp on his instep, but he jerked her backward, avoiding her effort.

"Lucky for me you went out for a stroll tonight," he spoke into her ear. "It's the last walk you'll ever take."

If only she could scream to draw her neighbors' attention. Her vision narrowed as she labored to suck air into her lungs. Going limp didn't help, either. He seemed attuned to her moves. But as he bent to secure his grip on her, she heard a sharp intake of his clove-scented breath and saw his gloved hand snake down to snatch the manila envelope from the ground.

Taking advantage of the opportunity, Marla shifted her stance and rolled him over her hip, shoving him to the ground in a move learned in self-defense class. He landed on his back, beady eyes glaring up at her. She couldn't see the rest of his face, hidden inside a ski mask. Nor did she care to linger. Screaming for help, she sprinted toward her house.

Doors opened, and neighbors poured into the street. This was one community where people didn't hide behind their own security. An engine revved, and a motorcycle whizzed past, wheels squealing as it rounded the curve.

Marla stood frozen. She hadn't even gotten a glimpse of the model.

"What happened?" called Craig as he ran toward her, his surf-blond hair in disarray. Lyn, his wife, remained uncertainly on their doorstep, holding the hands of their two children.

"Marla, are you all right?" Hector said, reaching her side just as Moss and Emma emerged from their place.

Brushing a trembling hand through her disheveled locks, Marla forced words from her mouth. "I . . . I was attacked. Spooks got loose. Has anyone seen him?" She glanced around, praying he hadn't been in the street when the motorcycle tore through.

"He's on your front doorstep, mate," hollered Moss.

"Thank goodness." Marla wrapped both arms around herself, suddenly feeling chilled to the bone. Her teeth chattered, and she couldn't stop shaking from head to foot.

Sirens wailed in the distance. "Do you want to come inside?" said Hector. "Amada called the police. She is quieting the baby, but she would be glad to help."

"No thanks, I'm all right." Taking solace in activity, she stooped to gather Goat's mail, which lay scattered on the sidewalk. Missing was the envelope containing articles on Martha Matilda Harper. *How interesting,* Marla thought. Had her attacker been after her or the mail?

She brought up the question to Detective Dalton Vail when he arrived to survey the scene. Despite their earlier disagreement, she couldn't help feeling a swell of relief at the sight of his brawny figure. Greeting him on her doorstep, she allowed herself a moment of respite by studying his angular features. Skimming over his peppery hair, parted neatly to one side, she noted his firm jaw with its five o'clock shadow, and his steely, determined gaze that bore a hint of disapproval directed at her over his hawk-like nose.

"Come in, Lieutenant," she said formally, thinking it seemed that they were destined to meet under less than favorable circumstances.

"How the hell did you let something like this happen?" he demanded, following her inside and shutting the door. He'd left his officers scouring the street for evidence against her assailant.

"How did *I* let this happen? Like I invited someone to attack me?" Fury shook her, or else she was still reacting to the assault. She couldn't seem to get a grip on herself. Spooks, freed from his leash, nudged her ankle. When she didn't respond, he trotted to Vail and sniffed his trousers.

Vail ignored the poodle, addressing Marla. "You're the one who belongs on a leash," he growled, drawing her into his arms and lowering his head before she could protest. He kissed her fiercely, as though wanting to drive home an understanding of his fear for her.

"You can't protect me from everything," Marla said after disengaging herself. Being in his arms turned her into a mound of styling gel. She needed her wits if she was to think clearly.

"I shouldn't have to be your protector. You're just too stubborn to stay out of trouble."

"I haven't done anything! I was in the salon all afternoon; then I came home. Someone must've been watching Goat's house."

"Oh yeah? Tell me why *you* were his target."

"I picked up Goat's mail. You must have missed collecting this afternoon's delivery from his box. Anyway, the man who attacked me took an envelope. Maybe he'd been expecting it, and I presented the opportunity for him to grab the item."

"Do you really believe that?"

She lowered her head, averting her gaze. "No. He said it was lucky for him that I was out for a stroll."

Vail's jaw tightened. "That sounds more like he

was watching you. I'm afraid you've stirred up a hornets' nest. If Cutter Corrigan is involved in Verkovich's murder, you've set yourself up with a big red bull's-eye."

"Have you confirmed the dead man's identity?"

"It appears you're right. We're waiting for an uncle to visit the morgue, but Verkovich didn't show up for work this week, and he fits the description a colleague gave us."

Giorgio's warning surfaced in her mind. Louise Cunningham, presumably a former classmate, had been a hit-and-run victim. Another stylist had drowned last month. Now she'd been attacked. Was there a connection, and if so, how did it relate to Goat's disappearance? Her assailant had taken the envelope containing articles about Harperites, she reminded herself. How could historical documents regarding a legendary hairdresser affect people today?

"There's something else you should know," Vail mentioned after they were seated at her kitchen table, nursing mugs of steaming coffee. "This is confidential. I found a stash of cash in Goat's house. Twenty-five thousand, in hundred-dollar bills."

"What?"

"You heard me."

"What would Goat be doing with so much money?"

Vail hunched forward. "Let's say he made a deal with this Verkovich fellow, and it fell through. Goat killed him, panicked, and ran out through the patio door."

Marla sipped the hot brew. "What kind of deal? I can't conceive of Goat killing anyone over a bad business proposition."

"They may have been involved in the pet-fur trade."

She shuddered with revulsion, remembering the thing she'd discovered in Goat's yard. "Tell me more."

His tone deepened. "It originates in the Far East, mainly China and Korea. People there don't value domestic animals like we do. Folks eat them, despite a law prohibiting human consumption of dogs and cats."

"Tally told me she saw skinned dogs hanging in a market when she and Ken visited the Orient. She saw the head of a dog with its legs stuffed into its mouth. Others were for sale in cages, still alive."

Vail nodded. "A Humane Society report told about dogs being skinned alive and cats being strangled for their fur. The article said it takes maybe twelve dogs or twenty-four cats to manufacture one coat. They estimated two million dogs and cats are killed annually for their pelts. In the United States, imported fur is used on clothing, novelty items, and stuffed animals. Major store chains plus smaller boutiques are involved. Just as an example, investigators found coats at a well-known store with fur trim that came from dog fur."

Bile rose in her throat. "Isn't it illegal in this country?"

He scratched his jaw. "There was a bill introduced in the Florida legislature to make the import and sale of this stuff against the law. As far as I know, the measure didn't pass the Florida House."

"So if this nasty business is considered allowable, why would anyone kill over it?"

"Because if the bill does eventually pass, penalties will be instituted. It could be a third-degree felony to kill cats or dogs to sell their pelts. There's a proposed bill in Congress that deals with the same subject. Meanwhile, we can get those involved charged with animal abuse."

"How can you tell you're buying these products?"

"DNA tests. Forensic analysis can determine the origin. Otherwise, you have no way of knowing. The cleaning and dying process makes cat fur look like it comes from a rabbit. Scuttlebutt says that a government minister in China said he would label it anything we wanted. Consumers should ask for a statement of origin if they buy these things."

"Yuck." She felt a surge of sympathy for rabbits and goats. They weren't on anyone's forbidden list.

"We've been concerned a cottage industry may be operating in the area, meaning dogs and cats are being used for this purpose. That's one reason why I'd like to get hold of your pal Goat."

"Goat loves animals. He wouldn't harm them."

"How do you know? Just because he keeps a few pets?"

"He took care of that goat that was in his yard."

"A scrawny thing it was, too. Maybe he kept it for a supply of milk."

She shoved her mug away. "Bless my bones, you're convicting him before he's proven guilty. If Goat was involved in this pet-fur trade, he wouldn't have left his bag of cash behind."

"Murderers don't think clearly. His only goal might have been to escape. I found some receipts in his place, too. From an exotic bird breeder made out to a local pet store."

"Maybe Goat buys his grooming supplies at the store. I'm sure when you find him, you'll learn the truth. I think he's running scared because he knows who killed Yani. He may have witnessed the crime."

"All the more reason to find him quickly." Vail rolled his shoulders forward, then pushed himself out of his chair.

Marla washed their mugs at the sink as an awkward silence descended. "When do you plan to talk to Cutter?"

"I'll get to him tomorrow. I want to finish interviewing your neighbors first. They may have something to add after your episode tonight. It also occurred to me that Yani may not have been the prime target."

Wiping her hands on a towel, she turned around. "How so?"

"If you're right, and Goat didn't do it, then either he was the intended victim or else he's being framed. You see," he said, grinning smugly, "I do consider all the angles."

Her heart flipped as his smile transformed his face. "That means you need to check into Goat's background along with the victim's. You'll be busy."

He folded his arms across his chest. "So will you, with your work at the salon. You're not to play sleuth anymore, understand?"

She gave him a sly glance. "You make your opinion very clear. Are you sure you don't need help with Brianna's party next week?"

"No thanks, we're all set. That reminds me, I have a gift for her. I'd appreciate it if you'd wrap it for me. I'm not good at that sort of thing. I've been carrying it around in the trunk of my car for the past week. Wait here."

Marla was surprised when he presented her with

a hand-carved wooden chess set. She'd expected something more personal or a new electronic gadget. "Does Brianna play chess?" she asked uncertainly. The girl hadn't struck her as the competitive type.

"Brie will after I teach her. Pam and I bought this on a trip to Switzerland," he explained, referring to his deceased wife. "Pam picked it out. I think it'll mean a lot to our daughter."

"Oh. Well, I'll do my best to wrap it up real nice." As she set the box on a side table in the living room, the diamonds sparkled on her amethyst ring. *Gads, I hope this didn't belong to his dead wife, too.* Shoving aside the uncomfortable notion, she thought about what she should buy for Brianna. Marla would rather buy the girl some hot designer duds, a Kate Spade bag, or the latest CDs. Something a teen could use, not a gift to store away as a sentimental treasure. She hoped Brie was going to appreciate Vail's gesture.

"About this Saturday night, I don't think I'm going to make our date," she said, facing him in her foyer. "Family obligations," she offered as a feeble excuse.

He stared into her eyes as though he could pierce her mental armor. "All right."

She shuffled her feet. "Brianna—"

"Is my daughter. I make the rules where she's concerned."

You make the rules for everyone. "Will you tell me if you learn anything new about Goat?"

"I may, if you stick to your business and let me do mine."

Marla fumed, curling her fingers. First Cutter had told her to mind her own business. Then

Giorgio cautioned her to steer clear of trouble. Dalton had added salt to her wounds.

"Keep in touch," she said coolly. "Thanks for the assistance tonight." Not that he'd done much except drink her coffee and accuse her neighbor of wrongdoing.

He opened his mouth to say something, then apparently changed his mind. Nodding curtly, he left.

Marla performed her nightly preparations in a daze. Still traumatized by the evening's events, she armed her newly activated security system after making sure all doors were locked. Then she allowed herself the luxury of a hot, soaking shower. While she was towel-drying her hair, the phone rang.

"What's up?" her friend Tally said at the other end.

Marla, fastening the sash of a terry-cloth robe around her waist, sank onto her bed. "Do I have things to tell you!" She proceeded to relate the day's events.

"Wow, you're just not content to stay put behind the salon chair, are you?"

"You sound like Cutter. I wonder if Dalton will find out any more when he interviews him tomorrow."

"Will the detective tell you what he learns?"

Marla gave a rueful chuckle. "I doubt it. I canceled our date Saturday night. We had a disagreement over Brianna."

"Oh no. What now?"

"Brianna wants to shave her legs and use makeup. Dalton won't allow it. He's afraid she'll start attracting men."

"Wait until she's older." Tally laughed. "So what's his beef with you?"

"I defended her right to make herself look pretty. Dalton can't face the fact that she's growing up. She told me she wants to go shopping and then her face got all red. I think she's approaching puberty and needs advice, not to mention intimate apparel and other feminine supplies."

"Why doesn't she ask Carmen, their house-keeper?"

Marla shrugged. "I don't know. Beauty is my business, so maybe she felt more inclined to seek my advice. Brie has a beautiful face without any cosmetics, but you know how teenagers are. They have to fit in with the crowd."

"It doesn't sound as though Dalton understands."

"He's too protective, and he won't listen to me. If he doesn't consider my opinions to be of any value, then there's no point in pursuing our relationship."

"You're overreacting."

"Maybe I was just rushing forward with my hormones instead of my head. It's time to reevaluate. At any rate, I'll see him next week at Brianna's party."

"How's your mom?"

Marla grimaced. "She invited Roger and Barry to join us for services Friday night. I wouldn't be surprised if Roger pushed himself to be included."

"He cares for Anita. Are you sure you're not jealous of the attention she pays him?"

"Of course not. I'd like her to be more cautious, that's all."

"Look in the mirror, friend. Were you cautious with David, or Dalton?"

"David wormed himself into my life. As for Dalton, I didn't jump into bed with him right away. It took a while."

"Uh-huh. Are you sure you're not getting cantankerous in your old age?"

"Ha! I'm only a few months older than you."

"Maybe we should rejoin Perfect Fit Sports Club. You need to work out that tension."

"No way. Besides, you'd be tense, too, after someone assaulted you. I'm too nervous to go to sleep."

"Maybe the guy was after Goat's envelope rather than you."

"I hope you're right."

"Did you see who sent it? You could try to track them down and ask about Goat."

Marla straightened her shoulders. "Tally, you're brilliant. I remember the sender's name and town on the return address. After we hang up, I'll call information."

"Be careful, will you?" Tally said, a note of alarm in her voice.

"A phone call can't harm me. When can we get together?"

"Ken will be out of town this weekend. Want to catch a movie on Saturday night? Unless you change your mind about seeing Detective Vail."

"Sounds good to me. Let's grab a bite to eat first, okay? I have a craving for clam chowder at Legal Sea Foods. Then we can go to the theater at Sawgrass."

A few seconds later, Marla dialed four-one-one.

"What city?" an impersonal voice responded.

"Mount Dora. The person's name is Jenny Stanislaw." She waited breathlessly for the answer.

"Here's the number."

She scribbled down the code before touching the flash button and keypad.

"Hello," a woman's sleepy voice answered.

"I'm so sorry. Did I wake you?" She glanced at the clock. It was only ten, early for her.

"It's all right. Who is this?"

"I'm a close friend of Goat's." Marla felt foolish that she didn't know his last name. "He, uh, mentioned your name to me on a couple of occasions," she lied.

"And you are?" The woman's voice sharpened.

"Marla Shore, his neighbor. I haven't seen him around for a few days, and I'm concerned about his absence. I was hoping you might know where he is."

"The police have already questioned me."

Marla's mouth dropped open. Vail had said nothing about Goat's connections. Apparently, he'd been one step ahead of her. Recovering her composure, she said, "I'm speaking to you as his friend. I'm worried about him, and I don't believe he's done anything wrong. I want to help him."

"What makes you think I know anything?"

"You sent him articles about Harperites. Why did he want them?"

"Look, Miss Shore, it's late, and I don't feel like talking about my brother right now."

Chapter
Five

"Your brother!" Marla repeated in surprise. "His real name is Kyle Stanislaw. He got the nickname of Goat because he could never grow more than a scraggly beard. I don't know where he is, but I can tell you one thing. Kyle may be involved in another of his scrapes, but he isn't a murderer."

"Why did Goat want you to send him those articles about Harperites?"

"I'm a librarian, so I assume that's why he asked me to research the topic. I thought it was odd, but I didn't question him. He's very bright in some respects, although he lacks common sense."

"We've been really concerned about him. I collected his mail, and while I was walking home, someone attacked me. Whoever it was stole the envelope you sent him."

A moment of silence followed, terminated by a sigh. "We have a place on Siesta Key. I'd hoped

Kyle might be there, but no one answers the telephone."

Hope flared in her chest. "Is it possible for you to give me the address?"

"I already gave that information to the police. I trust they've already checked it out and didn't find any sign of him."

"I've helped the police solve cases before. I don't know if Goat told you or not, but I'm a hairstylist. People tell me things they won't admit to anyone else."

"So?"

"So maybe if I ask around Siesta Key, someone might have spotted Goat, especially if you think he stopped off there."

"If you're who you say you are, come visit me. There are things about Kyle you should know if you truly want to help him."

Marla tapped her foot, mentally reviewing her schedule. "I'm not free until Sunday. Is this something we could discuss now? Your brother is in trouble, and he needs to be found."

Jenny's voice hardened. "You have it reversed. The person who killed that man in his house needs to be found. Only then will Kyle be safe."

"I pray that he's all right. I believe he took his pet snake with him. Its container was empty. Either that, or the creature is slithering around our neighborhood."

"I'd be careful if I were you," Jenny warned. "Kyle told me about the run-in he'd had with that guy next door. You don't know who you can trust."

"What do you mean?"

"I'll tell you when I see you."

"Did he say anything about . . . selling dog or cat fur?"

"What? Why on earth would Kyle mention such a thing?"

"Detective Vail believes he might be engaged in the pet-fur trade. He found an animal with . . . patches of skin showing." That was putting it mildly.

"I have no idea what you're talking about. If you're going to discuss such foolery with me when you come, then don't bother."

"I'm sorry," Marla hastily replied. "I didn't mean to imply Goat was involved in anything disreputable. It's just an angle the detective is checking, which may prove useful."

"We'll talk more when you're here," Jenny said. "Bye now."

After Marla hung up, she mulled over their conversation. Goat's real name was Kyle Stanislaw. His sister, Jenny, worked as a librarian. He'd requested articles about Martha Matilda Harper's followers, but Jenny didn't know the reason why he wanted them. Nor had Jenny heard any mention of his involvement in a pet-fur scheme. Perhaps he'd said something relevant, but his sister hadn't realized its importance at the time, Marla thought. She'd have to conduct a more thorough interview in person. Possibly Jenny didn't realize how strong the police's suspicions were concerning her brother.

Jenny warned me to be careful. What did she mean about Goat having a run-in with a neighbor? Which neighbor? Was there someone here to fear, in addition to Yani Verkovich's killer? Were they linked, and was Goat their patsy? What else could be at stake besides a shady business, not quite illegal, involving dogs and cats? *That's a question Cutter might be able to answer. He's mixed up in this—I know it.*

She got up to change into her nightshirt. Too many possibilities crowded her brain, so she took solace in routine actions. Nonetheless, her mind remained in hyperdrive. At this rate, she'd never relax enough to fall asleep.

A cup of coffee might help. She padded toward the kitchen, wondering if she had any sweets tucked away in the refrigerator. Passing the living room, her gaze zeroed in on Vail's chess set. It had fallen onto the carpet, cracked open, and some of the pieces had spilled out.

"Spooks!" she yelled, certain her poodle was guilty of a misdemeanor. Her heart sank after she replaced the carved chessmen into their felt-lined impressions. An open spot leered at her like an empty eye socket. "Oh, this is just great."

Charging into the kitchen where Spooks had his bed, she spotted him cowering under the table. As soon as he saw her, he dropped whatever was in his mouth. Marla stooped to pick it up, ready to scold the pooch. Instead, she gasped with dismay. The knight had been chewed to the extent that the varnish had come off, and teeth marks were visible.

Dear Lord, what would Vail say? "Spooks, what have you done? You've ruined his gift. Bad dog!"

Spooks whimpered. His tail down, he hung his head.

Vail had bought the chess set in Europe, many years ago. She'd have to find a replacement, but where? Marla opened her mouth to chastise Spooks again, but then recalled what Vail had told her about dogs being killed for their fur. Reaching for Spooks, she scooped him into her arms and snuggled her face against his soft, fluffy coat. *No one better hurt you, pal. I'll just deal with this new problem later.*

Easier said than done. Work consumed the next few days, and she was forced to push aside personal concerns. On Friday morning she arrived early at the salon to take inventory and place orders for supplies. That task accomplished, she set up the coffeemaker. So much to do, so little time. "I'm going to Bagel Busters," she told the receptionist, a temporary hire.

Hastening along the shopping strip, she approached the restaurant, already full with the breakfast crowd. "Hi, Arnie," she said to the man behind the cash register.

"Here's my *shayna maidel.* " Arnie beamed widely as he rounded the bend to embrace her in a bear hug.

"What are you so happy about?" she asked her old friend, whose dark hair increasingly showed traces of silver.

"Jill has decided to take Judaism lessons. I never suggested it to her; she made the decision completely on her own. Needless to say, I'm thrilled."

She smiled, touching his forearm. "That's wonderful. Did you tell Josh and Lisa?"

His eyes twinkled. "They think it's cool."

"We'll have to double-date again. I'll talk to Dalton."

Arnie, a widower with two children, had courted Marla before he started dating Jill. While Marla held a special fondness for him, she'd made it clear friendship was on her slate, nothing more. She didn't want to be burdened with children, although now she'd gotten involved with Dalton Vail and his daughter, Brianna. How far their relationship would go, she'd yet to find out. Marla doubted the staid detective would ever consider converting to her religion. But it wasn't an issue for her.

Ma still hopes I'll marry someone Jewish. After divorcing Stan, Marla had felt less inclined to honor her family's wishes. She'd learned to follow her own heart, more or less.

"Is my order ready?" she asked Arnie, aware of his perceptive gaze on her face.

"Yep. Here you go." He retrieved a large bag from behind the counter. "Everything okay? Any word on your missing neighbor?"

"I haven't spoken to Dalton lately, nor have I had a chance to look into Goat's disappearing act myself. It's been a busy week."

"No further unpleasantness?"

"Well, there is one thing. I have a problem."

"You know you can count on me, *bubula*. What's wrong?"

Rummaging in her purse, she pulled out the mangled chess piece. "This is part of a gift Dalton is giving to Brianna for her birthday. He wanted me to wrap it. Spooks thought this was a meal."

"*Oy vey.*" Arnie peered at the damage. "What will you do?"

"I can't tell him I ruined his present. He bought this with his late wife on a trip to Switzerland. I'll have to find a replacement."

"You could try the toy stores."

"And the hobby places. I'll look around. Just another chore to add to my list."

"When is her party?"

"A week from tomorrow."

"You've got time. Let me know if you need help."

Warmed by his thoughtfulness, she gave him a quick kiss on the cheek. "You're a savior. Say hello to Jill for me."

Back at the salon, she handed the bagels to the receptionist. "Giorgio should be here soon, and Nicole will be coming at nine. I'm going out for a little while."

Marla approached the stucco facade of the Sunrise Academy of Beauty with a feeling of déjà vu. No wonder; she'd spent forty weeks here studying cosmetology, earning the required twelve hundred hours toward her diploma. The building didn't show its age, thanks to a fresh coat of coral paint. She wondered if the interior had been spared the ravages of time. If memory served her correctly, this place had been here since 1975.

Inside the air-conditioned lobby, she faced a receptionist's desk done in generic office motif. Rows of plastic chairs lined the opposite wall. A couple of senior citizens lounged there, leafing through old hairstyling magazines.

"Hi, I'm Marla Shore," she introduced herself to the middle-aged redhead behind the desk. The secretary's name badge identified her as Janine.

"Are you here for hair or nails? You'll need to sign in," Janine said before Marla had a chance to explain her purpose.

"I'm not here for any services." She was aware students practiced on real clients in an adjacent lab, and members of the public could walk in and register for treatments. A sign on the wall said a wash and blow-dry was only three dollars. Huh!

That was a lot cheaper than the twenty dollars she charged. And where else could you get a pedicure today for five dollars?

"I'd like to speak to someone about your program," she announced firmly.

"Which one?" Janine's gray eyes scrutinized her as though she were an overgrown cuticle. "We have courses in cosmetology, facials, nails, and skin care. We've recently added a health department where you can study to become a medical, dental, or nursing aide."

Marla lifted her eyebrows. "I didn't know you had expanded your curriculum."

Janine's ample bosom swelled with pride. "Our enrollment keeps increasing. Dorothy May founded the academy in 1975. All we had to offer early students was nail and skin care technology. Then we moved into hair, and now we have cosmetic specialties in fields like sculptured tips and permanent makeup."

"I'm interested in cosmetology."

She pursed her lips. "You'll have to attend our orientation program which runs every Tuesday, either in the morning from eight until ten, or in the evening from seven to nine. You're required to take a placement test to measure your math, reading, and language levels. It takes about twenty minutes on the computer. Then a counselor will describe the required classes."

Grinning, Marla shook her head. "That's not why I'm here, although I'd like to learn more. Just to see how things have changed, you understand. I'm a licensed stylist."

"Oh, then you're here about a renewal? We don't do the HIV/AIDS course here or the other things you'll need. It's tough to get part-time instructors, and we have too many regular students. One of the other schools may be able to help you."

Marla stood her ground. "I need to speak to a director."

Challenged, the receptionist tilted her head. "Maybe you're here to register for one of our advanced-products seminars?"

"I'm seeking specific information on my former classmates. Do you keep records from several years ago?"

Janine's expression deflated now that she realized Marla wasn't applying as a student. "You'll have to speak to Virginia. She's the cosmetology department chief. I'll ring her up and see if she's in." A few moments later: "You're in luck. Go down the hall; it's the third door on your left."

Marla marched proudly along the corridor, appreciating how far she'd come since she'd walked these halls so many years ago. No longer a novice, she now had the benefit of many years of experience. She glimpsed into the laboratory on her left, smiling at the scene. Students wearing blue uniforms worked on mannequin heads while others practiced on actual clients clad in maroon smocks. Although part of her felt a wave of nostalgia, she was glad her year of basic training was long finished.

When Marla reached the office indicated, she knocked on the solid wood door.

"Come in," rang out a strong female voice.

Marla entered. An auburn-haired woman, sitting behind a mahogany desk, glanced up and smiled. Her china blue eyes looked vaguely familiar.

"Please come in," the director said. "I'm Virginia Hawkins."

"Hi, I'm Marla Shore. I graduated from here a number of years ago, and I need some information."

"Please have a seat. I remember you, dear. I believe I was one of your instructors."

After sharing nostalgic memories, Marla stated her case. "Do you keep class rosters? I'm interested in looking up a former classmate."

"We keep a database on all our former students. Names, addresses, phone numbers, résumés, job placement. We don't normally give out this information."

Marla thought fast. "I'm planning a reunion."

"A reunion, how exciting!" Virginia grinned in delight.

"I think we lost a member," Marla said in a sad tone. "I'd read in the newspaper about a stylist drowning in an accident. I couldn't remember whether she was in my class or not."

The director clucked with sympathy. "Just let me bring up that window." Turning to her computer, Virginia typed in a few commands. "You're talking about Eileen McFee."

"May I see?" Marla craned her neck to peer at the monitor. What she saw made her blood run cold. Louise Cunningham, the recent hit-and-run victim Giorgio had mentioned, was on the same list. "This is my class! Can I possibly get a print-out?"

"Well, since you're a former student of mine . . . I'll make an exception, but only if you invite me to the reunion." Virginia pushed the PRINT button.

"It's difficult retaining students with our transient population."

"Tell me about it. I have the same problem with my staff."

The director's eyes lit with curiosity. "How long have you had your own salon?"

"Eight years. I actually used my portfolio design from class." It had been part of her graduation requirements. The portfolio included a floor plan for an imaginary salon, projected costs, outfitting, and price lists for services, among other items. "I'd be interested in seeing what you do now. Things have probably changed since I studied here."

She needed time to think about the connection between the dead stylists and herself. Were their deaths accidental as reported in the news, or had she almost become the third victim of a crazed killer who hit on hairdressers? Though if this were the case, why would her assailant take Goat's envelope?

Cutter Corrigan had been their instructor. She should pay him another visit, with or without Dalton Vail's approval.

"I think one thing you'll find different than when you were here is that now we have defined lesson plans," Virginia said, rising. She handed Marla the printout of her class roster, and a bunch of other documents. "As you see, the curriculum is much more structured, with set objectives and a course syllabus. Students must pass a basic skills test. We also have field trips to various shows."

Marla shuffled through the papers in her hands. Lecture subjects ranged from bacteriology to business skills, sanitation to science, Florida state law to salon management. She noted classes on electricity, anatomy, chemistry, and disease. The requirements weren't much different than when she'd gone through school. Hairstyling, cutting, coloring, chemical waving, and other services still had the same performance sheets, with a few modern additions.

"We're always looking for substitute teachers," Virginia said, noting her interest. "Let me give you a tour. Perhaps I can motivate you to become one of our instructors. Have you taken any specialized courses since you obtained your license?"

"Well, sure." Marla mentioned some of the seminars she'd attended. They began their tour in the lab, the sound of blow-dryers competing with the students' chatter. "It looks pretty much the same as when I was here," she said, noting the worn linoleum on the floor and the plastic ceiling panels overhead.

"Terms three through five spend two days a week in the laboratory. The rest of the time is in the classroom. We're working with Broward Community College to try to get college credit for our courses and maybe have some high school students join us. The health section is in our new building. We're slated to renovate this one next year."

"Are classes still just in the mornings?" When she'd gone to school, Marla had worked part-time as a shampoo girl in a local salon during the afternoons.

"We run three sessions six days a week. You can start at eight in the morning, three in the afternoon, or six in the evening. Labs are Wednesdays and Fridays. So if you're considering being a substitute, just about any time you're available except Sundays would work."

They passed a row of green vinyl chairs with old-fashioned dome hair dryers. She figured a lot of senior citizens came in who still liked to get a wash-and-set. "How many students are enrolled?"

Virginia waved an arm. "We have upwards of one hundred twenty in here at a time. That's an average of thirty students per classroom, with four rooms, including this lab. Then there are the facial rooms and the pedi-spa."

Marla smiled at the familiar sight of one girl setting a mannequin head with perm rods while another combed out a head of curly brown hair after doing a foil frosting. *Gads, look in that corner!* She hadn't used an electric oven for comb-pressing hair since training. Chuckling, Marla turned her attention to another student doing a demi-perm coloring on a real customer. Products spilled from rollabouts standing in the aisles; cut hairs littered the floor; and trailing wires from various implements tangled on the counters. In the center stood a row of sinks for mixing chemicals. Her former mentor would be horrified by the mess. Cutter's place exemplified order amid high style.

"Do you remember Cutter Corrigan? He was another one of my instructors. Cutter owns a salon on Las Olas now. Do you keep in touch with him?"

Before answering Marla, Virginia called out, "Not that way," to a student doing a piggyback perm. "You've put the rods too far in the back. Move them over here." After demonstrating the proper technique, she turned her attention back to Marla. "Cutter is always looking for promising graduates. I saw him at the Wella show a few weeks ago. He'd brought his friend."

"Oh? Male or female?"

"The same guy as before."

Marla gave her a curious glance. "Light or dark hair?"

"Very dark, with those Latin good looks."

"Hmm." Couldn't have been Yani Verkovich; and, besides, you had to be a licensed professional to get into the shows.

"There's one of Carolyn Sutton's girls." Virginia pointed to a student fixing a fancy updo on a mannequin. "You used to work for her, didn't you?"

"Carolyn gave me my first job after I graduated."

"She sponsors students here. Some of them don't speak much English, so I don't know where she gets them. She employs them in her salon after they graduate."

Marla put a hand on Virginia's arm. "Carolyn is opening a salon in the same shopping strip as my place. I thought her previous location looked rundown, and our rent is probably higher. How can she afford to move, plus sponsor any students? How much is tuition today, by the way?"

"It costs twenty-five hundred for the year. That includes fees, books, uniforms, and a personal styling kit. Field trips cost extra."

Marla dropped her hand. "I think someone must be financing her." Marla's ex-spouse, Stan, had tried to undermine her lease at one point in Carolyn's favor, but she'd defeated his efforts. After she helped solve the murder of his third wife, they'd become allies if not friends. He wouldn't back her rival this time, so who would? *Get back on track.* Dealing with the competition wasn't her priority right now.

"Do me a favor," she said to Virginia. "If you see Cutter again, don't mention that I was here."

The director's eyes widened with glee. "I know!

You're planning to surprise him with the reunion, aren't you? How delightful. It's so unusual for people to keep in touch these days."

"I appreciate your help," Marla said before taking her leave. Celebrating Cutter's stint as her teacher was the last thing on her mind. She needed to learn what Cutter knew about Goat, if the deaths of these two stylists were coincidental or not, and where the history of hairdressing fit into it all.

Chapter
Six

Marla didn't get a chance to ask Cutter Corrigan about her classmates, because when she reached Heavenly Hair Salon at five P.M., he was just leaving. She followed in her Toyota as he strode along the sidewalk, then turned right at the corner. Thinking he must be going for a bite to eat, she was surprised when he climbed into a black Mercedes in the rear lot and headed off.

It might be better if she spoke to him at home anyway; the salon wouldn't be very private for the questions she wanted to ask. But instead of aiming toward the part of town where he lived, according to the address she'd looked up, Cutter veered west on Broward Boulevard—all the way west, to Flamingo Road. Gritting her teeth, she followed, hoping they wouldn't end up on Alligator Alley for a trip to Naples.

Staying several cars behind him, she passed the WELCOME TO DAVIE sign after the I-595 underpass going south on Flamingo Road. Plant nurseries, herb farms, and palm-tree growers lined either side of the long stretch, interspersed by vast open spaces studded with pines, palms, and native shrubs. As they crossed the intersection at Southwest Thirty-Sixth Court, Marla spied a couple of tour buses in the parking lot at Flamingo Gardens on their left. Not much farther up the avenue, Cutter turned where a sign said WILD BIRD RANCH. He charged down a bumpy dirt road into the dusty distance.

Marla made a U-turn and parked in the free lot at Flamingo Gardens. It wouldn't be smart for her to trail directly behind Cutter's Mercedes down a private road. Nor was it wise for her to continue on this course of action without backup, she realized with a spurt of doubt. But curiosity got the better of her, and so did her need to find Goat. Cutter knew something, and it was possible that tailing him might help her find her neighbor.

Glad she'd dressed for comfort that morning in dark pants and a lightweight pullover sweater, she trod down the dirt road in her sturdy work shoes. They'd never win a style award, but eight hours of standing in pumps or even strappy sandals would have left her legs hurting. Treading on small pebbles, she was grateful it hadn't rained, or she'd be sloshing in mud. Probably she should've left her handbag locked in her car, but you never knew when a nail file, can of hair spray, or metal pick would come in handy.

What kind of ranch was this? The dirt road abruptly ended at a tropical hammock. She spotted Cutter's black Mercedes parked on a patch of grass. No sign of her quarry showed anywhere in the thick foliage ahead. A glimpse of various buildings gave her a goal. Cutter must have gone in their direction. Shifting her purse from one shoulder to the other, she started through the foliage toward the closest structure. It wasn't long before she realized the grounds consumed considerable acreage and the distances were deceiving.

Her hair lifted in a breeze too warm and humid for March. Carried on the wind came a cacophony of sounds: strident bird cries, twittering songs, squawks, and loud honks. Wait a minute. Hadn't Vail said he'd found receipts in Goat's house from a bird breeder? Could this be the place? According to his report, the receipts had been made out to a pet store. It logically followed that the breeder sold birds to that store. She wondered if Vail had visited either place to inquire about Goat.

Grimacing as her feet crunched on twigs and dead leaves, she steadily proceeded into the jungle along a meandering path. Shafts of sunlight illuminated pink and white impatiens nestled among broad-leafed green plants. A cluster of bamboo creaked next to a stand of spindly red crotons. On either side of the trail, trees rose skyward, forming a canopy. Species she had seen only in parks had her craning her neck to spy the tops: hundred-year-old live oaks, shady Indian jujube trees, sapodillos, and arjun trees with thick, odd-shaped trunks. She recognized a peeling melaleuca as the wind tickled her skin and brought a musty smell of humus.

Steering around a bread-nut tree, she narrowly avoided colliding with a glistening cobweb. A black spider hung in the center, crouching for prey. Her nerves tensed as she imagined its sticky web catching her unaware, and a shudder racked her spine. She advanced forward, treading carefully to avoid roots and rocks in her path. Wary of creatures dangling overhead, she ducked under an overhanging branch.

A mosquito buzzed past her ear, and she swatted it away, cursing. Water trickled down a rocky ledge into a nearby pond, providing breeding grounds for more of the pesky insects. Bugs and spiders were not her thing, nor were the strange, piercing bird calls that rattled her composure. She almost missed the low murmur of voices ahead, but drew herself up short just in time.

"What's happening?" Cutter said in a harsh tone.

"You go on ahead. I'll join you in a few minutes," said another man.

"Who's this?" grated a third fellow's voice.

"Cutter is my cousin. Cutter, this is Wake Hollander. Wake and I have some business to finish."

"Sure, Evan. Is this business that pertains to me?" Cutter's nasal voice inquired.

"Wouldn't I tell you if it did? Wait in the lab. I'll be right there."

"If you don't mind, I'll stand my ground."

"Suit yourself. Wake, I told you, the shipment was delayed. It should be in early next week."

"I paid you to have it ready today."

"I can't control what happens on the other side. You'll have to be patient."

"Be patient, my ass. My sponsor is expecting them tonight."

"Look, I'll throw in some extras. I've got an Anegada Island iguana coming in. Should be some new macaws, too. You tell him he can have his choice."

"No way. We had a deal. You don't deliver on time, you don't keep the cash, buddy."

"What is this?" Cutter broke in. "Listen, cuz, you told me you'd finished with this stuff."

Marla crept closer to where she could discern their outlines through the trees. Squinting, she wished her vision allowed her to see more clearly. Maybe it was time to visit the eye doctor. Beside Cutter stood a brawny fellow. Together they faced a shorter, wiry figure.

"I have your parakeets, Wake," said Cutter's cousin. "I promise I'll call you as soon as our other shipment comes in. It's not my fault. I've always been reliable, you know that."

The short man clenched his fists. "I'll discuss it with Tiger. We'll get back to you." Abruptly, he turned on his heel and left.

Afraid he'd come in her direction toward the exit, Marla slinked back against a prickly tree trunk. Instead, he walked the opposite way, making her think there must be another entrance to the property. That made sense, especially if the rancher lived here. He'd want to drive up to his house. Did this place belong to Cutter's cousin?

"You'd better not mess up our project," Cutter warned the man named Evan when they were left alone.

"Don't worry. I can handle those guys."

"You're risking our enterprise by screwing with Tiger. If he decides you're a liability—"

"He won't. I'm his main supplier. He won't cut off the hand that feeds him. Now follow me to the lab. The results of our latest tests are exciting."

"You're able to proceed without Verkovich?"

A heavy sigh. "It's necessary. Have you had any success tracking our friend?"

"Nope, but I have in mind someone who might lead us to him."

As they strode away, Marla strained to hear more, but she couldn't make out their words. Darn! She sidestepped along the path, intending to trail them, when she stepped on a particularly large twig. A loud crack made the two men glance over their shoulders. Marla froze, praying she blended in with her surroundings. After a moment suspended in time, they shrugged and resumed their pace.

She watched a lizard scurry up a papaya tree, waiting until the coast was clear before she proceeded after her quarry. She came upon a few buildings that looked like work sheds. Peacocks strutted across the grass, eyeing her warily. Rounding a corner, she stopped, confused. The two men were nowhere in sight.

She stepped onto a concrete path and entered an alley between huge wire enclosures. Each mesh cell was labeled and appropriately designed for its occupants, with rocky prominences and tropical foliage. But this was no zoo, and Marla wondered at its purpose.

Her nostrils wrinkled as she stepped carefully around a splotch of bird droppings. The stench reminded her of dead lizards she sometimes found at home. Curiosity compelled her to peer into some of the enclosures. At least the labels helped to identify the residents. Two red-tailed hawks kept each other company next to a cage harboring prairie owls. A Mississippi kite, with a gray body and black tail, gave a high, keening cry. Marla hoped its noise wouldn't draw attention. Osprey, eagles, and a collection of vultures stared at her as though they knew she was an intruder.

Were these creatures for sale, or were they part of a private collection?

The air grew hot and still. Just as she considered clapping a hand over her nose to filter out the odor of death, someone else did it for her.

"Whaddya doin' here?" hissed a male voice in her ear, a strong hand clamping over her mouth. When she mumbled between his fingers, he transferred his grip to her shoulder. Turning her around, he maintained hold of her arm while giving her the once-over.

Marla swallowed as she faced what appeared to be a thoroughly disreputable character. Hunched over with a twisted spine, the man stank worse than their surroundings and looked as if he'd been groveling in the dirt. Torn jeans covered mud-splattered boots. A ratty T-shirt hung over his beer belly. Much of his face was hidden by a scruffy black beard, but it didn't distract from the man's bulbous nose or his sharp gaze. He licked his lips, waiting for her answer.

She swiped her mouth where he'd touched her. "Uh, I . . . had some trouble with my car and was looking for help." Her excuse sounded feeble even to her own ears. She glanced at his hairy arm. "Please let me go. I'll just head back to Flamingo Gardens and call the motor club from there."

"No, ya won't, missy. My boss will wanna see ya." His grip tightened. "This way."

"Wait!" Panic flared at the thought of Cutter finding her here. "My friends know where I was headed. They'll be looking for me."

He halted, squeezing her arm painfully as he

drew her close enough to smell his sweat. His gaze flickered downward, resting on her bosom. "I think you're lying. You behave, or it'll go the worse for ya."

"You're making a mistake!"

She struggled futilely as he shoved her toward a pair of double wood doors with chipped, peeling paint. Swinging one open, he pushed her inside a dank, dark room. "Mr. Fargutt will decide what to do with ya. When he's done, maybe he'll give ya to me. He knows ole Jimbo is hunkerin' for a woman."

Slam went the door, followed by the thud of a bolt sliding into place.

Marla whirled around. She faced a small space with a dim lightbulb overhead. Her gaze fell to the wall where a series of glass tanks were filled with branches, leaves, and rocks. And something else. A long black snake slowly uncoiled.

"Yikes! I'm outta here, pal."

The next instant found her shoving open the double doors at the other end of her cell. She pushed outside into moisture-laden air that smelled like dung. Glancing around, she noted with dismay that the entire area was enclosed by heavy wire mesh. Great, she'd landed in an aviary, trapped like a bird.

Mashing a mosquito that considered her arm to be a handy ledge, she stepped forward onto sandy ground. The sound of water slipping over rocks reached her ears as she strode forward through a swampy preserve. Ducks held a quacking competition that increased in volume as she passed by. She spied a yellow-crowned night heron beside a cluster of spiky sawgrass. Other birds sat with their beaks tucked into their feathers like silent guards, watchful and wary. Brightly colored creatures flashed overhead among tree branches that veiled them from clear view. Ahead on her path, a dirt-covered turtle lumbered across the sand as though its life were a burden too heavy to bear. Or maybe she was projecting her own feelings onto her cell mate. Crossing a slippery wooden bridge, she cursed when something splattered onto her hair. Dammit, just what she needed: bird poop on her head.

There had to be a way out of this place. *Schmuck. You shouldn't have left your cell phone in the car. You could have called for help.* Ma would worry when she didn't arrive for dinner, but that might be too late. With no way to summon friends, she'd have to escape on her own. *If only I'd brought a pair of wire cutters!* she thought, mentally reviewing the contents of her purse. Nothing useful in there. Quickening her pace, she decided to prowl the edge of the screening. Maybe she could pry a section loose from the ground.

Brushing through a clump of bamboo creaking in the breeze, she encountered a cobweb that imparted a sticky residue on her skin. With a cry of disgust, she scraped it off. *Never mind; just hurry.* Twigs and other debris stuck to her sweater, while her neck dripped rivulets of sweat. Ducking her head, she aimed for a clearing beyond a cluster of tall green fronds with jagged edges. A branch caught her hair, tearing at its roots. Tears wet her lashes as she yanked herself free, leaving behind a few strands as she sprang forward.

Crouching at the perimeter, she used a stick to clear away a mound of yellow feathers at a point where the mesh wire didn't quite seem to touch the ground. Sure enough, a small gap was just large enough to slide her hand underneath.

Retreating, she cried out when the protruding wire gashed her wrist. Blood welled while she fumbled awkwardly in her purse for some tissues. She didn't have time to apply pressure. Giving up the effort, she grabbed a rock and began digging. Time flew by while she labored, her breath coming in short bursts, perspiration dripping down her face and blinding her eyes. In desperation, she held the rock in both hands and banged at the screen. Her heart leapt in joy when it bent outward. Between pounding and digging, she finally created a hole big enough to slip through. She barely scraped past the barrier, ignoring abrasions on her skin and broken fingernails.

Exhausted, she lay prone on the other side, mindless of the insects crawling inches from her nose. *Get out of here,* an inner voice prodded. Her muscles quivered, resisting her mental order. She felt as if all the adrenaline had drained from her body. *They could still find you. Move!*

Gritting her teeth, she forced herself to her feet. Her vision narrowed, and her head swam dizzily. Hunger pangs struck, nauseating in their intensity. All that effort had required extra fuel. She lifted her purse from the ground and rummaged a shaky hand inside. A moment later, she'd stuffed a Lifesaver into her dry mouth. Those things had a literal meaning, she thought wryly as she headed for the entrance.

Hoping her car would still be where she'd left it, she limped down the dirt road. She hadn't gone far when a human cry of outrage reached her ears.

They must've discovered her absence. Fear gave her the impetus she needed to charge ahead until her Toyota came into view. Refuge, at last. She dove inside, slamming down the locks before sticking the key in the ignition.

Trembling from head to foot, she didn't allow herself the luxury of rest. Her pursuers might come after her. She drove off without another minute's hesitation.

Taking her cell phone from its charger, she dialed her mother's house. Her hand shook so badly, it took her several tries to punch the numbers. "Hi, Ma. I'm running late, but I'm on my way. Don't get upset when you see me. I can explain."

Right. How will I tell her why I'm bleeding, covered in dirt, and stink like an unkempt zoo?

After she got cleaned up, she'd be able to think more clearly. A calm, orderly dinner would be balm for her wounds.

Or not.

"What in heaven's name happened to you?" Anita demanded upon opening her front door.

"I'll tell you as soon as I get washed." Utterly fatigued, she dragged herself across the threshold.

"Use my bathroom. I'll get you some clean clothes."

"Something that fits, I hope," Marla muttered, watching her mother's petite figure disappear down the hall. Stopping in the kitchen to get a glass of water, she paused when she heard voices coming from the living room. Oh no! She'd forgotten Ma had invited Roger and Barry for Shabbat dinner.

Her attempt to slink by them unnoticed failed. "Good God, woman, were you in an accident? You're a wreck," Roger stated bluntly, shoving his large bulk from a chair. Marla noticed he'd been enjoying the appetizers. Only one cracker remained on the chopped-liver platter, and the herring dish was empty.

Barry jumped to his feet. "Can I help? Do you need to lie down?" His ocean blue eyes reflected astonishment mixed with concern.

"I'll be fine once I wash away this filth. Go ahead and start the meal without me," she urged her mother when Anita returned with a towel and washcloth.

"I hung your suit in the bathroom. You gave it to me for our Hadassah chapter rummage sale, but I'm sure you can squeeze one more use out of it. You can't go to services wearing pants."

Her scowl of disapproval got on Marla's nerves. "I would have gone home and changed if I hadn't gotten locked in that aviary. There's probably bird glop in my hair. I'm lucky I got out, or I would have ended up as feed for their next meal."

"What aviary?" Anita asked with a worried frown. "I hope another killer wasn't chasing after you again."

"Again?" Barry queried, raising an eyebrow.

"It's a long story." Marla trudged toward the lavatory, looking forward to a quick shower. As she soaked away her fears along with the grime, she said a silent prayer of thanks for her narrow escape.

"Your mother says you need to settle down," Roger said when Marla joined them at the dining table. "She's told us all about your encounters with criminals. It's her opinion that if you had a husband, you wouldn't go chasing around town looking for excitement. You'd find it home in bed." He guffawed loudly, patting his belly.

Her scornful gaze swept over the paper napkin

he'd tucked into the collar of his blue shirt under a lemon yellow sport coat. The latter looked about to burst its button over his girth. *You'd think his son would have told him to wear something other than dark green pants with that yellow shirt,* she thought with an inner shudder. His colorful outfits reminded her of the parakeets in the aviary.

"My mother thinks she knows what's best for me, but she isn't always right." Unable to suppress her hunger, Marla helped herself to a few slices of roasted chicken, a heaping spoonful of kasha varnishkes, some tzimmes, and green beans with pimento. Breaking off a piece of challah, she said a quick *Hamotzi* prayer followed by the Kiddush for her kosher wine.

"So tell us why you showed up looking like a *schlepper,*" Barry said, his eyes twinkling.

"Ma already told you," she answered blithely. "I'm tracking another criminal, maybe more than one. They caught me snooping, but I got free."

"Aren't you concerned about the danger?" His handsome face sobered. "If they know who you are, they could come after you again. Shouldn't you let the police handle things?"

"My neighbor Goat is missing." She regarded him beyond the burning Shabbat candles. "The detective believes Goat may have murdered a man found in his house. I think Goat was a witness and is hiding from the real killers."

"So why is it your responsibility?"

"It's not; I just want to help a friend."

If that ranch hand, Jimbo, described her to Evan or Cutter, she could become their next target. That is, if she wasn't already singled out by virtue of being a former member of Cutter's class.

As Ma would say, *az me shloft mit hint shtait men oif mit flai*. If you lie down with the dogs, you get up with the fleas.

It was a chance she was willing to take.

Chapter Seven

"**D**o you see any possibilities with Barry?" Tally asked Marla after they were seated at Legal Sea Foods in the Oasis at Sawgrass Mills. There had been a short wait for a table, unlike the crowds at the Cheesecake Factory or Wolfgang Puck. Saturday night was bound to be busy anywhere in Broward, but with the cinema here, shoppers competed with moviegoers for restaurant tables.

"I like him. He's good-looking, quiet in a dependable sort of way, and sincere. It's his father who I can't stand."

"That your mom's problem."

"Roger does seem devoted to her. I wonder what would happen if I fixed Ma up with someone else?"

Tally laughed. "That would be a switch!"

"I know Ma approves of Barry. Here I thought she had begun to accept Dalton. I guess deep down she still wants me to marry a nice Jewish boy." Her ex-spouse, Stan, didn't count. While he qualified by being Jewish and a lawyer, he wasn't nice in any sense of the word.

"Barry is an optometrist, and he's never been married. That makes him a good catch," Tally said, tucking a stray blond hair into her French twist.

"Whose side are you on?"

Tally tilted her head. She looked svelte in an ankle-length flowered dress with a cranberry sweater tied stylishly around her neck. "Well, you told me you were mad at Dalton because he's too strict with Brianna, and he wouldn't listen to your advice. Children won't be an issue if you go out with Barry."

Marla shifted in her seat, tugging at her long black skirt. It had felt oddly comfortable to sit next to Barry at services last night, chanting hymns and reciting verses in unison. His broad-shouldered figure beside hers seemed to belong there. He'd looked debonair in a navy sport coat that brought out the deep hue of his eyes, and often she caught him glancing at her. His interest made her feel softly feminine.

Or maybe she'd just been grateful to the Almighty for sparing her harm, and her sensitivities were on overdrive.

"Let's change the subject," she said to Tally. "I went to the Sunrise Academy of Beauty to look up those names Giorgio had given me." She paused to sip from her glass of chilled chardonnay. "Remember how he mentioned Louise Cunningham was a hit-and-run victim? Another stylist drowned last month. Her name was Eileen McFee. They were both in my class taught by Cutter Corrigan."

"Interesting." Tally watched her expectantly.

"Yani Verkovich was Cutter's client. Yani's body was found in Goat's house, and Goat is missing. Along with his pet snake, I might add." She shut her eyes, remembering the snakes at Evan Fargutt's ranch. It might be wise to take Spooks out on his leash for the next few days, rather than let him run loose in her fenced backyard.

"Are you okay?"

She snapped her eyes open at her friend's solicitous tone. "I'm not done. I decided to ask Cutter about my classmates, but he was just leaving when I reached his salon. I followed him to a ranch owned by his cousin, Evan. From what I could gather, Evan breeds exotic birds. He probably sells them to pet stores or local tourist attractions. Evan was arguing with some guy named Wake Hollander about a delayed shipment."

"So he imports specimens as well."

"Yeah, and I don't think they're all legal, either."

Their soup arrived, and they paused to dig in. "What does Evan's business have to do with Cutter?" Tally continued between spoonsful of clam chowder.

"I have no idea, but they mentioned Yani's name and some friend they were tracking. I wonder if they meant Goat."

"If so, that means they don't know where he is."

Marla waved her fork. "I'll bet he's afraid of them, and that's why he's hiding. Goat didn't kill Yani, but he knows who did."

"Cutter or his cousin? Or are you being blinded by your friendship for Goat, as Vail believes? Maybe Goat murdered Yani, and that's why Cutter and Evan are after him."

Marla shook her head. "Goat wouldn't harm anyone." Her gut feeling might be irrational, but she'd learned to listen to it.

Tally leveled her gaze on Marla. "You said Goat looked up information on Martha Matilda Harper. Tell me more about her."

Marla leaned forward, warming to the subject. "I wrote a paper about her for a college history class, so I can tell you more than you want to know. Harper started out in Canada as a servant in the late 1800s. She worked as a housekeeper for a doctor who taught her about hair growth. He shared his secret formula for a hair tonic. When she moved to Rochester, New York, she worked for a childless couple who encouraged her to produce the tonic in their toolshed."

"Is that all? What made her so special?"

"Her enterprising spirit." Marla wagged a finger. "In those days, hairdressers attended clients in their homes. Harper saw this as another form of servitude, so she opened her own salon. It wasn't easy finding a location. She approached a landlord who believed cosmetics were inappropriate for ladies. He was afraid her shop would attract undesirables. She had to get a lawyer in order to rent a room."

"How did she get customers?"

Marla grinned. "Next door was a music teacher. While the mothers waited for their kids, Harper offered her salon as a waiting room. The women were impressed by the professionalism of her staff. Harper promoted healthful hair treatments instead of styling and products like we do today. She cared more about her customers' well-being than about how they looked. In her view, beauty came from good health, not from services that enhanced your image from the outside."

Tally's eyes twinkled. "Is that why your new shampoo girl gives clients such a good scalp massage?"

She nodded. "People want to relax when they come into a salon. Massaging the scalp helps to relieve tension."

"So Harper was your model for customer service."

"That's not all. She helped women open their own salons and provided training. By expanding her range, she began the first business franchise system in the country. Harper ended up with over five hundred salons worldwide. We owe her bigtime."

Marla leaned back while the waitress delivered their entrees. She ate several bites of grilled salmon before resuming her train of thought. "I'm not clear about how any of this relates to what's going on at Evan's ranch. Or why Goat needed those articles about Harper's followers."

"You said two stylists from your class were dead, and you were attacked."

"It may be coincidental, or not. I'll talk to my classmates who still live around here. They may know more."

Sunday afternoon, Marla found two of the stylists at home, neither of whom remembered much about their school. Not yet discouraged, she tracked down Tina Yarborough at the chain salon franchise where she worked.

"I really like it here," Tina said, brushing cut

hairs off her chair. "The benefits are good, and I can just go home and relax. I don't want the responsibility of my own place. We get a brisk business, especially on weekends." The salon was open seven days a week.

Tina still maintained a petite figure, Marla noted enviously, glancing at the younger girl's miniskirt and open-necked blouse. She switched her attention to the modular units. This type of cookie-cutter design plan didn't appeal to her. A hair salon should reflect the personality of its owner. "I have a place in Palm Haven," she said. "You should come visit sometime. Remember our instructor, Mr. Corrigan? He has a fabulous place on Las Olas."

"I don't like Cutter. I saw him at a show and said hello, but he ignored me." Tina tossed back a strand of bleached blond hair that framed her face in a pixie cut.

"You ever hear any dirt on him?"

"Not really, why?"

"A couple of gals from our class had fatal accidents within the last few months, and I was attacked the other day. The incidents might be unrelated, but I'm still worried."

Tina's mouth dropped open. "Like, you think there's a Jack the Clipper doing in hairstylists?"

"I don't know. I wanted to touch base with the people in our class, see if everyone's okay."

"So why are you asking about Cutter?" Tina popped a piece of gum into her mouth.

"He taught our group, that's all. A few people from our class have dropped out of sight." She mentioned their names.

"Man, I haven't kept track of anyone. How about that bunch you used to hang out with? You were a tight group. I'm surprised you didn't keep in touch."

Marla shrugged. "Everyone went their separate ways."

"Go see Darcy King. She's working at some little place in Lauderhill on University Drive. It's next to a Mongolian barbecue restaurant. I'll bet she can give you the scoop."

A smile lifted Marla's lips. "You're right; Darcy always kept on top of things. Thanks for your help."

She found the salon where Darcy worked without much trouble, but it was closed until Tuesday. Recalling her other urgent business, she spent the rest of the afternoon driving to toy stores looking for wooden chess sets. None of the pieces she saw matched the one Spooks had destroyed. Neither did hobby shops nor department stores possess the item she sought. Maybe she could find it in a gift catalog at home.

Speaking of gifts, she still had to get Brianna something special for her thirteenth birthday, so she ended up at Macy's jewelry sale. After purchasing a sterling silver and marcasite bracelet, she wandered toward the clothing section. By the time she exited the Fashion Mall, her stomach was growling for dinner.

That's the trouble with you, Marla. You get distracted too easily. How would she locate Goat if she spent her time shopping? Putting the bags in her Toyota, she remembered Brianna's plea to come along. Guilt pulled her heartstrings. Just because she was mad at Vail didn't mean she should ignore his daughter. The girl needed her advice.

Upon calling Vail's house, she heard Carmen's voice answer. "This is Marla. Is Brianna home?"

"Sorry, she is over a friend's house. You want to speak to Senor Vail?"

"No thanks. Could you leave Brie a message for me? I'd promised to take her shopping, and we should go before her party next week. Please have her call me."

"*Sí.*"

"You'll write her a note?"

"I tell her before I leave. She'll be home soon."

"Please don't forget. It's important." A glimmer of an idea had hit, and she couldn't wait to share it with the soon-to-be teen. Vail didn't have to know what she had planned.

Tuesday rolled around fast, but unfortunately Marla wasn't able to get away from work to track down Darcy. She mentioned her research to Giorgio while waiting for her customer's perm to set.

"I looked up the girl who drowned last month. She was in my class at Sunrise Academy of Beauty. So was Louise Cunningham, who you'd mentioned was killed in that hit-and-run accident. Then I was attacked in my neighborhood. Your warning hit home."

The handsome Italian thrust a hand over his heart. "Were you hurt?"

"No, just scared. But I'm beginning to wonder if it's coincidence or not."

His dark eyes studied her. "Have you found your missing friend?"

"Not yet, but I'm following some clues."

He wagged a finger at her. "You should take a vacation, leave town. This is not a safe place for you. Leave the police work to your boyfriend."

Nicole edged into their conversation. "Yeah,

how is the hunk? I haven't seen him around lately. He usually pretends he's passing by and stops in."

"Huh! I'm sure he's too busy."

"Come on, I thought you'd be over your argument by now."

Joanne, the new shampoo assistant, saved Marla from having to answer by calling for her to come over. As Marla responded to her summons, she thought how lucky she'd been when the girl and her sister had walked in for interviews. They'd fit the bill perfectly for what she had been looking for in replacement staff members. She nodded at Jennifer, a small-framed blond stylist, on her way to the rear. After answering Joanne's question about which conditioner to use on a client, Marla returned to her station. She finished her last customer at five-thirty, then tore out of the salon.

Darcy was just getting ready to depart when Marla arrived at her beauty parlor. "Marla Shore, what are you doing here?" she called in an overly loud voice. A dyed blonde with a frumpy figure, Darcy looked as though she had gained considerable weight in the interim since beauty school. She wore a bright red turban, flowing caftan, and frayed sandals.

"You look great," Marla lied, thinking she appeared more like a fortune-teller than a hairdresser. "How's it going? I'm looking up members of our class. You weren't updated on the roster, but Tina knew where to find you."

"Tina's a pip. I run into her at Sally's Beauty Supply all the time."

"Can I buy you a cup of coffee? I need some information, and I was hoping you could help." Darcy had been the class yenta, and Marla didn't think the woman would pass up a chance to gossip.

"You don't mind if we get something to eat, do you? I'm absolutely starved."

If a free meal would loosen her tongue, so be it. After they were seated in a deli at Lincoln Park West, Marla stated her case. "Two girls from our class are dead," she began, forced to pause while Darcy ordered a bowl of beef barley soup, salad, and a roast turkey platter. *Don't forget dessert.* Hopefully, she had enough cash to pay for this unexpected repast.

"I read the news," Darcy snapped.

At least Marla didn't have to give her the details. "I'm wondering if these accidents were related. Have you kept in touch with anyone from school?"

"Only Harriet and Julie."

Marla couldn't suppress her disappointment. "How about Cutter?"

Darcy slurped her Miller Lite. "What about him?"

"Heard anything about who he's hanging with these days?"

The woman grimaced. "How should I know? Probably some cute guy."

"I figured he's gay."

"No kidding. I could tell when he hit on Wyeth."

"Oh my, I'd forgotten about him. He's not on the roster." Grabbing her purse, she withdrew the sheet of paper Virginia had provided. How peculiar. She scanned the chart but didn't see Wyeth listed. "What was his last name?" Maybe a typo accounted for the omission.

"Wyeth Holmes. How can you forget after what your gang did to him?"

Marla stared at her. "You know about that?"

"He whined about it for days. I'd be worried if I were you. Maybe he's out for revenge."

"After so many years? Give me a break."

Their conversation left her with a sinking feeling. Perhaps there was more to Darcy's theory than she'd thought. The so-called gang was her group of friends in class. They'd eaten lunch together, endured the lectures, shared the same lab assignment, and performed a prank that had slipped her memory until now. Eliminating the rest of her classmates, that presented two more names to check. Five of them had completed the circle: Marla, Lori Webber, Kenya Dobson, Louise Cunningham, and Eileen Joyce McFee. The latter two were dead. How could that incident have eluded her memory?

Lori Webber Snow and her husband were out of town on vacation when Marla called later in the week, using the roster from the beauty school. Lori's mother answered; she was baby-sitting for their kids. Marla left a brief message and promised to call back the following week. She had better luck when she looked up Kenya Dobson. Kenya worked at a salon in Lauderdale Lakes.

Marla drove over during a break on Friday when a client scheduled for a highlights canceled. She caught Kenya teasing a woman's hair into a beehive style. Her critical eye scanned rows of domed hair dryers opposite shampoo sinks that belonged in antiquity. The clientele, mostly white-haired, suited the old-fashioned environment. "Can I have a few minutes of your time when you're through?" she asked after they greeted each other. Kenya still appeared youthful, her rich mahogany skin stretched smooth over a face contoured with high cheekbones and full wine-glossed lips. She moved with the grace of a jungle cat, her royal blue smock covering a pair of tight black jeans.

"I don't think anyone knows what happened to Wyeth," Kenya said after her customer departed. Marla stood by while the stylist cleaned her counter. "Maybe his hair never grew back."

Flushing hotly, Marla regarded her. "He'd achieved a short fuzz by the time we graduated. We all thought the stuff worked, but it wasn't a miracle like we'd expected."

Kenya gave her a frank stare. "We were dumb to try it on him. New drugs are usually tested on animals first."

"The formula wasn't new, nor was it a drug." Kenya's words nagged at something in her memory that troubled her, but it wasn't as bad as the disgraceful reminder of what they'd done.

During her research for the paper on Martha Matilda Harper, Marla had unearthed a diary written by a chemist from Harper Laboratories in Rochester, New York. The man, John Kagan, mentioned a nourishing tonic that rejuvenated hair. Presumably this was the formula Harper had acquired from the doctor whose household she'd served.

Kagan opened his own lab and continued to refine the tonic. He'd actually created a compound to grow new hair, but the formula was flawed. His diary contained the mixture of components. He'd died before he could complete his work.

As a prank, Marla and her classmates had prepared the solution and applied it to Wyeth during a session on hair coloring. They figured it should make his hair grow thicker. It didn't work that way. Wyeth Holmes, who prided himself on his virile looks, went bald. The formula caused hair loss, not growth. At least on a first trial, that's what happened.

Had Wyeth's hair grown in after that episode? She hadn't seen him since graduation, when a short fuzz covered his head. Maybe the formula was effective, but it needed to be applied on a regular basis. Or maybe that's all the hair growth it produced. Considering that Wyeth's baldness was due to their intervention, would the compound work with age-related hair loss? If someone in her group had developed it in that regard, the tonic might have become extremely valuable.

Her thoughts returned to Cutter Corrigan. As their instructor, he'd had access to everyone's notes. What if this was something he had decided to pursue? Holy highlights, what an idea! But it didn't explain how Goat was involved, why Yani was killed, or if the deaths of the two stylists were related.

She presented her theory to Kenya, who appeared to regard the whole notion with mirth. "Better watch your back, girlfriend," Kenya said, chuckling. "Wyeth's ghost is coming back after all these years to haunt us."

"You may not be far from the truth. Why is his name gone from the class roster, and where is he now?"

"Find your missing friend, and you might find him."

Marla shook her head. "I have the feeling everything is connected, but I don't understand how. Maybe Detective Vail has more information."

She'd probe him for answers tomorrow at Brianna's party. In the meantime, finding a new chess piece became her priority. Otherwise, she'd be in more hot water. Having a possible killer after her was bad enough; having Vail as an enemy would be worse.

Chapter Eight

Marla was nearly late for Brianna's party. She arrived at Dave and Buster's at ten minutes past seven, rushing into the dinner theater where several tables were reserved. Vail's daughter, surrounded by friends, looked grown-up in a black sheath dress. Her dark brown hair curled softly onto her bared shoulders. Spotting Marla, she smiled, giving a thumbs-up signal.

Dalton wore a flustered air as she approached. "It's about time," he told her. "I was hoping you weren't going to abandon me to this troop of teenagers. What am I supposed to do now?"

"You could try to relax and enjoy yourself." He looked spiffy in a polo shirt and Dockers, she thought. He must've taken pains to blow-dry his hair, because the texture was soft and fluffy. *His part could be a tad straighter, though.*

"You took Brie shopping today," he said after she'd put down her gift-wrapped packages. She didn't miss his accusatory tone.

"She picked out that dress, along with some other necessities. Didn't Brianna give you the charge slips?"

His mouth tightened. "I'll need to limit her spending. I didn't expect to get a bill for over a hundred dollars."

Marla grinned. "Things are expensive, and teenagers like to go shopping. Get used to it."

"You did something to her hair."

"We stopped off at the salon. Her ends needed trimming, and I curled her hair a bit. Those waves give her a softer look, don't you think?"

His gaze narrowed. "Brie's eyebrows look different."

"They're just more defined." *My, aren't we observant.*

Vail leaned inward, lowering his voice. "Her legs are smooth, and I forbade her to shave."

She gave a smug smile. "Well, after I shaped her eyebrows, we used some depilatory cream on her legs. You might consider buying your daughter an electric razor." She paused. "I'm only saving you from later grief. If you don't allow her some freedom, she'll rebel, and then you'll lose her altogether. Have you noticed her makeup? It emphasizes her eyes and cheekbones."

He raised his hands as though in supplication. "She's only thirteen; she doesn't need makeup. It'll clog her pores."

"Gads, are you old-fashioned. What time does the show start?" she asked, to distract him.

"Eight o'clock."

Let's lighten things up here. She sashayed closer, giving him a coy glance. "I'd rather have a private show, just for the two of us. It's been a while."

"So it has." He placed his large hands on her hips, drawing her against his hard form.

Marla wiggled her body, eliciting a groan from his lips. He kissed her with a brief, crushing press of his mouth on hers. Through her skirt, she became aware of just how powerfully her presence affected him. It was as though the antagonism between them had never existed.

He introduced her to Brianna's friends. It wasn't lost on her that Brie had no other relatives present. Vail had been an only child, and both sets of grandparents lived out of state. Marla gave the girl an effusive hug, glad she'd made Brianna feel better about herself.

Dinner and the mystery play that followed kept them entertained for several hours. When the kids were about to disperse to play video games, Marla suggested Brianna open her gifts. Brianna's expression vacillated. Clearly she wanted to run off with her friends but wasn't sure of the proper protocol.

"I'll keep a list," Marla said, grabbing a notepad and pen from her purse. "I'm sure your pals would like to see what you got. Read me off the names on each card."

When Brianna reached for Vail's chess set, Marla clenched her teeth. If this worked, Vail wouldn't notice the mangled knight. She watched the girl rip the foil paper she'd carefully wrapped. Brianna's face cracked into false delight when she spied the wooden box.

"It's a chess set," Vail explained. "Your mom and I bought it on a trip to Europe. I thought you'd like to have it."

"Daddy, it's wonderful." Brianna slid open one of the drawers containing the carved pieces.

"Wait." Marla snatched the box from her grasp and closed it. "If you don't mind, I'd like to take this home. These pieces are so beautiful, but they need a decent matched board. I'll get you one, honey. Here, open my package next." She thrust the gift into Brianna's hands. Not once did she glance in Vail's direction, afraid he'd be glaring at her suspiciously. She focused on her notepad, pretending to be scribbling madly.

"Marla, I love it!" Brianna exclaimed happily, holding up the sterling silver and marcasite bracelet.

"Let's put her loot in your car," Marla said to Vail after the teens collected tokens and ran off to play games.

Outdoors, she detoured to her Camry to stick the chess set inside before accompanying the detective to his vehicle. "Any leads on Goat?" she asked in a casual tone.

"We have a few trails we're following," he commented, his eyes gleaming darkly under the glow of a street lamp.

"I'll tell you what I know if you'll share your findings."

He pulled her into his embrace. "Do we have to talk? The kids are occupied. I can think of better things for us to do." Kissing her soundly, he made her resolve melt away. Almost.

"Dalton, I'm worried about Goat." Stepping away, she regarded him seriously. "I fear he's mixed up in things beyond his control."

"You don't say. Dare I ask what you've found out?" His face, half shadowed, appeared all stark angles and craggy prominences.

She shook her head, tendrils of hair escaping to caress her cheeks. "You first."

A muscle moved in his jaw. "Very well. Yani Verkovich worked as a biochemist at Stockhart Industries. Familiar name?"

Her mouth dropped open. The very place where her friend Jillian held a position, and where they'd had dire dealings before. Wait a minute. The dead man had worked in a laboratory? Cutter and Evan had spoken about a lab at the ranch.

"Go on," she said encouragingly.

"He was a spokesman for the citrus canker eradication program."

"That doesn't have anything to do with hair products."

Vail peered at her curiously. "Why should it?"

"Can we go back inside? We should keep an eye on the kids." After they found a quiet spot where they could watch the teens, Marla spoke in a low tone. "Did you check out Cutter Corrigan? He has a cousin named Evan Fargutt who owns a bird-breeding ranch in Davie. Evan deals with a man, Wake Hollander, in a manner that may not be quite legal. Maybe Goat got wise to their scheme and they tried to off him, but they got Yani instead."

Marla didn't believe her theory even as she said it. Too many loose ends still flapped in the wind.

Vail didn't buy her story, either. "What does your neighbor or Verkovich have to do with Cutter's cousin and this man Hollander? And how do you know they might be doing something illegal?" Settling back in his chair, he crossed his legs. "I'm anxious to hear how you came by this information. It's sure to be an amusing story."

"Another time. Just consider extending your investigation to Evan. His place has a Web site: wild bird ranch dot com."

"Hmm."

"I'll call Goat's sister again to see if she's heard from him."

"The gal who lives in Mount Dora?"

"Right."

"I already spoke to her. She has no idea what happened to her brother."

"She's more likely to confide in another woman. I should take a drive up to see her. Wanna go for a ride? I'm off tomorrow."

"Can't. I have an obligation." He squared his shoulders. "Why don't you wait until I can go with you?"

"Go where?" Brianna's girlish voice said from behind.

Marla twisted her neck to face Brianna. "I was thinking of taking a ride to Mount Dora tomorrow. It's a neat place to visit for the shops and restaurants, if they're open on Sunday."

"Why don't I come? I'm caught up in my homework, and Dad will be gone all day. I don't want to stay home by myself."

Marla queried Vail. "What is this obligation you have that's so important? Can't you bring your daughter?"

A lock of black hair streaked with silver fell across his forehead as he shook his head. "I'm giving a crime-scene workshop at SleuthFest."

"What's that?"

"SleuthFest is a mystery writers' conference sponsored by the Florida chapter of MWA. They have it every year in March. This is the first time they've asked me to participate."

"It's an all-day affair?"

"My seminar is in the morning, but I've agreed

to stay until the concluding ceremony. They're judging an interactive murder game they've had running all weekend. I agreed to play the detective. Despite what she says, Brie has been wanting to stay home alone, so this is her chance."

"I'd be glad for the company on the road."

"You might run into Goat, and he could be dangerous."

"Don't be absurd. Goat needs our help. I'll call Jenny first to ask if she has any news." If Jenny had learned that her brother had gone to the beach house on Siesta Key, Marla would go there instead. But if Jenny was reluctant to talk, it would be best for Marla to confront her face-to-face.

"Marla, take me with you," Brianna pleaded when Vail left to round up the kids whose parents had arrived.

"I can't. You heard your father. He'd rather you stay home by yourself. Isn't there a friend you can ask to come over?"

"I'm not afraid to be alone, but it's boring." Her dark eyes misted. "I'd love to go to Mount Dora. We never go away on weekends. My life sucks."

Marla hugged her. "No it doesn't, honey. You just had a great party, and your dad loves you."

"He loves his job more than me."

"That's not true, and you know it."

Brianna used an expletive that made Marla's face go white. "He treats me like a baby. Where does he ever take me besides G-rated movies? Daddy used to pay me more attention after Mom died, but now it's like I don't exist."

Her heart swelling, Marla patted the girl's shoulder. "Maybe he just doesn't know what to do with you since you've become such a lovely young lady."

"Since I grew tits, you mean."

Marla's hand dropped away. Clearly, the teen needed a guiding light. They should devise a plan together on how to approach Vail. He had to accept his daughter's transformation before his restrictions chased her away. She didn't dismiss his reasons for concern, but he went too far.

"Sorry, but we have to obey your dad's rules. Most of them, anyway. It's enough that we got you to the salon today."

Apparently, Brianna found a way to circumvent Vail's rules, because Marla got a phone call from her early Sunday morning. "Dad said I could go with you. I hoped to catch you before you left."

Marla, still in bed, glanced at the clock. "I was planning to leave at nine. Let me talk to your father."

"He's already left for the conference."

"Oh. Are you sure he said it was okay?"

"Uh-huh."

Stretching, Marla considered her plans. "I'll get dressed and then come by to pick you up. It'll take us a few hours to get to Mount Dora. After we talk to Goat's sister, we'll have lunch and go shopping. It should be fun."

But when Marla went to start the car, her battery was dead. She called Anita on her cell phone. "Sorry to wake you so early, but my car needs a new battery, and I don't think Sears is open yet. I planned to go to Mount Dora today."

Anita's sleepy voice answered, "Call Triple A and drive to Sears after they give you a jump-start. I'll pick you up there." She hesitated. "You can take my car today. I don't need it; Ruby is driving me to the Hadassah luncheon. I'll stop off at Sears later and get your car fixed."

"I'd appreciate that. Thanks." She hated to burden her mother, but days off were so rare that she had to make the best of them.

An hour and a half later she cruised in front of Vail's house, driving her mom's several-years-old Lexus sport utility vehicle. Brianna, alerted to their delay, ran out the front door.

"Jenny expects us," Marla said after they had turned north on the Florida turnpike. "I called her earlier." She paused, glancing at the silent teen beside her. "Maybe we'll find a game board in one of the gift shops today." Secretly, she hoped to find a carved wooden chess set with a piece that closely matched the mangled knight in Brianna's box. Mount Dora boasted some unusual boutiques with imported items.

"I hope your talk with that lady won't take too long."

"It's important that I find her brother." Speeding along at seventy miles an hour, she spared a glance at the girl. "Has your father mentioned any new developments in the case?" Maybe he'd revealed more to Brie than to her.

Brianna's ponytail swished as she turned her head. "He spoke to that hairdresser downtown."

"Oh, yeah?"

"Daddy said something about where Cutter met the victim."

"I thought Yani was Cutter's client."

"Right, but they'd met somewhere before. Dad was interested in looking up more of the dead man's contacts."

She hadn't realized Yani and Cutter had an earlier history. She'd assumed their relationship took off after Yani started coming to Heavenly Hair Salon as a customer.

"I understand how you want your father to spend more time with you at home, but he gets involved in solving his cases," she told the girl. "That's what makes him such a good detective. It doesn't take away from his love for you, though."

Their subsequent discussion ranged from Vail's work to his disciplinary practices to Brianna's concerns at school. Marla could tell the girl needed someone to confide in, and she was glad to have been chosen. Miles sped by as she offered her best advice. Funny, she'd never seen herself in this role. Listening to her customers was one thing; bearing up under teen angst was another. Despite Brianna's mood swings, wherein first she snapped irritatingly at Marla and the next she whined about not having the right socks, Marla felt strangely fulfilled.

"What do I do if I get my period in school?" Brianna asked.

Startled, Marla glanced at her. She'd just begun changing into the left lane to pass a slow car in front. "Be prepared. That was always my motto." She craned her neck to check her blind spot on the left even though she'd already scanned the mirrors. A white car shifted into the same lane, nearly on top of them!

Marla swerved to the right, but she swung too sharply. The Lexus veered straight for the shoulder. To correct the imbalance, she yanked the steering column to the left. Her heart raced when their car careened into the next lane at high speed. "Lord help us," she cried, fighting to regain control, but it felt like the SUV tilted off-balance. *I need to slow us down, but if I step on the brake, we might spin around to face oncoming traffic.*

Her grip slippery from sweat, she swung the steering wheel again in an attempt to straighten the wheels. Tires squealed as they sped toward the shoulder. Marla glimpsed what appeared to be a parallel flat stretch of grass. Maybe she could slow the car off the road, where they wouldn't crash into anyone else. Again, the car veered too sharply to the right.

Directly ahead of them, a white pole rose out of the ground. "Hold on!" she yelled. Her mind quickly calculated the odds of clearing the obstacle if she steered to the left. The wheels were already twisted to the right, so it made sense to go in that direction.

Fate no longer resided in her hands. Whatever was going to happen, would happen. There was nothing else she could do. Her heart pounding wildly, she felt an icy calm. This was it.

She twisted the wheel toward the right. They cleared the pole. Tapping the brake, she meant to reduce speed, but then the world tipped. She heard a scream. Hers? Brianna's?

Images collided in front of her. Thrust against the seat belt, her body seemed detached from her brain as she was tossed in different directions. It all happened so fast that her mind reeled. Something cracked the left side of her head.

In the next instant, the car halted, ignition still running. Sitting upright, she stared at the shattered windshield. *This didn't happen. It's a nightmare. I didn't crash the car.*

"Are you all right?" a small voice asked.

In slow motion, Marla turned her head. Miraculously, Brianna's side of the car seemed perfectly intact. The teen didn't have a single scratch and looked to be moving all body parts. Marla tested her limbs. "My head hit something," she said, exploring her left temple. "Otherwise, I'm okay. How about you?"

"I'm fine." Brianna's lower lip trembled.

Faces, two men and a woman, appeared at their windows. Brianna recoiled, but Marla realized they were Good Samaritans coming to help. She fumbled for the window controls and remembered to unlock the car doors.

"Ma'am, are you all right?" said the younger man when she'd rolled down their windows.

"You might want to turn off the engine," the woman added.

She twisted the key, but the ignition wouldn't shut off. "I don't know what's wrong," she said, frowning in puzzlement.

"Try putting the gearshift into park."

"Oh." She noticed the car had shifted into neutral on its own. No wonder she couldn't kill the engine. Her mind must be blurrier than she'd realized. She pushed the knob into PARK and turned the ignition key. The engine went silent. Her gaze took in the cracked windshield and crumpled frame. How amazing that neither of them had been cut by shards of glass.

"I can't believe this happened. It's my fault; I should have looked more carefully before changing lanes. I didn't see that car." She spoke aloud to no one in particular.

"At least you didn't hit anyone else," said the second man.

"Thank God." She pressed a shaking hand to her head in the spot where it throbbed. A goose-egg size lump met her touch.

"Did you know you rolled over?"

"What?"

"Your car went over, once or twice, I'm not sure. I was behind you, and I saw the whole thing. You flipped over down a ditch, hit a small tree, and that's what stopped you."

They must have crashed into it on her side, she realized, surveying the damage. Although the cabin was intact, her door was dented in, and the frame was mangled by her side of the windshield. Oh no. What would her mother say? How would she explain to Vail that his daughter had been in an accident?

"I called for help," said the second man on the scene, holding up a cell phone. "Do you want to go to the hospital?"

"I guess I should. I hit my head. It needs to get checked out." She knew enough about medical ailments to realize it could turn into something more than a bump, like an internal bleed. Marla shuddered, realizing less detectable injuries might be present. "Are you sure you're okay?" she asked Brianna anxiously.

When the girl nodded, Marla gave a silent prayer of thanks. It could have been worse. They'd landed upright. The cabin interior stayed intact. There had been no water in the ditch. Most importantly, they were alive and mobile.

It could have been much worse.

Chapter
Nine

Marla had enough presence of mind to remove her earrings and hand her purse to Brianna along with her cell phone. She still couldn't conceive of the fact that they had been in an accident, much less wrecked the car. Her mother would be glad they could walk and talk, but Vail would go through the roof when Brianna called him.

Let's hold on the walking part, she told herself when a wave of dizziness struck. With gratitude, she gave herself up to the ministrations of rescue personnel, who stopped her when she attempted to rise.

"Don't move, we'll get you out," said a uniformed medic. "You could end up being paralyzed if you've injured your spine."

Marla didn't think anything was wrong with her neck, because she'd twisted it to look at Brianna. Besides, the side of her head hurt, not her nape. Nonetheless, the possibility of paralysis loomed real enough that she obeyed the rescuer's commands. He fastened a collar around her neck and, with the help of another man, lifted her onto a stretcher. Under the open sky, she had her first look at the ditch they'd rolled down. She hadn't even seen it from the road. A red truck with flashing lights stood parked on the shoulder.

I was never unconscious. That's a good sign, she considered, reviewing her mental files on head injuries. On the other hand, her slightest movement made the world spin. She heard a medic questioning Brianna, who replied in a calm voice that she was unhurt.

"Your daughter can take whatever you want her to bring from the car. She'll ride in the truck with us."

Marla didn't correct his assumption. She felt a surge of pride for the way Brianna was handling the situation.

"Here's my business card," said one of the bystanders, "in case you need a witness." He handed it to Brianna.

Marla swallowed her thanks as the medics pushed her gurney up an incline. Images swirled as she bumped over mounds of grass. Closing her eyes against rising nausea, she kept them shut until they reached level road. Someone squeezed her hand. Cracking open her lids, she gave Brianna a wan smile.

While the girl headed for the passenger's seat up front, the two medics slid Marla's stretcher into the back of the rescue truck. One of them jumped in, fastened the door, and crouched beside her. He straightened her arm to check her blood pressure.

"I shouldn't have eaten so much for breakfast," she complained. "I can feel the food sitting in my stomach."

The mustached tech gave her a curious glance, as though he was assessing her cognitive abilities. "Don't worry; it's a short ride." He scribbled some notes on a chart, then covered her with a blanket. A stethoscope dangled around his neck.

"Have you got any ice?" she asked, touching the lump on her head. You'd think he would know to apply ice to an injury to reduce swelling. It might help stop any further bleeding, too.

"Sure," he agreed, offering her an ice bag.

She endured the ride in silence, stifling the queasiness in her stomach. This wasn't really happening, she said to herself for the umpteenth time. *How can we have been in an accident? I should've looked more carefully. I would have seen that car.*

They arrived at the hospital. In a blur of action, she was wheeled into the emergency room and brought to a stop in front of the nurse's station. After murmuring to the rescuers, a white-coated doctor hastened to her side.

"Hi, my name is Doctor Segal. I'm the emergency room physician. Does your neck hurt?" He probed around the stiff collar, examining her shoulders and neck.

"No, nothing hurts there. I hit the side of my head."

"Okay, we'll look at that in a minute." Very carefully, he removed the collar while observing her reaction. "How does this feel?"

"Better."

He tested her limbs, prodded her abdomen,

and evaluated her neurological signs. So far so good. But when he raised the head of the stretcher to a slight angle, dots swam before her eyes.

She shut her lids against the overwhelming dizziness. "I can't . . . I'm light-headed."

Supporting her shoulders, the doctor lowered her into a flat position. "I'm going to order an X ray." He walked away to confer with a handsome male nurse.

"Brie, are you here?"

"I'm sitting on a chair right behind you."

"You'd better call your father. He won't be so worried if he hears your voice. Use my cell phone."

"I have to go outside. There's a sign that you can't use cellular phones in here."

"Go ahead." Her eyelids sank shut. She felt shaky and cold, no doubt from the shock. Her body trembled like a seedling in a storm.

"Ma'am?"

She opened her eyes to see a police officer bending over her. "Yes?"

"I'm sorry to bother you, but if you feel all right, I have a few questions. Who is the owner of the car?"

"My mother. The registration is in her glove compartment."

"Do you have automobile insurance?"

"Yes, with Allstate. The card is in my wallet. My health insurance cards are in there, too. Brianna has my purse."

"She's your daughter? Was she injured?"

"No, she's not my daughter, and Brie says she's all right. I'm dating her father, Detective Dalton Vail with the Palm Haven police force."

His expression didn't change. Cool blue eyes

maintained their distance. "Can you describe the accident?"

Marla repeated the sequence of events. "I could swear I looked in the mirrors. That car wasn't there. I checked my blind spot when I started to change lanes, and I saw a white car nearly on top of us. I swerved to avoid it and couldn't regain control. It felt like my car was off-balance."

"Were you wearing seat belts?"

"Yes."

He thanked her and moved away to confer with the rescue personnel. Her ears picked up the words *phantom car* and *rollover*. She gritted her teeth, wondering how Brie was doing on the phone with her dad.

She watched the nurses bustling about the station until an orderly came to take her to the X-ray room. She submitted to the procedure, hoping the outcome would be favorable. Evidently she wasn't deemed to be in serious enough condition to occupy a cubicle, because after the test she resumed her previous position in the hallway. *I hope it's nothing more than a conk on the head,* she told herself. *If that's the case, we're very lucky. We could have been killed.* Her face blanched. She would have become the next hairstylist to meet with a fatal accident. Maybe it wasn't an accident after all.

"I spoke to Daddy," Brianna said, sidling up to her stretcher. The girl's face looked pinched. "He's on his way. The police officer talked to him."

"Oh joy." She anticipated his greeting with a flutter in her already queasy gut.

The doctor reappeared. "Your X ray is fine. You've had a mild concussion. You may have some residual dizziness or headaches, but I expect you'll be okay. You need to rest at home for the next week or so, and I'll prescribe some medicines."

Marla's heart sank. What would she tell her customers? How could she follow up on the trail with Goat? But then she rallied: Heck, she might not be able to raise her head, but she could talk with a clear mind. There was always the telephone until she got back on her feet.

Meanwhile, a more important urgency gripped her. How would she make it to the bathroom? Whenever she moved, her head spun and her stomach revolted. The nurse offered her two Antivert tablets so she could stabilize enough to stumble into the lavatory and do her business. When she was finished, she climbed gratefully back onto the stretcher and lay flat. She still wore the slacks and sweater she'd put on that morning. Slivers of glass stuck to the cashmere. *Brianna's clothes must be messed up, too,* she thought idly. That was the least of their concerns.

Vail's reaction was every bit as horrendous as she'd expected. He came charging into the emergency room looking like a bull in a fighting ring. When he spotted her supine position, his face crumbled. "Are you all right? Where's Brianna?"

"Right here." His daughter's eyes flashed defiance. "Don't be mad at Marla. I told her you gave me permission to come."

"What?" His expression darkened. "I'll have plenty of time later to deal with both of you. You could have been killed. What does the doctor say?"

"I have a mild concussion," Marla said, reassured by his presence but not his words about "later." "I should be okay in a week or two, not that I can afford the time off from work."

"I notified your mother. She's waiting to hear from me."

Marla turned her face away, a motion that she immediately regretted as she shut her eyes momentarily against the spinning images. "I wrecked her car."

"She doesn't care about the car. She's worried about you, and so am I. Brie, were you injured at all?"

Brianna shook her head, swishing her ponytail.

Marla gazed up at him. "She's been wonderful. You should be proud of how she's handled the whole thing." She noticed his black suit and smelled his spice cologne. "Did you finish your workshop at the conference?"

He nodded, his face somber. "Let me talk to the doctor. If he releases you, I'll take you home, but you can't stay alone. You'll have to come to my house or Anita's."

Marla didn't protest. She couldn't even get up, let alone care for herself. She'd never felt so helpless in her life. *You're alive, and you didn't break any bones. Be grateful. This, too, shall pass.*

Brianna held Marla's hand while her father pursued the physician. "I'll take of care you if you come to our house."

Her offer brought moisture to Marla's eyes. She squeezed the tears back, afraid that if she let one slip, a deluge would follow. "You go to school, and your Dad has to work. It'll be better for me to go to Ma's place. Someone will have to bring Spooks over." A stray thought surfaced. "Jenny is still expecting us. Can you call to let her know we're not coming?"

After Dalton and Brianna left to get the car, and

Marla was left alone, a flood of worries inundated her. She pushed them aside, wanting only to get better. Right now, she was in no position to deal with anything else.

Their ride home was an uncomfortable ordeal, with Marla reclining in the backseat and feeling queasy. When they arrived at her mother's house, Anita rushed out to greet them. Marla didn't hear the words she exchanged with Vail, but he ended up wheeling her inside using a desk chair. She couldn't stand without the floor rushing up to meet her on a collision course.

Reaching the guest bedroom, she rose to walk a few feet to the bed. That simple effort made the room spin crazily. She collapsed onto the twin bed and leaned over the side to vomit.

Under her mother's tender care, she managed to achieve a level of comfort. One day stretched into several more until she could finally walk upright again. A neurologist examined her, confirming her diagnosis and reassuring her that her symptoms would clear with time.

"This is my punishment for bringing Brianna against her father's wishes," she told her mother late Thursday afternoon. She'd taken the week off from work, hoping to resume her duties next Tuesday. Muscle spasms in her neck caused headaches that still debilitated her. "I should have verified with Vail that Brianna could go. I just took her word for it."

"You believed Brianna because you want her to like you," Anita said. "If you had been in another car, the accident might not have happened. SUVs are known for their instability. Newer models have things like traction and stability control." She arched her eyebrows. "I hope the insurance people will tell me my car is totaled, so I can get a new one. In the meantime, they're providing a rental."

"I'll pay for anything the insurance doesn't cover."

"You just worry about getting stronger."

"When I'm better, Dalton is going to be really angry."

Anita patted her arm. "If it helps, your detective wants to call the witness for a report. He said something about you being cut off by another car." She was interrupted by the doorbell. Jumping off the side of the bed where she'd been sitting, Anita fluffed her short white hair. "I'll just see who that is."

Marla wondered who could be dropping by. She'd already had visits by her salon staff, concerned friends and neighbors, and Vail, who'd come twice, along with Brianna. Anita, who hadn't met his daughter before, seemed charmed by the child.

"Hi ya, doll," said Roger from the bedroom doorway. His florid face broadened in a smile. Carrying an enormous arrangement of flowers, he entered without waiting for an invitation. "Barry is here, too. We've come to visit the invalid." He put the vase on her mother's vanity chest.

"Gee, thanks." Although her legs still felt wobbly, she'd showered that morning and pulled on a pair of slacks and a blouse. Her face had minimal makeup, but that mattered less to her now than it might have last week.

Barry followed his father into the room. He must have come from work, she surmised, because he wore a collared shirt and tie. "I was hoping to see you again, although not under these circumstances," he said, his blue eyes sweeping over her.

"Are you gonna be all right?" Roger asked. "Your mom is taking good care of you, but she's liable to wear herself down."

"I can stay by myself now. She doesn't have to baby-sit me. I even made it into the kitchen today to fix myself a sandwich." Yeah, and she'd been so winded, she had lain in bed ever since.

"Would you mind if I take Anita out to dinner? Barry will be happy to keep you company."

His son grinned, as though delighted by the prospect. She couldn't help smiling in response. It got boring lying here all day. Her head hurt enough that she couldn't watch television, and she couldn't concentrate to read. Although the doctor had given her muscle relaxants, she didn't like to take pills.

Barry hadn't entertained her for long before someone knocked at the door. It was Lieutenant Vail. His craggy face didn't look pleased when he entered her room. She hadn't heard their introductory remarks to each other in the hallway, but whatever Barry said must have disturbed Vail.

"I have news," he said curtly.

"Go ahead. Barry knows about the case involving Goat."

Vail cast him a dark look. "If you don't mind, I'd rather keep this private."

"Marla is still recovering," Barry said, unfazed. He leaned against the wall, hands in pockets. "She shouldn't hear anything upsetting."

"This is police business. I'll decide what she can hear."

Marla bit her lip to keep from smiling. "Barry,

I'd really like a cup of coffee," she told him pointedly.

"Oh. Well . . . whatever you wish." He darted a glance at Vail. *"K'nacker,"* he muttered on his way out. Marla heard banging pots and pans when he reached the kitchen.

Vail speared her with a suspicious glare. "What did he call me?"

A wise guy. "Nothing you need to know."

He squared his shoulders. "Barry calls himself your friend. Just how close are you?"

"He's Roger's son. I've seen him a few times, when Roger and Ma were together."

"What does he do?"

"Barry is an optometrist. What does it matter?"

Vail folded his arms across his chest. "It doesn't. I have no say over what you do, just as you have no say over how I raise my child." A pained expression came into his molten eyes, and he lowered his voice. "I had thought, though, since you and I became close, that you had a commitment to our relationship."

His words stirred her in places she'd rather ignore. "I'm not dating Barry. Anyway, I thought you were mad at me."

He kicked the door shut, came over to the bed, leaned over and kissed her. "We'll discuss my being mad another time. How's your head feel?"

"It still hurts."

"Dizziness?"

"Gone, but I'm weak when I walk around."

"That's from staying in bed too long. I picked up your Toyota from Sears. It's parked at your town house."

"Thanks. How is Spooks doing? Are he and Lucky okay together?"

"They're fast friends. Brie is getting a kick out of training your poodle to do some new tricks."

"I'm glad she's all right. Is that your news?"

"No. I spoke to the witness from your accident. He said that white car cut you off. It pulled into the lane just as you were switching."

"That doesn't prove anything. It was an accident."

"I'm not so sure. If you'd been killed, you would have been the third stylist from the Fort Lauderdale area to die within the past couple of months. Strikes me as an odd coincidence."

Wanting to chase away the memories, she closed her eyes. "Did you learn anything new from Cutter?"

"He told me his cousin Evan breeds birds and sells them to local pet stores and tourist attractions. He denies any partnership between the two of them. Nor does he acknowledge a relationship with the dead man except in a professional capacity."

"He's lying. One of the staff members told me they were close. That means either they had a gay relationship or they were scheming."

"I learned something else that's interesting. I asked Jill to sniff around at Stockhart Industries since she works there. She said Yani often consulted with another researcher, a Chinese man. I spoke to him. He acted nervous during our interview."

"So?"

"Many of the dog- and cat-fur items come from the Far East."

Her head throbbed from the effort of memory recall. "You still believe Goat was involved in a pet-fur caper? I don't believe he'd stand by while animals were hurt." Something niggled at her brain. "The director of my beauty school said she'd seen Cutter at a hair show with another male stylist. Remember Goat's interest in Martha Matilda Harper? I visited some of my school classmates. They reminded me of an episode where we played a prank on one of our own. It makes me wonder if someone from my class is working on a hair-growth formula."

Vail frowned. "Explain."

"You know how you've seen dead animals with patches of fur missing?" In addition to the skinned creature in Goat's backyard, he'd told her of finding a cat with part of its coat shorn. "What if it has nothing to do with shady products? What if it has everything to do with animal testing?" She sat up excitedly. "Cookie Calcone taught me about it when we were working on Jolene's case. The skin-irritancy test is often done as part of the approval process for cosmetics and household products. To test whether a substance irritates the skin, researchers shave sections of an animal's back. The test chemical is applied to the skin. They look for signs of redness, swelling, or blisters to determine toxicity."

"I don't get your point."

She leaned forward. "Rabbits are usually used for these tests, but what if someone is trying an experimental compound on dogs and cats?"

Vail rotated his shoulders. "Tell me more about this prank you played." His tone of voice told her he didn't believe it could be anything serious.

When Marla finished relating her tale, she regarded him curiously. "Wyeth Holmes was not listed on the class roster the director gave me. How do you think his name disappeared? Could he have anything to do with the attacks on myself and the other two hairdressers?"

"What would be his motive? You screwed with his hair years ago. But for all you know, it might have grown back after that episode. Or even if it didn't, why would Holmes wait until now if he held a grudge?"

"Good question. Or maybe Cutter is the guilty party. He could be working on the formula. If it's valuable, he wouldn't want anyone else to stake a claim. Suppose he did away with Wyeth before going after Louise and the rest of us."

Vail snorted. "If so, what does this have to do with Goat?"

"Goat must have found out something significant, and that's why he was reading up on Harper. But I can't figure out the connections. How did Yani end up at Goat's house?"

"We're still missing a lot of pieces," Vail acknowledged. "I'll check on those two stylists who were killed in accidents. As soon as you're better, let's take that ride to visit Goat's sister. Your neighbor is the key to whatever is going on."

Chapter
Ten

"Don't think you're getting off the hook so easily," Vail said to Marla on the drive to Mount Dora. "You nearly got my daughter killed. I realize why you brought her along, but you have to understand something. Brie needs a parent more than a friend."

Marla compressed her lips. She'd had enough aggravation getting her life back to normal without having to deal with the guilt Vail's words brought. "I know I should have checked that you'd given her permission to come with me. If you can't accept my apology, then maybe you should turn around and take me home."

His brooding silence pierced her heart with fear. Although he'd been solicitous during her recovery, had she totally blown any chance for further intimacy between them? Then again, did she even want to get closer, knowing how pigheaded he was about his daughter? But maybe, as a father, he truly knew what was best for his child.

He gave a long sigh, then cast her a look filled with regret. "I realize you meant well. You tend to be impulsive, and that brings to mind a question I've wanted to ask you. How did you know about Evan Fargutt?"

Marla swallowed. "I needed to talk to Cutter, but as I approached his salon, he was leaving. I followed him to Evan's ranch." Her glance caught the view in the side mirror. Orange groves stretched into the distance, rows of trees laden with small green fruits.

"So did you talk to him there?" Vail's steely gaze was fixed on the road.

Marla fortified herself with a deep breath. Confession time. "No. He was talking to his cousin and another man, Wake Hollander. I overheard Evan mention something about a shipment being delayed. Wake wasn't happy, said his boss Tiger would be upset. Evan offered several birds as an incentive for them to be patient."

Lines of concentration creased Vail's forehead. "What kind of shipment?"

Whew, Marla thought. *At least he isn't yelling at me for trespassing.* "Exotic birds? He breeds them, but maybe the ones he ships in are illegal varieties. Cutter didn't seem to approve of his cousin's activity. After the others left, Evan offered to show Cutter his progress in the lab."

"A lab on the ranch? Or related to Yani's work at Stockhart Industries?"

She raised an eyebrow. "I assumed he meant a place on the ranch. I went to look for it, but Jimbo got me." A shudder ran through her. "Don't worry, I escaped before Cutter or Evan learned I was there."

"Who's this Jimbo fellow?"

"One of the ranch hands." Her throat constricted. "If Cutter figured out it was me, do you suppose he could've been the one who ran us off the road?"

"Possibly."

She plowed on despite his disapproving scowl. "If the deaths of those other stylists are related, it's logical Cutter is responsible. But the only motive I can gather harkens back to that prank my classmates and I pulled. If Cutter is developing the hair-growth formula, that would explain Yani's involvement. Cutter doesn't have the scientific background."

"And what about Goat?"

"He could have been protecting the animals they used as test subjects."

Vail squinted. "How did Cutter and Yani become associated with Goat?"

"Hopefully his sister can tell us."

"I ran a background check. Kyle Stanislaw has a rap sheet. Mostly stuff like check forging and conning old ladies out of their money."

"No!"

He gave a wry smile. "Your neighbor isn't the innocent lamb he appears to be."

"Maybe so, but he's not a murderer."

"We'll see."

She resisted the urge to swat his smug smile away. "Jenny mentioned something about Goat having a problem with one of our neighbors. Do you know more about it? You spoke to everyone in the neighborhood."

"Most of them think Goat is a crackpot. Hector was the only one who sounded less than amused. I thought he might be holding something back by the way he kept scratching his jaw during our interview."

She chortled triumphantly. "You see? Something must have happened between them."

"If Jenny says her brother might be on Siesta Key, what do you want to do?" He glanced at the dashboard clock. "It'll be lunchtime when we arrive in Mount Dora. Visiting Jenny might take more than an hour. We wouldn't be able to swing over to the West Coast, then come home at a reasonable time."

"You said Brianna was sleeping over a friend's house tonight. She'll be in school tomorrow. I don't have to go into work, so there's no rush to return." Sundays and Mondays were her days off. "What do you have in mind?"

He kept his glance straight ahead. "We should stay overnight and drive to Siesta Key in the morning. There's another stop to make on the way home. Yani Verkovich's family owns a vineyard on Route Eighty. His uncle is the one who ID'ed the body. I have more questions to ask him."

"I didn't bring anything for an overnighter."

His grin made her heart flutter. "You can buy a toothbrush. You don't need any extra clothes."

Heat rose from her toes to her scalp. Despite their differences, he still wanted her. That knowledge imbued her whole body with a heightened sensitivity. Every movement he made for the rest of their trip made her squirm. Each glance he sent in her direction made her breath come short.

Stop it, she told herself. *You're here on a mission.* Yet if she could use this occasion to earn back his regard, she'd jump at the chance.

By the time they neared their destination, it

took every ounce of willpower not to touch him. She craved proof of his forgiveness, but he wasn't ready to give her that satisfaction. Instead, he teased her with studied glances at her figure and verbal innuendoes.

She straightened her blouse and slacks as they approached the town via State Road 46, an eighteen-mile stretch of road west of I-4. Plant nurseries yielded to miles of undeveloped land dotted with palms and pine. A "Bear Crossing" warning sign made her peer into the Seminole State Forest, but the trees were too thick for her to spot wildlife. Cow pastures, horse-rental stables, and lakeside vistas met her wistful gaze. She rarely encountered rural Florida and was appreciating what she'd missed.

Mount Dora delighted her as they cruised past residences dating back to the 1800s and entered a downtown area filled with enticing boutiques and restaurants. Mindful of Brianna's chess piece in her purse, Marla hoped they would have time for shopping.

"We're too early for our appointment," Vail remarked. "Let's find a place where we can eat."

She didn't feel like wasting time at a sit-down restaurant. "How about stopping at the Dickens-Reed Books and Café? We could probably grab a snack there, and it wouldn't hurt to ask around about Goat before we see Jenny. Someone in town might have spotted him."

"You're right." He drove through the streets searching for a parking place. Spaces were free, unlike metered Fort Lauderdale, Marla noted with approval.

"Look, there's Lake Dora," she said, pointing to a large expanse of water glistening in the sun. Its surface reflected live oak branches garnished with Spanish moss that gave the town a lazy, Southern ambiance. Alligators and raccoons inhabited Palm Island Park, an elevated boardwalk through an adjacent swamp replete with cattails wrapped with spider webs. Getting a glimpse of the brown murky water, she shuddered.

"I'll see if we can get a room at the Lakeside Inn," Vail said as they passed the hotel. "Pam always wanted to stay here. Friends told us about it."

She studied the yellow buildings with their verandas, paddle fans, and rockers but would never admit to Vail that the place looked inviting. "There's a railroad depot with train rides," she said to distract him from thoughts of his dead wife. "That white building with black shutters is on the National Register of Historic Places. It was built in Nineteen fifteen for the Atlantic Coast Line." Across the street was the Gables Restaurant and a row of shops. "This town would be fun for a couple of days."

"Uh-huh." He pulled into a free space and shut off the ignition.

She spared a moment to study him before they started on their way. Rarely did she see him out of his customary suit. He wore a plaid cotton shirt, long sleeves half rolled up his sinewy forearms, and hip-hugging blue jeans. His mouth curved as he caught her regarding him.

"Maybe we should check into the hotel and skip the interview," he suggested with a wink.

"Tempting, but not a good idea. Let's go." Moistening her lips that seemed too dry, she quickened her pace to keep up with his faster stride.

The bookstore café was located on Fifth Avenue in the heart of the downtown shopping district. Its cozy atmosphere included a mixture of old and new books with an area set aside for dining. Marla ordered a tuna salad with potato chips while Vail got a barbecued pork sandwich. Sitting across from him, she couldn't help her expression of distaste.

"What is it?" he said between greasy bites.

She swallowed a forkful of tuna. "I don't eat pork. It's not kosher."

His eyebrows lifted in surprise. "Since when do you follow the rules? I've seen you order shrimp at restaurants."

"I don't eat pig products. I grew up in a kosher home, and even though I don't keep kosher myself, I can't eat pork or ham." She hesitated, wrapping her hand around her mug of coffee. "I won't have them in my house, either. Would that be a problem, if you and I ever, you know, got together?"

"I suppose Brie and I could manage, if you're thinking about moving in, although I sure do like a juicy pork tenderloin. Pam used to cook—"

"Look, do you realize how it affects me whenever you mention her? This is not about your former marriage; it's about us."

His gaze chilled. "Pam will always be part of my life and Brianna's."

Marla's meal settled like lead into her stomach. "I know," she said quietly, "and it's right for you to honor her memory, but if you want to have a relationship with me, you have to stop comparing us."

"It's not an issue of comparison." He put his fork down.

"Well, I feel it is. Just as things get more serious between us, you mention her name more often. As for me moving in with you, your house is like a mausoleum. I don't think you've changed anything since she passed away. Could you accept it if I wanted to replace her antiques with more modern furniture, or store her collections? You need to clean out the cobwebs of the past before you're ready for the future, in my opinion."

Throwing his napkin on the table, he rose. "This conversation is getting nowhere. Let's go see Jenny."

Marla almost wished she hadn't come. Why did she always make things worse between them? Maybe Ma was right, and their differences were just too great for it to work.

They walked silently along Fifth Avenue, past the Princess Antique Mall and a stained-glass emporium. At the corner of Donnelly Street, she pushed the button for the crossing signal. The sound of birds chirping puzzled her until she realized it accompanied the green "Walk" sign. Traffic zoomed by, fumes mixing with the scent of gardenias in front of a restaurant.

"Wow, these are real hills," she remarked as her heartbeat increased with the incline. They turned left on North Baker Street and passed City Hall, a Mount Vernon-type white colonial structure. She watched her footing on the cracked sidewalk, grateful for the shade from leafy century trees, palms, and oaks dripping with moss. Her sense of peace broke with the hiss of a pressure cleaner from a man cleaning his car.

Finally on Tremaine Street, they found Jenny Stanislaw's address. The single-story house, painted sandy brown with dark green shutters, had a covered carport that led to a screened patio. Like the neatly manicured lawn landscaped with blue plumbago and ferns, the front door appeared well maintained, boasting a recent coat of varnish.

Jenny opened the door at their first ring as though she'd been waiting behind the vestibule. Marla grinned at the woman's prim appearance as she made introductions. The librarian looked the total opposite of her brother. Images of Goat's scraggly beard, wild outfits, and odd demeanor came to mind.

In contrast, Jenny wore her straight blond hair plunging down her back. Little makeup adorned her square-jawed face and Viking-blue eyes. Her basic black slacks and sweater indicated a life of practicality with few embellishments. She swept them inside to a living room decorated in generic contemporary style. Her furnishings reflected her personality even less than her clothes. Or maybe simplicity was her style.

"May I get you something to drink?" she asked in a tight voice.

"No thanks. We just ate lunch." Vail plopped himself down on the sofa, taking up half its width. Marla and Jenny chose armchairs. He pulled out a notepad and regarded their hostess. "I hope you don't mind that I came with Marla. I have some more questions to ask you."

"Go ahead, Lieutenant."

"Have you heard from your brother since I last spoke with you?"

Jenny clasped her hands in her lap. "I did get a call. Kyle was in a rush, and his voice sounded strained. He warned me not to talk to strangers."

Vail leaned forward. "Did he mention any names?" When Jenny shook her head, he posed another question. "Where was Kyle phoning from?"

"I heard music and background noise, like he was in a bar or restaurant."

"Do you have Caller ID?"

"Sorry."

"At least he's all right," Marla said reassuringly, "and he's worried about you. Has anyone other than Detective Vail contacted you about him?"

"Not so far. What else can you tell me? All I know is that Kyle was involved in a murder." She glanced at Vail. "You told me a man's body was found in his town house. Kyle may have witnessed the crime, in which case the bad guy might be after him. That could be why he's running scared. I don't believe he's guilty. Kyle has gotten in trouble before, but nothing so serious. He wouldn't hurt anyone."

Marla nodded. "I agree. I feel bad about not getting to know Goat—Kyle—better. I'd like to help him."

"Kyle means well; he's just keeps falling in with the wrong crowd. I suppose this is what happened again."

Glancing at Vail, Marla noted his impassive expression. Apparently, he was content to let her carry the ball. "Tell us about Kyle's background."

Jenny hung her head so that her hair fell like a veil, framing her face. "He loves animals, but I'm sure you already know that much about him. His big goal in life is to buy a farm up north, a place where his pets can roam free and where he can raise livestock. But getting the money for it is the problem."

"How so?" Vail queried while scribbling in his notebook.

"He wasn't able to finish college. I'm older than him, so I was out by the time Mom died. Dad had a heart attack two years earlier. We didn't have enough for my brother's tuition and other expenses, so he dropped out to get a job. I don't think Kyle would've stuck to his studies anyway. He always wanted the fast buck."

"What did he do then?" Marla asked gently.

"He got a job with a lawn service. That only lasted a few months, or until they got busted. Apparently, they were pulling bills from people's mailboxes, erasing who the payment went to, and making the checks out to themselves."

"You can do that?" Marla said, surprised.

Vail smirked. "It's a popular ploy. He also got in with a group who preyed on the elderly, didn't he?"

Jenny pursed her lips. "He's looking for quick money so he can follow his dream. I think he learned that landing in jail won't help him accomplish his goal. That's when he opened his pet-grooming business. It's legit, but he'll be working for a long time to build up his nest egg."

"Did he ever mention Yani Verkovich?" Marla ventured.

Jenny gave a pained glance at Vail. "That's the man found in his place, right? No, I don't recall him talking about the guy before."

"When was the last time, not counting this latest phone call, that you spoke to Kyle?" Vail said.

"A few weeks ago. Actually, he seemed somewhat excited. But I told you all this already, Lieutenant."

"What was he excited about?" Marla blurted. "Did he indicate he'd be getting a lot of money soon?"

Vail shot her a dark look, and Marla realized she should have left the question more open-ended. Too late. Oh well, he might have more practice interviewing people, but she knew how to encourage confidences.

"I didn't get any impression that Kyle expected to get rich. It was more like he was keeping a secret, you know?" Jenny replied. "He did say something about a payment, but not as though it were a good thing."

"Sometimes it helps to get secrets off your chest." Marla tilted her head expectantly. "If he couldn't tell his sister, who else would he share things with?"

Jenny clucked her tongue. "He took something from those other people he worked for. Something valuable. He did it to protect the animals, he said. Do you think they got mad enough to frame him for this murder?"

"Who else did he work for, ma'am?" said Vail. "I thought he just had the pet-grooming business."

"Why, I thought you knew he worked at that ranch part-time. He picked up extra cash to sock away in his bank account."

Marla's heart thudded faster. "A ranch, you say? With horses, or cattle?" Some cow pastures remained in Broward County, although not many.

Jenny's even features scrunched in a frown. "Now that you mention it, I asked him if it was a farm. Kyle said there weren't any big animals, just birds and snakes and such. I thought it sounded a bit peculiar, but he seemed happy to be working there."

Marla and Vail exchanged a glance. "Evan Fargutt," she muttered. "Goat worked at his ranch.

Evan and his cousin, Cutter, were mixed up in something involving Yani Verkovich."

"That's the connection you were looking for, isn't it?" Jenny asked Vail.

He rose to pace the room. "Your brother may have met Verkovich at the ranch. I'll check it out when I talk to Fargutt. If that's the case, and your brother took something belonging to them, it could be they were after him to return it. Something went wrong, and Verkovich got killed "

Marla stood, rocking on her heels. "The hair tonic. It could be that Cutter approached Yani to help refine the formula derived from my history-paper research. Let's assume they created a make-shift lab on Evan's property. Goat got wind of what they were doing while he worked there."

Vail regarded her steadily. "There's more to Verkovich's background that figures into this case. I'm hoping his uncle will shed more light on things."

She put her hands on her hips. "Don't tell me— you want to know about Yani's Chinese colleague because you're still fixated on that pet-fur trade idea. It's more likely Goat was protecting animals from skin tests conducted by the dead man in his attempt to develop the formula."

Jenny shot to her feet. "Are you saying Kyle killed a man to save a few pets?"

Marla hastily reassured her. "Not at all." She returned her attention to Vail, ignoring his waggling eyebrows meant to shut her up. "Here's something else to consider. When I was at Evan's place, I overheard the rancher talking to Wake Hollander about a shipment. They mentioned a person named Tiger.

Do you suppose this could be the Chinese associate? If so, perhaps we're dealing with a smuggling ring. They may be bringing in exotic animals, not pet-fur products. Goat spied on their activities, threatened to expose them. They meant to eliminate him, but they got Yani instead." She shook her head. "I'm so *farmisht* . . . confused. There are too many possibilities."

Shaking his head in resignation, Vail stuffed his notebook and pen into a pocket. "We still have a lot of angles to investigate. You've been very helpful," he said to Jenny. "At least now we have a possible connection between your brother and Yani Verkovich through the ranch owned by Evan Fargutt." He paused. "I'd still like to check out your place on Siesta Key. Your brother might be nearby, or someone may have spotted him."

"I'll give you my spare key, and you can mail it back. There's one more thing." Jenny stepped closer to Marla. "I'm thinking of cutting my hair. What style do you suggest?"

Chapter
Eleven

"What should we do now?" Marla said after they emerged from Jenny's house.

"I'll make a reservation at the Lakeside Inn. Why don't you go into the shops and ask if anyone has seen Kyle lately."

"I'm so used to calling him Goat. I think it's what he prefers."

"Whatever." Vail glanced away as though distracted. "I'll meet you later." Jangling his car keys in his pocket, he strode toward the center of downtown.

Marla hurried to catch him. "Are you sure we can't head to Siesta Key? It's only three o'clock."

"It's a long drive. I'd rather spend more time here, see what we can dig up. I'm not certain Miss Stanislaw was sharing all she knows."

"What do you mean?"

"Did you notice how she never looked me in the eye? I think she either knows where her brother is hiding, or she has a good idea."

"You may be right. I'll see what I can find out. Where shall I hook up with you?"

His flinty gaze met hers. "How about in the hotel lobby at five? We can cover more ground by splitting up."

Right. You can avoid talking to me about personal issues that way, too. "Okay. Until later, then." Clutching her purse, she veered toward the main shopping street. This would also give her the chance to look for a matching piece to Brianna's chess set.

She began at a corner shop that sold an eclectic assortment of gift items. Just inside the entrance, she stopped to admire a blue ceramic coffee jar, sets of brightly colored kitchen towels, and a rack of regional cookbooks. She reached out to pick one up when she stopped herself. *Schmuck, you don't have time for shopping.* Lenox collectibles, Peggy Karr glass plates, pewterware, and fancy stationery tempted her. Not a wooden chess set in sight, although she saw one with colored crystal pieces.

Scooping up the coffee jar that she just couldn't resist and a package of dish towels, she approached the counter. "Excuse me," she said, digging into her purse for her credit card.

A white-haired woman with a short, layered cut smiled at her. "Shall I ring these up?" she asked in a pleasantly modulated voice. Over her shirtwaist dress, she wore an apron that Marla noticed came from a selection on sale hanging on a set of hooks.

"Go ahead," Marla replied, reminding herself of her mission. "This is my first time in Mount Dora. It's a lovely town. I came to visit my friend, Jenny Stanislaw. Do you know her family?"

"Sorry." The saleslady shook her head. "I only

work here part-time, and I live across the lake. Don't know the folks from these parts. Besides, we get mostly tourists in the store."

Marla had similar encounters in the next few places: an art gallery, jewelry store, antique shop, and bakery. She tried another gift shop, with toys in the window, but they didn't have any chess sets in their inventory.

"You know where you could look, dearie?" warbled the cashier, an elderly woman with a round face and owlish eyes. "I've seen wooden ones in gift catalogs."

"Oh, yeah. I meant to sift through my pile, but I got too busy. I'll remember when I get home."

"Or try doing an online search. You can find anything on the Internet these days."

"You're right." If she had been thinking clearly, Marla thought, she might have accomplished this task already. "Do you know anyone I could ask about a friend of mine who lives here? I haven't been able to contact him. His name is Kyle Stanislaw."

"Go see Alma in the Gourmet Kitchen. She makes it her business to know everyone in town. Now, can I interest you in one of these brain teasers?"

Feeling guilty about asking questions without buying anything, Marla purchased a puzzle as a gift for Brianna and a Cameo Girl vase for herself. Her arms grew weary from carrying shopping bags after she added a few delicacies from the gourmet food store.

"I've known Jenny and her brother for years," said Alma, grinning at Marla from behind the cash register. "Just saw her in church this morning. Funny you should mention Kyle. He stopped in last week to stock up on his favorite jelly beans." She held up a cellophane package. "Kyle likes the Key lime-flavored ones. Wanna try some?"

"No, thanks." Her nose sniffed a strong aroma of coffee beans. She'd rather have a cup of java. "You say Kyle was here? Did he seem okay?"

Alma leaned forward. "The boy looked as though he'd stuck his finger in an electric socket. His hair was all askew, and his clothes, well, they needed a good cycle in the washing machine. Told me his sister would fix him up, and then he was heading out of town."

"Did you happen to see what kind of car he was driving?"

"How would I know? He used to drive a van. Maybe he left it parked at Jenny's house."

"What does she drive?" Marla asked, a glimmer of suspicion rising in her mind.

"She got herself a new Buick. Nice little white car."

"Did Kyle say where he was going after he saw his sister?" She almost mentioned Siesta Key, but held her tongue. Vail's interview techniques were rubbing off on her.

"Can't help you there. Something was troubling that boy, though. I hope Jenny was able to straighten him out."

"Thanks so much for the information. Goat— Kyle—is my friend. If he drops by again, please tell him Marla is looking for him."

Lugging shopping bags that seemed to grow heavier by the moment, Marla hightailed it back to Jenny's house. It took an effort to plaster a bright grin on her face when the woman opened the door.

"Hi. I'm sorry to bother you a second time," she said, breezing inside before Jenny could shut the door in her face. "I've been shopping, and I didn't want to stop in a restaurant. Would you mind very much if I use your bathroom? The one without Kyle's snake, of course." She held her breath, waiting to see if her bluff worked.

"Oh, I keep Junior on the patio. Can't abide the thing myself, and I wouldn't let Kyle put it in my new car." Jenny's face pinched as she glimpsed Marla's expression. "My heavens, you didn't know, did you?"

"I guessed. Your brother stopped off to leave Junior here, and you traded cars. Why didn't you tell the truth?"

Jenny gestured for Marla to follow her into the living room. "He's my brother, what else could I do?"

She took a seat on the couch. "I understand you want to protect him. So do I, especially if the people who killed Yani Verkovich are after Goat as well. We need to catch them to guarantee your brother's safety."

Jenny sank into the same armchair she'd occupied earlier. Her posture slumped, she regarded Marla with a morose expression. "I don't know where he is. He came by in a hurry, said he was in trouble, and dumped his snake here. We exchanged cars. He told me I had to keep his vehicle in the garage."

"He didn't bring his work van. By any chance, was he driving a dark Corolla?"

Jenny nodded. "How did you know?" Her gaze bespoke fear mixed with anxiety.

"One of the neighbors told me he saw that car

parked beside Goat's van in his driveway the same night as the murder." *Vail never told me the actual time of death or how the guy was killed,* she realized. *He will now, in exchange for the information I'm learning here.*

"I wondered where he got it, but I was afraid to ask. It's stolen, isn't it?"

"It's likely the Corolla belonged to Yani." *Another thing to ask Vail.* "The only person who can tell us what really happened that night is your brother. That's why it's imperative that we talk to him."

Jenny clasped her hands. "He asked me if anyone was using our place on Siesta Key. I assumed that was where he meant to go, but when I phoned there, no one answered."

"Maybe he didn't want anyone to know he was there," Marla said. "We'll check it out. Did he mention anything else about his associates at Evan's ranch?"

"Nope."

"How about suppliers for his pet-grooming business? Do you know where he buys his shampoos and such?"

Jenny's facial lines creased as she concentrated. "He gets them wholesale from a pet-store owner. Not one of the chains, like Pet Supermarket, but a privately owned place. I remember it's named after a book. Animal Kingdom? No, that's a Disney park."

"Does he keep an address book for his customers? He'd have to have notified them that he was out of town."

"I'm sure he canceled his appointments. Kyle seemed to be making a genuine effort to succeed at this business. If only he hadn't gotten involved with the wrong people again."

Marla shifted in her seat. One of her shopping bags toppled over, and as she bent to fix it, she noticed a ring glinting on Jenny's hand that hadn't been there before.

"Um, did your brother mention anything about receiving a large amount of money?" she asked. Goat may have dipped his hand in the pie before running away and shared it with his sister. Or maybe that hadn't been his first payoff.

Jenny's face flushed, and she averted her eyes. "He said he didn't get the windfall he'd expected, but he gave me some money to offset expenses for taking care of Junior. I got the impression Kyle had more than enough for his immediate needs, because for once, he didn't ask me to loan him any cash but instead gave me some."

"You told me on the telephone he'd had a run-in with one of his neighbors," Marla said, redirecting their conversation. "Who did you mean?"

Jenny pulled at a long strand of blond hair. "He had a disagreement with the Colombian man living next door. The guy complained that he had ants in his house. He said they were coming from Kyle's yard, but my brother wouldn't spray. He has too many pets to use insecticide. Well, one day Kyle comes home, and one of his cats is dead in the backyard. He sees granules on the lawn."

Marla leaned forward, aghast. "The neighbor killed the cat? You must mean Hector. I can't believe he would spread poison on someone else's grass."

"That man has a temper. He yelled at Kyle for

spreading ants through the neighborhood and boasted that he'd taken care of the problem."

"What did Goat do?"

"My brother isn't a violent sort, but he doesn't like being made a fool. He gave Hector another problem to worry about. It wasn't the smartest thing, considering the neighbor has small children. He dropped a few tarantulas into the guy's house through an open window."

"Bless my bones, I'm surprised I never heard about this."

"The outcome was that the neighbor promised to get back at Kyle. I doubt anyone would kill another person over a bug problem, though."

You'd be surprised, pal. "I appreciate your honesty. Do you mind if I share this information with Detective Vail? He may come across as harsh, but he's dedicated to learning the truth."

"I'm afraid for my brother. What he knows may get him murdered."

"If your brother is scared, we understand. But coming forward is the only way we can help him. Please tell him so if you speak to him again."

"Kyle mentioned your name, and he said you're in danger. From the context, I thought he meant you should watch out for your neighbor, but now I'm not so sure."

Thanks for the warning, Goat. You're a little late. "You've been very helpful, Jenny. Please contact me if you have anything to add." She rose and stretched. "I really would like to use your bathroom."

A few minutes later, she strolled toward downtown, shlepping her packages. With time left before her appointment to meet Vail, she wound through a series of eateries and stores. No new information came her way, but she found a great boutique where she lost thirty minutes along with two hundred fifty dollars for a red suede jacket, a matching purse, and a slipover black and silver velvety top by Rafaella.

"What a steal," she told Vail in the lobby of the Lakeside Inn. "The suede jackets in Macy's cost that much alone."

He gave her a wry glance. "You're a dangerous woman to leave to your own resources. Either you end up getting attacked by bad guys, or you take out your angst on the nearest credit card. I'd better watch my wallet."

"Very funny. Did you get our room keys? I'd like to put these packages upstairs."

"Sure. We have a lakefront view. I think you'll enjoy the accommodations."

It wasn't until he opened the door that she realized he'd used the plural pronoun. "Don't we . . . have separate rooms?" she asked, her tone a bit breathless.

Carrying her bundles in both arms, he shoved the door open with his hip. "I should have put these in the car," he muttered. "And, no, this was the only thing available. The Renninger Antique Fair is this weekend. Everything else is booked solid."

"Is this a good idea?" She tossed her purse on the queen-size bed and turned to face him. "I mean, things seem to be at odds between us right now. Maybe we should—"

"Maybe we should kiss and make up, at least for tonight."

His heated glance roused body parts traitorous

to her logic. "You want my body—and my brains, when it pertains to solving your cases. But when it comes to including me in household decisions, you shut me out. Why should I go to bed with you if you're unwilling to compromise?"

Stepping forward, he drew her close and gyrated his hips against her. "I might be persuaded to your viewpoint," he said, nuzzling her neck. He smelled like herbal shampoo and spice cologne.

Does it matter what happens tomorrow? Seize the moment! Are you going to deny yourself this luscious male because of the uncertainty of your future together? Lust has a place in life, too. Go for it.

Bolts of pleasure shot through her as she responded by rubbing her breasts against his chest. He groaned as his rising need became evident. A surge of female power emboldened her. Raising her arms, she rifled her fingers through his soft, thick hair. Reveling in its silky sensuality, she pulled down his head until his lips met hers.

Sorry, folks. Lights out. See you in the morning.

They got an early start the next day. Barely coherent until she'd downed two cups of coffee in the hotel dining room, Marla ate little from her dish of fresh fruit offered with their continental breakfast. Her mind reflected on their leisurely dinner at the Goblin Market last night followed by other activities that had kept them occupied into the late hours. If she contemplated moving into Vail's house, she'd have to get used to his presence. It was a distinctly attractive proposition. It felt good to be with him, a man who knew how to give pleasure as well as accept it. But there was no rush on things, not when they still had a lot of issues to work out.

"Where do we go from here?" Vail asked when they were in the car en route to Siesta Key.

"Keep heading west until we hit I-75," Marla said, relaxing in her seat for the long drive.

"That's not what I meant. What's going to happen between us?"

She glanced out the side window. "Last night was special, but that's not enough to build a relationship on. You won't listen to me regarding Brianna's restrictions, and you're still in love with your late wife. I wonder where I enter into your equation."

"I'll always love Pam, but that doesn't mean I don't have feelings for you. For example, people with kids don't focus their attention on just one child—they love each kid for their individual traits."

"Gee, thanks." She resisted the impulse to dig her fingernails into her palm. "If you really care, why don't you show it by listening to me? Brianna just wants to make herself more attractive. Grooming is a natural impulse for girls her age. Teenagers are group animals; they need to fit in. You can still have rules about curfews and such."

His lips thinned. "I'll think about it."

"There's more. If we agree to have a trial period together, how do we do *it* with Brianna around?" Her face flushed. "You and your wife must have had a method, but Stan and I never had that problem."

"There are ways." He flashed her a grin. "If you're using that as an excuse not to move in, it's a pretty feeble one."

"I might want to change how your place is decorated," she said, testing the waters. His furnishings reminded her of an antique barn. If she and Vail ever got hitched, she'd like to get rid of half the stuff but didn't know if he'd be able to part with anything of sentimental value. His loyalty to his dead wife was admirable, but she wanted proof that he was ready to move on.

That brought up another issue. Part of her wanted the warm security of his affection, but the other part craved independence. *What's for dinner tonight? When will you be home? Who are you talking to on the telephone?* Stan's insistent demands echoed in her mind. Moreover, he'd coaxed her to comply with his wishes with continuous put-downs. After the divorce, it had felt wonderful to make her own choices without fearing his disapproval. She didn't want to answer to anyone else now that she'd tasted freedom. But was it fair to ask Vail to compromise without making an effort herself?

"Do you really hate the things in my house?" Vail said after a long silence.

She gave him a sidelong glance. "It's not that I hate your stuff, but I prefer a different style. I like contemporary designs. No offense, but your place reminds me of a museum, with its heavy drapes and dark-wood pieces. My choice would be for lighter woods, simpler lines, and fabrics with brighter colors. Would it bother you if I brought in some of my own furniture?"

His expression brightened. "Not if it means you are seriously thinking about a permanent move."

"We'll see." She took a deep breath and let it out in a long sigh. Relationship talks were so difficult. "I hope this trip to Siesta Key is worthwhile. Jenny said her brother mentioned their place on the is-

land, so she figured he'd go there. He's not answering the phone, though."

Vail's face folded into a frown. "When did Jenny
say this?"

Her smug smile caught his notice. "When I went
back to talk to her after we split up. I'll share my
information, if you tell me how Yani Verkovich
died and when it happened."

"He was shot around eight-thirty that Friday
evening. Neighbors say they saw a black Corolla in
his driveway, and one of them heard a motorcycle.
The car belonged to Verkovich."

"I'll bet nobody traced the Corolla, and I know
where it is. It's parked in Jenny's garage." She told
him how Jenny had traded cars with her brother.

"Why the hell didn't you tell me this yesterday?"

"I'm sorry, but I was afraid it might ruin our
evening if we talked business."

"This is important information. You should
have mentioned it right away." Vail used his cell
phone to put out an alert for Jenny's white Buick
and to contact the police in Mount Dora.

"Will Jenny get in trouble for shielding a suspect?"

"I'm not going to make a case of it, but Yani's
car will have to be examined for evidence. What
else did you learn?"

"Goat had an argument with our neighbor,
Hector." She related what Jenny had told her about
their disagreement.

"A neighborly dispute over bugs has nothing to
do with Verkovich," Vail said thoughtfully.

"Jenny said Goat gets his supplies from a pet-
store owner. Have you checked into his business
practices?"

Vail nodded. "I didn't find his appointment book, but I tracked down his checking account. Got a bunch of deposits that I assume are from customers. Also checks made out on a regular basis to a place called Animal Farm. Maybe that's his supplier."

"You could look up those customers to call and ask if they've heard from Goat."

"I'm ahead of you. He canceled appointments, telling people he had to go out of town. No one has heard from him since."

Chapter
Twelve

Siesta Key turned out to be exactly what its name implied, a sleepy island just south of Sarasota, Florida. Veering off I-75 to head west for six miles, they crossed the north bridge onto the key and cruised south along Midnight Pass Road. Joggers trotted along a sidewalk bordered by tall shrubs. Marla wondered if they were year-round residents or snowbirds as she studied the facades of beach-front motels, pastel condos, and apartment rentals. White sand beckoned from the west, quartz crystals glittering in the midday sun.

Her stomach rumbling, she eyed Granny's Corner Café, which stood opposite Captain Curt's Crab & Oyster Bar. She didn't think Vail wanted to grab a bite to eat just yet. Like a bloodhound, his nose followed the scent of his quarry. He peered at the scrap of paper scribbled with Jenny's beach-house address, then refocused his attention forward. *So much for our romantic interlude.* Hunger wouldn't divert him, neither hunger for sex nor for food.

When on the trail, he concentrated on only one thing: tracking a potential witness.

In a peculiar sense, that reassured her. While they often had diverging viewpoints about suspects, Marla respected his dedication to learning the truth. If he'd become jaded about the justice system, it wasn't evident to her.

"Here it is," Vail said, pointing to a sign indicating Sara Sea Circle.

As they turned in, she scanned the curved driveway lined by single-story buildings in a tropical setting where lush foliage sucked moisture from the air. Coconut palms, spiky crotons, crimson and pink hibiscus, and banana plants shaded a maze of gravel paths through a central park. Tangerine-colored fish swam in a koi pond, part of a cascade of shaded natural pools below a trickling waterfall.

Vail parked in front of a lemon-painted duplex. A salty sea breeze ruffled the hairs on Marla's arms as she emerged from Vail's car. Grappling for her sunglasses, she snapped them on her nose before proceeding to the given address.

Knocking on the beach-house door and ringing the doorbell produced no response, so they tried the adjoining neighbor. Deadsville. The house must belong to snowbirds who'd already gone north.

"We'll check the exterior for signs of forced entry before I use the key Jenny gave us," Vail said. "I'd rather not have any unpleasant surprises waiting for us inside."

Marla swallowed, remembering the scene in Goat's town house. That memory encouraged her to let him go first. Their trek through the yard yielded nothing remarkable, except that she gained some sticky green things on her sandals.

"You go ahead," she told him when they returned to the front lawn. She waited until he called for her to enter.

Cushioned wicker furniture, potted silk plants, and Haitian paintings gave the house a completely different look than Jenny's place in Mount Dora. Marla's mouth dropped open in admiration. What a fantastic hideaway. A quick survey told her no one had brought any food into the kitchen recently, and the beds were neatly made. A stale, musty odor hung in the air. Tracking the hum of an air-conditioning unit, she found the thermostat. Jenny wouldn't mind if she turned it down a notch to prevent mold.

If Goat had been here, he was long gone, she concluded. *There goes our best lead, although this is exactly where his enemies would have looked for him, too, if they knew about it.*

"Let's go," Vail said. His voice held disappointment that didn't show on his stony face.

Marla gasped as they exited through the front door. She could have sworn she'd seen a hand on that Surinam cherry hedge, but the branches had fallen back into place. Was someone watching them? Her skin prickled with unease.

"I thought I saw something," she said to Vail. "Over there." Indeed, sandy footprints marked the ground behind the hedge. Squinting, she surveyed the path to the Sara Sea Inn. That wasn't the way to the oceanfront. The other direction, then.

"What is it?" Vail asked, his gaze boring into her. She craned her neck around to answer him. "I

saw a hand through those bushes, as though someone had pushed them aside to watch us. No nail
polish," she said irrelevantly. "Maybe I'm just imagining things."

"Maybe not." He gripped her arm for an instant, then let go. "We'll ask people if they've seen
Goat."

"Let's try the beach. If anyone was watching us,
they'll have sand on their shoes." She pointed to
the evidence.

"Good point. I knew there was a reason why I
brought you along." His mouth curved upward.
"We can work our way around to a restaurant. I'm
getting hungry."

She grinned. "That's why you're eager to move
on. Your nose sniffs a meal, not a suspect."

"Let's hope we find both." Taking her elbow, he
steered her toward the beach at the end of the
drive.

Waves crashed ashore, swirling onto white, pow-
dery sand before dissolving into foam. Marla
stopped for a moment to watch a pelican flap its
wings, soar into the sky, cruise into a graceful
glide, then dive into the water. The bird dipped its
head to pluck a hapless fish into its long beak.
After a hard swallow, the pelican floated with others of its kind before repeating the act.

Among a flock of seagulls on the sand stood a
lone white bird with yellow feet, a long neck, yellow-
ringed eyes, and a black short beak. As they approached, Marla shuffled away strands of dried
seaweed and white, tubelike debris that were underfoot. She could almost taste brine on her tongue.

"I don't see anyone who looks familiar," she said,
examining the sunbathers.

Vail's lips thinned. "I doubt anyone here has seen our friend. These are mostly tourists. It's possible he's staying nearby, though. The locals might know."

"Too bad most salons are closed on Mondays. That's the best place to pick up gossip. I would have talked to Jenny's hairdresser yesterday if it hadn't been Sunday."

"Let's get in the car and find a place to eat."

"Look, Bob's Boathouse has a crowded parking lot," Marla said a few minutes later as they drove along Old Stickney Point Road. "That's a sure sign of good food, but what a weird building." She stared at the structure shaped like a silver airplane hangar with portholes.

Inside, it was decorated like a boathouse with flags hanging from the high ceiling and even a yacht labeled *Megan and Michael.* A fireplace pit took up the center of the room. Loud rock music distracted attention from the decor: plaid carpets, square wooden tables with blue woven placemats, and a view of the water.

Seated by a hostess, Marla bristled when Vail ogled the brunette's cowgirl outfit. "My goodness, I didn't know you get turned on by jeans and belts that jingle. Maybe I should dress up in Western gear."

He turned the full force of his gaze on her. "Nifty idea. You'll try on different outfits, and we'll see what turns my hot switch."

"Why bother, you'd only want me to take them off."

Her throat suddenly dry, Marla ordered a bushwhacker while Vail settled for a bottle of Miller Lite. "What are you going to eat?" she asked him after perusing the menu.

His mouth curved in a suggestive smile that made heat rise to her face. "This potato-crusted grouper sounds good," he said with a wink. "It comes with a salad and herb bread. Why don't you order for me? I'm going into the men's rest room. Besides hair salons, lavatories are good places to pick up information."

That man always knows how to get to me, Marla thought, watching him stride away. Even the way he walked, with a determined swagger, made her breath come short. She distracted herself by reading a newsletter on the table called *Bob's Gazette.* She was impressed by the number of activities the restaurant sponsored: fund-raisers for charities, karaoke night, live reggae entertainment. *Take the elevator,* she read. *Come see our dine-in boats upstairs for parties of six or more.*

No, thanks. She had better things to do. She busied herself spreading smoked tomato and pepper jelly on a piece of crusty bread. Wondering what was taking Vail so long, she glanced in the direction of the rest rooms. No sign of him there, but from the corner of her eye, she spotted someone waving near the front entrance. Her heart lurched. The face looked like Goat's, but the hair didn't match. This man had long, black hair and a beard to match. A scraggly beard, though, no mistake, which, despite the color, could only belong to one person she knew: Goat. He was looking directly at her, signaling as though he wanted her attention.

She shot to her feet so fast that her chair tilted backward. Sparing a moment to upright it, she charged after him. A waitress holding a tray of plates blocked her path. As she sucked in her stomach to pass, she noticed a panicked look transform Goat's features.

"Wait," she yelled, seeing him turn away.

When she reached the entrance, he was gone.

"Where'd he go?" Vail said from behind her shoulder.

Ignoring him, Marla pushed past other customers to open the outside door. A motorcycle zoomed past, close on the heels of another vehicle. *Jenny's white Buick, by the looks of it.*

Vail cursed. "I'll go after them. You stay here and wait for me."

"Hell no." Marla ran after him, but she wasn't fast enough. He'd slammed the car door and squealed out of the parking space before she got near. Stomping her foot, she glared after him. "You arrogant toad. See if I share any information with you anymore."

Retreating inside, she picked at her meal while waiting for him to return. She'd sent his lunch back to the kitchen, urging the waitress to keep it warm. Meanwhile, she indulged herself in a hot fudge sundae. Nothing like a dose of chocolate to make you feel better.

"I was afraid you were going to stick me for the bill," Marla grumbled when Vail finally sank into the seat opposite her. "Did you get them? Where is Goat?"

His glum expression told her the answer. "Goat must know these streets backward and forward. He's probably tucked neatly away in his hideout, unless he left the island. That would be the logical thing to do, now that he's been spotted. As for your friend on the motorcycle, he got clean away after nearly sideswiping a couple of other cars. I stopped off to speak to the local authorities. They'll let me know if they locate either one. I've alerted them to keep a watch on Jenny's place."

The waitress brought his meal, and he dug into his grouper with relish. The chase seemed to have increased his appetite rather than lessened it, Marla thought wryly. She remained silent, considering the lost possibilities. At least Goat appeared alive and well.

"Do you suppose Goat was watching the beach house?" she asked when Vail had taken his last bite. "He could have followed us from there. Unless he was lying on the beach. I wouldn't have recognized him with his dark hair."

"He wouldn't expose himself so readily, not with bad guys after him. I think you're right about the beach house. He probably picked us up there. Damn, if only we'd gotten to him first." His mouth tightened. "We'll talk to some more people, look around town, but then we have to move on. I still want to stop at that winery." He signaled to the waitress for the bill.

"Huh?" Marla gathered her purse, ready for a visit to the rest room herself.

"Orange Blossom Winery belongs to Yani Verkovich's uncle. We'll be passing by on the way home. I've already spoken to him. He's waiting for us to stop by this afternoon."

They picked up Route 80 heading east toward LaBelle just above Fort Myers. The rural road gave way to orange groves on either side as they proceeded inland. It wasn't long before they came upon the broad white structure with a wraparound porch that looked like an old Floridian-style house. A sign out front proclaimed this was the winery. They turned down a gravel drive and parked in the front.

Inside, a tall white-haired gent greeted them from behind the counter. He wore a friendly smile on a suntanned, lined face. His denim overalls and calloused hands indicated he didn't shy away from hard labor. "Yo, folks, welcome to the Orange Blossom Winery. We have samples here for y'all to taste, or you can look around." He gestured to shelves laden with wine bottles and related gift items.

Vail showed his identification. "I guess you don't remember me. I'm Detective Vail. This is my friend, Marla Shore."

"I'm Igor Verkovich," the man said to Marla. He came from behind the counter to shake their hands. "Sorry, Lieutenant, I should have recognized you. But when people are out of context, you know how it goes. I don't have the greatest memory."

"Thanks for seeing us," Vail said.

"No problem. Have you found my nephew's killer?"

"We're following some good leads. I have a few additional questions, if you don't mind."

"Shoot."

Vail glanced at Marla. "We understand Yani was friends with Cutter Corrigan. Do you know how they met?"

"That's the hairstylist fellow, right?" At Vail's nod, he continued. "Those two got right close, if you get my drift. Didn't seem like they'd ever see eye to eye, coming from opposite poles like they did."

Marla pretended to examine a bottle of grape-fruit wine while listening intently. This was Vail's ball game. She'd step in to play if intuition guided her to do so.

Vail hung his thumbs off his belt. "Cutter said Yani became his client, and that's when they first met each other."

"Not true. Come out here with me a moment. You'll understand better if I show you what we have." He shuffled to a rear exit, walking with a slight limp. Pushing open the screen door, he led them outside into the bright afternoon sunshine. Rows of orange trees stretched into the distance.

"I didn't realize your property extended so far back," Marla commented. "You actually grow your own fruit for the winery." She'd been at another Florida winery in St. Petersburg that had merely been a building selling fruit wines.

His face crinkled into a smile. "We grow about a dozen different types of trees. The usual citrus, plus coconut, lychee, and jackfruit varieties. Even so, my business barely puts a dent in the state's citrus industry."

"What was your nephew's share?" Vail inquired, shading his craggy face from the sun.

"Our daddies started up this place. They owned equal shares. When Uncle Regus died, Yani got his half."

"Who inherits from him?" Vail asked, although Marla suspected he knew the answer.

"My sons. Yani was an only child, and you know he favored other men." Igor gave an embarrassed cough. "My boys help me run the orchard. I do the wines, and they work the groves. We sell a good bit of our produce. That brings me back to where Yani met Cutter. They were at a public hearing for the citrus canker eradication program. My nephew is ... was a spokesman for the government. His lab is contracted for testing plant specimens. Cutter led the opposition, a group of homeowners who've filed lawsuits to stop the program."

Vail kicked up dust as he strode along a dirt path to examine a Valencia tree. Having shed most of the ripe fruit, it had sprouted blossoms that sweetened the air with a honeyed fragrance. "What's your take on the situation?"

"I'll support anything that will prevent the spread of disease," the senior Verkovich replied. "If it gets worse, canker will be disastrous for citrus growers. You're talking about a nine-billion-dollar industry. I don't want to lose my grove, but I'll do what's necessary."

"You're willing to see your trees destroyed?" Marla asked in surprise.

He chuckled. "Some of my pals are switching to freshwater-shrimp farming. We've had declining citrus prices for the last ten years. Between the loss of income and the tree diseases, many of us are thinking about changing crops. We're small potatoes compared to the big companies."

"Try tilapia," Marla murmured. "I can put you in touch with a tilapia fish farmer if you want to learn more about it." The way Reverend Jeremiah Dooley liked to lecture, he'd be happy to set Igor up in the business. Marla and Vail had toured his fish farm near Tarpon Springs not long ago.

"So your nephew favored cutting down people's backyard trees?" Vail asked, to verify the victim's position.

Igor jabbed a finger in the air. "He sure did.

That rule about cutting down healthy trees within nineteen hundred feet of infected ones may be unpopular, but it's effective."

"You may be right, but I don't agree with the government's tactics," Vail said. "I came home from work one day, and all my citrus trees were cut down. I couldn't go into the backyard for some time. It looked like a desert." Turning to Marla, he said, "Wouldn't you object if workers trespassed on your property, and destroyed your trees without permission?" Then to Igor, "If that wasn't bad enough, they trampled my grass and put toxic chemicals on the stumps."

"They're supposed to follow proper procedures," Igor countered. "Survey crews come out to inspect your lawn. They usually knock on your door or leave a notice. When they find a questionable tree, they paint a white mark on it. A pathology crew comes next to determine if the disease is present. If the trees are infected, the plant pathologist paints a red X on them. Then homeowners receive a final order before control crews return to remove the trees. You should have had plenty of warning."

"My trees were healthy. The tree that was infected was way down the end of the block. I know the signs: small, round lesions on the fruit, twigs, and leaves. The lesions are surrounded by an oily margin and a yellow ring. My trees didn't have any of those symptoms. Who decided it was necessary to cut down adjacent trees in the first place?" Vail queried.

"I reckon government studies were done."

"Oh yeah? What studies? Seems to me this is the basis for those lawsuits against the government. I can understand the need to remove diseased trees, but not healthy ones just because of some arbitrary decree made up years ago."

Igor hunched his shoulders. "There is no cure or other method of prevention."

"How about chemical sprays?"

"They'll kill surface bacteria, but they don't penetrate to the colonies. Removal and burning of infected and adjacent trees is the only effective means of control."

"What a shame," Marla said with a sad shake of her head. "It's similar to what happened to our coconut trees back in the seventies."

"If canker keeps going north," Igor told her, "scores of groves will be in danger of getting wiped out. The disease causes trees to weaken, lose their leaves, and drop fruit prematurely. The crop is no good."

"How does it spread?" she asked. "I've read that canker is a bacterial disease that thrives in warm, moist conditions. But how does it go from yard to yard?"

"The bacteria live in crevices in the bark." Igor's eyes glowed brightly. "Wind, rain, insects, birds, and people with contaminated clothing and tools can spread it across short distances. It crosses larger areas when infected plants, seedlings, and fruit are moved. That's why we have regulations about transporting citrus fruit out of state."

"How about the folks who come into my yard from a neighbor who's got a diseased tree?" Vail asked.

"Inspectors are supposed to disinfect themselves and their tools before moving on to the next property or even the next tree."

"But they don't always do it. I read in the newspaper that workers were videotaped walking from yard to yard, and they failed to spray disinfectant on their shoes."

Igor shrugged. "An isolated case."

Marla glanced at Vail, searching for a way to bring their conversation back to Cutter. The detective shot her a narrowed glance in return. Igor was more than willing to talk, just not on the subject they wanted. Time was a-wasting, and they needed answers.

"How did the disease get started?" she asked, unable to think of any direct questions regarding the murder.

"Canker has been around since Nineteen ten," Igor said, signaling for them to follow him back inside. "It's gone through several eradication programs, but it keeps popping up. Nearly two million trees statewide have been destroyed so far. We have to stop it now, but your average homeowner won't cooperate."

"If you're the homeowner, your fruit trees mean a lot to you," Vail stated.

"That's a selfish attitude. You're risking the livelihood of Florida for a few backyard trees. You're not seeing the whole picture."

"All I see is my property being destroyed without regard to my rights as a citizen," Vail retorted, squaring his shoulders. "I can see why Cutter would oppose your nephew."

Marla gave a sigh of relief when they entered the air-conditioned shop. Feeling hot and sweaty, she propped herself directly under a vent to get a cool blast. Vail needed to keep his cool, too, she realized. Or was he being purposefully contentious to provoke Igor?

"Yani understood the need to protect our industry," Igor said, standing rigidly behind the counter as though it were a barrier separating opposing sides of the issue. "What's a few orange trees compared to a business that provides nearly ninety thousand jobs? People like you just don't understand the stakes involved."

"Maybe your nephew was merely trying to protect his interest in this grove," Vail suggested, a sly gleam in his eye. "No wonder he didn't want canker to progress north. It might wipe out his extra source of income if you lost your trees."

"He had bigger concerns at heart. That's why I can't fathom how Yani and that hairdresser ever got together in a personal way. Cutter led the homeowners' lawsuits against the state. His actions blocked the work crews from doing their job. He didn't realize the damage he caused to the industry. To Florida's welfare. Yani was only trying to preserve our state's valuable citrus groves."

"How far did Cutter go in his efforts?"

Igor leaned forward, elbows on the counter. "My nephew was murdered, Lieutenant. You figure it out."

Chapter Thirteen

"So Igor believes Cutter killed his nephew," Marla said to Vail during the drive home.

The detective raised his bushy eyebrows. "The first time I interviewed him, Igor said things hadn't been going well between Cutter and Yani. He didn't supply details, because Yani hadn't said much about it."

"It could've had nothing to do with the citrus canker issue." She shifted restlessly in her seat. Her leg was cramping from sitting too long.

"It could have had everything to do with Goat interfering in their relationship," Vail offered.

"You always come back to Goat. Did you ever find the murder weapon?"

"Not yet."

"Maybe you should broaden your search. I still think my classmates are involved. Things might not be as simple as they seem."

"We'll see." He cast her a sidelong glance. "Do me a favor, and refrain from doing anything stupid on your own to get information. This is my case, and when I need your help, I'll ask for it. I don't want you to put yourself at risk again."

Like I'm going to listen, pal. You should know me by now. She wouldn't be dumb enough to return to the ranch alone, but another interview with Cutter was in order. He couldn't do anything bad to her if she showed up at his salon.

Her efforts to carry on the investigation during the rest of the week were frustrated by an overloaded work schedule and personal business. Tally wanted to meet her for dinner; Nicole invited her to a barbecue at her boyfriend's house; and Anita reminded her of family obligations.

"Don't forget the Passover seder is next Thursday at Cynthia's house," Ma said during a telephone conversation. "What are you bringing? I think we're having about thirty people."

"I'm making the Haroset and hard-boiled eggs. What about you?" Marla said, sitting at home in her kitchen.

"I'm cooking brisket and farfel. Have you gone shopping yet? I could give you a box of matzos."

"I've been too busy to do anything." She'd barely had time to catch her breath since returning from the trip with Vail on Monday.

Anita clucked her tongue. "You never told me the results of your excursion with the detective."

"We found the murdered man's car. Goat had driven it to his sister's house in Mount Dora. Jenny told us about Goat's argument with Hector, one of our other neighbors, but it doesn't seem important. The next morning, we drove to Siesta Key. We were eating lunch in a restaurant, and I noticed Goat waving from the entrance. He appeared to be trying to catch my attention. All of a sudden, he looked scared, and then he took off. Vail chased him. Another guy was on Goat's tail, presumably whoever had spooked him. Poor man. All he wants is a farm up north, but he keeps following the wrong path to get money."

"Those wrong means could get him killed, and you too. If you ask me, you should focus your mind on something else, such as a good man. Did you sleep with the detective?"

"What?"

"You heard me."

"That's none of your business."

"It is if you're going to lead Barry on. Roger will be upset if you ditch his son. Choose one or the other, but make up your mind."

"Thanks for the advice. I'll see you next week. Bye." Clenching her teeth, she hung up.

The prospect of seeing her relatives on Passover did little to lighten her mood. When Friday evening arrived, she hadn't heard from either of her two beaux. She'd declined her mother's offer to attend services, unable to tolerate Roger's obnoxious presence. Briefly, she toyed with the idea of phoning Vail to see if he were free, but decided it was better to cool things off between them for a while. She missed Brianna, though. It was odd how they'd started off with such a stormy liaison, and now she felt more warmth from the daughter than from the father. *The sturdiest relationships often start on rocky ground and build onto a solid foundation,* Anita had once told her.

So you're right about one thing, Ma.

Brie was busy this weekend anyway. She'd been invited to two bat mitzvahs and had called Marla to discuss appropriate gifts. Their conversation had gone on to include clothing options, makeup, and advice on dealing with school pressures.

Drifting into her office, Marla settled in for a night of paperwork. She should be glad to be alone for a change but felt strangely bereft. Focusing on her correspondence, she picked up a form for her favorite charity when an idea flashed through her mind. Here was the perfect excuse to visit Cutter Corrigan.

Cutter was cleaning his electric shaver when she walked into his salon late Saturday afternoon. Fortunately, she'd finished with her last client in enough time to dash to his place before it closed. Even luckier, she'd caught him between customers. Marla winked at Jax, busy with a blow-out, on her way to Cutter's chair.

Noticing her, Cutter scowled. "What are you doing here?"

She plastered a sweet smile on her face. "Hey, I thought you'd be happy to see me again. Don't look so sour. I'm here for good reason."

"I'll bet."

"I work for the Child Drowning Prevention Coalition. We're collecting items for a silent auction at our spring luncheon. Would you like to donate a gift certificate? It'll get your name in our program book as a contributor. Free publicity," she added as an incentive.

Putting down the razor, he gestured to her, an

evil grin on his face. "Come into the back with me. I'll write you a check for your organization."

"I'm not sure it's safe to be alone with you." She spoke in a teasing tone for the sake of his staff but noticed an answering gleam in Cutter's eyes. Jimbo must have told Evan and Cutter about the intruder on the ranch. Shortly after that incident came her car accident. Was one of them responsible?

"I heard you were in an auto accident," Cutter said as though reading her mind. "That's what happens to people who ask questions in the wrong places."

"A white car cut me off. You wouldn't happen to know who owns one, would you?"

He smirked. "A lot of people own white cars in Florida, but you didn't come here to ask me about that." Signaling to another stylist doing a layered cut, he shouted, "Bring it up another inch in the back, Heather. You'll give her more lift." His scornful glance snagged Marla. "These people know nothing when they come out of school. They must look to a masterful designer such as myself for guidance."

"But not for modesty," Marla murmured, half under her breath. Loudly, she said, "I hoped you could help me on another issue. I've had plant inspectors come out to my yard. They put a white mark on my orange trees. My neighbor Hector said he met you at a Department of Agriculture workshop where you represented homeowners' rights."

"That mark doesn't mean your trees will be cut down. A plant pathologist has to examine them first."

Marla sank into the unoccupied chair at the next station, amid pungent aromas from sprays and chemical solutions. Farther down the room, a manicurist clipped her own fingernails with audible snaps. Whirring blow-dryers competed for noise with radio music and background chatter. *The sounds and scents of home,* she thought, intending to throw Cutter off guard before asking him more pointed questions.

"I thought they'd stopped cutting down healthy trees," she said, relieved when Cutter didn't insist on getting her alone. "Aren't things tied up in the court system?"

"It's an on-again, off-again situation," Cutter explained, giving her an assessing look.

"Tell me about it."

"Why do you care?"

"I don't want my trees cut down if I have any say in it."

A play of emotions crossed his face, as though he were debating how much to reveal about his involvement. "The problem is the nineteen-hundred-foot rule. The State Department of Agriculture can't justify destroying healthy trees just because they're within a certain radius of an infected one. They've never proven the science behind the ruling, nor have they done cost studies. Now they're repressing our rights further by issuing county-wide search warrants."

"How did that become an issue?"

"We filed suit in Broward Circuit Court challenging the right of workers to enter our properties without a search warrant. There's no justification; citrus canker doesn't threaten public health or welfare. Unfortunately, along with a bill that passed the legislature regarding the nineteen-hundred-foot rule, judges were authorized to issue blanket search warrants for an entire county. Now law officers and other authorities may be able to search places without getting a warrant for a specific address."

You'd be up a creek, pal. Vail would have a field day searching your property. "That violates our constitutional rights. How did this mess get started?"

He hunched his shoulders. "As I understand it, a group of scientists and citrus industry representatives got together and recommended the nineteen-hundred-foot destruction radius."

"So it was just an arbitrary decision to cut down all trees within that distance?"

"You got it. Through a series of court injunctions and appeals, we fought the state department over their right to cut down our healthy trees. The ball bounced back and forth between federal and state courts until an administrative judge found the directive for cutting down trees within the nineteen-hundred-foot radius to be too vague."

"I don't get it."

"The original rule called for the destruction of exposed trees that were likely to harbor bacteria because they were near infected plants." He snorted. "Imagine! They could declare the entire state of Florida to be exposed under that definition. Anyway, this hearing stopped the state from destroying more healthy trees. It meant the department had to hold public workshops in accordance with formal rule-making procedures. We took advantage by filing a formal legal challenge."

"So you halted the destruction."

He grimaced. "Are you kidding? To circumvent

the judge's ruling, the Agriculture Department issued an emergency order that all trees within nineteen hundred feet of infected ones would be cut down. Supposedly, once you file something like this, you can act on it immediately." He raked stiff fingers through his thin wheat-colored hair. "Those foxes used a phony agricultural emergency to get what they wanted."

"So did they get away with it?"

"Hell no," he retorted, pale blue eyes narrowing. "We filed a petition to challenge the order, saying it violated our constitutional rights. Look what happened to me: I wouldn't allow the workers on my property, and I got arrested. Half those guys don't even speak English. They invade our yards and destroy our trees without proper legal grounds. I'd had my citrus trees for years, and I grew attached to them like pets. I wasn't about to allow some goons who work for the state to destroy them. You know what you get for it? A one-hundred-dollar Wal-Mart garden voucher for the first tree destroyed and fifty-five dollars per tree thereafter. That doesn't compensate me for years of the best fruit you've ever tasted."

You value trees over animals? You don't seem to object to the experiments going on at your cousin's ranch, if that's what they are. "When people get sick, we don't kill them or others within sneezing distance," she said. "Healthy trees should be allowed to live, too. You'd think citrus growers would offer to compensate homeowners."

"They don't understand our viewpoint. All they think is, why should they let folks who own a few backyard trees threaten a multibillion-dollar industry? They may have gotten their law passed, but we aren't through yet. Our constitutional rights as citizens are being abused."

"So you've been active in organizing lawsuits against the state, and you've spoken at public workshops. Is that where you met Yani Verkovich?"

He scrutinized her expression, and she hoped her eagerness to hear his answer didn't show. "Yani was one of the scientists involved in the testing program for the Agriculture Department. They called on him as an expert witness to testify in favor of the nineteen-hundred-foot rule."

"How did you two grow so close if you started at opposite sides on an important issue?"

His eyebrows drew together. "I don't see how that's your concern."

"Yani's body was found at my neighbor Goat's town house."

"So?"

"Goat is missing. Maybe you know where he's hiding, or why he's running scared."

"Maybe you should leave."

"This appears to be a touchier issue for you than the citrus canker program."

"Get out, Marla." He took a few paces toward her.

She knew when her welcome had ended. Time for a tactic switch. Rising, she gave him a coy glance. "You can mail me your donation check if you still want to give a contribution to the Child Drowning Prevention Coalition. It'll help get your salon some favorable publicity. By the way, I stopped over at our beauty academy. They've expanded tremendously. You'd be impressed by the new programs, but perhaps you've already been by for a visit. Virginia, the director, said she'd seen you at a hair show with a companion: a Latino with dark hair. Anyone I know?"

Grasping her elbow, Cutter steered her toward the front door. "Asking questions about me, were you? Remember, curiosity killed the cat, or was it a dog? Better watch your pooch."

Her fingers curled. *Touch my dog and you're dead meat.* She kept her voice level. "I talked to some other girls in my class about a reunion. I was just trying to track down everyone on the roster. Unfortunately, a couple of gals had met with accidents lately."

"Like you when your car crashed," he sneered, pinching her nerve point.

Her arm ached, but she gritted her teeth. "Wyeth Holmes was not on the list. Would you know what happened to him?"

He stopped abruptly, letting go of her. "Why do you bring up his name?"

She shrugged. "We didn't part on the best of terms. Wyeth was mad at me and my friends for putting that solution on his head that made him go bald. He had a slight fuzz growing back when school finished. Did you ever find out if he regained his hair?"

Cutter's face dissolved into an angry scowl. "Old business is best left to rest, if you get my meaning. Otherwise, the past can come back to haunt you . . . or worse."

Was that a veiled warning? Marla pondered their conversation on her way back to the salon, where she wanted to make sure things were locked up. She didn't understand the vibes emanating from her former teacher. You'd think any threats would come from Cutter and his cousin, Evan

Fargutt. Was he hinting someone else menaced her? Surely not Goat.

Her brain addled with theories, she didn't at first notice the folded newspaper at her styling station. When she reached to pick up a stray comb, her glance fell on the highlighted article.

Lori Snow, a Palm Haven resident, was the apparent victim of a freak electrocution. The mother of two, a hairstylist just back from vacation, received a fatal shock when she plugged in her curling iron at work. A short in the system was blamed for the accident.

Blood rushed to Marla's face. Lori had been a member of her gang at beauty school. First Eileen McFee had drowned, then Louise Cunningham became a hit-and-run victim. Now she and Kenya Dobson were the only two left, not counting Wyeth.

Marla flew to the telephone. After looking up the number of Kenya's salon, she dialed, but no one answered. She must have finished work for the day, meaning she wouldn't be back until Tuesday. Darn! Rummaging under the counter, Marla scrounged for a directory and searched for Kenya's name in the white pages. She had to be warned, but against what and whom?

Unable to find a listing, she shut the book and put it away. Her sense of personal jeopardy heightened, she wondered what to do next. What she lacked was a connection between the different puzzle pieces: her colleagues being knocked off, Yani's death, Goat's involvement, and Cutter's scheme with his cousin.

Best to deal with those problems tomorrow.

Right now, she had to get ready for a barbecue at Eddie's house. Nicole's boyfriend liked to entertain, and he'd invited the salon staff to his place for ribs and chicken.

Nicole is lucky she found someone who likes to cook. Now if only Eddie would be as committed to their relationship as he was to the outdoor grill, Marla thought while securing the salon.

She tried to empty her mind of the day's events during her drive home, concentrating on what to wear for the evening. Her sense of caution made her glance into the rearview mirror more often, but nothing seemed out of the ordinary.

After taking Spooks out, she changed clothes and wrapped the barley and wild rice dish she'd promised to bring. Hopefully, tonight would provide more than a good meal in friendly company. Nicole was an avid mystery fan. Marla was hoping she'd offer some fresh insights on recent events regarding Goat and friends.

Seven o'clock found her knocking on Eddie's door in Davie, where he lived in a single-story ranch home. He greeted her with a friendly smile that seemed a permanent fixture on his face. Eddie had curly black hair, puppy-brown eyes, and a short mustache. His colorful island shirt hung loose on his tall frame over a pair of faded jean shorts. A strong whiff of Old Spice wafted her way, mingling with the mouth-watering aroma of sizzling beef ribs.

Outside on the patio, Nicole rushed to greet her. The cinnamon-skinned beauty wore a flattering sarong dress and had braided her raven hair down her back. "Marla, I was afraid you'd be late. Where did you run off to this afternoon?"

Marla smoothed her belted black slacks. The air felt cool, as a light breeze stole under her royal blue blazer. "I went to see Cutter. I'll tell you about it later," she said, spotting other staff members mingling with the couple's friends. "Did you by any chance leave a newspaper lying open on my station?"

"Not me." Nicole gave her a curious glance. "Why?"

"Because someone wanted me to see a particular article. If it wasn't you, who left it there?"

Nicole nodded at a passing acquaintance. "I don't know," she said to Marla. "What did it say?"

"Another stylist was killed, supposedly by accident. She's the third one in my group from beauty school. There are two of us left."

Her friend's eyes widened. "You said someone at Cut 'N Dye left this article for you to see?"

"It may have been a customer. Or maybe not. Anyone could have entered through that back door. I'm always forgetting to lock it during the day."

"I'd have spotted a strange face."

"Not if you were occupied."

Nicole gasped. "You don't think it's one of us? That new shampoo girl, Joanne, or her sister Jennifer? They've only been working with us a couple of weeks."

The new staffers had been invited to the party. Marla glanced in their direction, reluctant to believe someone from her salon could be involved in a conspiracy against her. *It happened before, remember? You can't trust anyone.* The women were flirting with two men not of Marla's acquaintance.

Maybe her rival, Carolyn Sutton, was trying to

scare her. *She* might have paid one of these gals to leave that news article on her chair.

Marla clenched her fists. She wouldn't put it past Carolyn to plant people to spy on her, but damned if she'd become paranoid. She trusted her own judgment to a good extent, and she liked the Cater sisters. They just couldn't mean her any harm.

Then again, another possibility entered her mind. Maybe the article had been left on her chair as a friendly warning, not as a threat. Could Goat be in the vicinity, keeping an eye on her? If so, she wished he would turn himself in. Surely Vail would find a way to protect him from the killer still on the loose.

When she had the opportunity, Marla brought Nicole up to speed on the case. She related her conversation with Cutter, her trip with Vail, and her growing fear that she might be a target for an unknown murderer.

"It's very strange," Nicole agreed as they sipped Bahama Mamas on the patio. "I don't understand how these events are connected. One thing I can tell you: your friend Goat probably has all the answers if you could only locate him."

"I'll bet he left Siesta Key after he was spotted. I have a feeling he's closer at hand. But why won't he reveal himself? Who or what does Goat fear?"

Chapter Fourteen

Marla spent most of Sunday catching up on housework, doing some food shopping, and visiting Miriam Pearl. She described her exploits to the old lady, who delighted in her adventures. They'd become close friends after Marla helped solve her granddaughter's murder a few months ago.

"What are you going to do next?" the matriarch asked, as Marla pushed her wheelchair along a shaded path on the family's extensive estate. Miriam reached up a bony hand to fluff her newly set hair. Marla always gave her a wash and blow-out when she came.

"I'll let Detective Vail find Goat. I've been away from the salon too much, and it's time for a staff workshop. I like to do them once a month. Besides, this week is Passover, and I have to get ready. I need to take care of things on the home front." Not to mention friends like Tally who required attention. That didn't even count her problems with Dalton, or Ma trying to push Barry on her.

"What are you doing for the seders?" Miriam asked.

Marla sniffed the pine-scented woods that surrounded them. "We're having our big family gathering on the second night. I'm going to my friend Arnie's house for the first night. His girlfriend, Jill, is setting things up. It was nice of them to invite me."

"You're always welcome here. Barbara and the kids are flying in later this week."

She heard the note of sadness in Miriam's voice. "You must miss them terribly."

"I don't blame them for leaving after what Morris did. My son got what he deserved."

"You still have Stella and Florence." Not that Miriam's daughters were much use. *See what happens when you interfere? You wrecked this entire family structure by investigating the granddaughter's murder. If you would let Vail do his thing alone, you wouldn't feel so responsible.*

Marla tightened her resolve to mind her own business later that afternoon when she took Spooks for a walk. Someone was taking an unhealthy interest in her activities, and if she stuck to her own affairs, perhaps they'd back off.

A shiver snaked down her spine. She couldn't disregard what had happened to the other three stylists. Regardless of her desire to end her participation in Vail's case findings, she might not be able to withdraw so readily.

Spooks pulled on his leash as he caught a whiff from the next lawn. She stood by patiently, admiring a cluster of brilliant crimson and fuchsia impatiens while he did his business. The cool air was redolent with the scent of orange blossoms. Overhead, few clouds disturbed the clear March sky. Her thoughts turned to Goat, who'd never returned to water Moss's flowers as promised. Her shoulders sagged with discouragement at the lack of progress in locating him.

"Come along, precious," she said to Spooks. Emotion clogging her throat, she crouched to pet him. He lapped at her hand, grateful for the attention. She found comfort in snuggling against his warm, silky coat.

"Hey, Marla."

She jumped upright, whirling to regard Hector bearing down on her. "Hi, what's up?" Her gaze darted nervously down the street.

"Haven't seen you in a while. Everything okay?"

"Sure. How's Amada?"

"Muy bueno, thanks."

He stepped in front of her path. *Dark hair, with Latin good looks.* That's how Virginia had described Cutter's companion at the hair show. Hector fit the bill perfectly, except he didn't have a cosmetology license. *Cutter would know how to get around that problem.*

Spooks sniffed Hector's ankles, growling ominously. "Uh, did you want something?" Marla's pulse raced, her flight-or-fight response activated against her will. Surely she had nothing to fear from her neighbor in broad daylight. She was getting paranoid.

Hector jerked a hand toward Goat's house. "Anything new in the detective's case? Goat still hasn't come home."

She followed his gesture. "As far as I know, our

neighbor is alive and well but is eluding the authorities. Lieutenant Vail is checking out the victim's relatives and acquaintances. Why? Did you have something to add?"

He kicked at a stone on the sidewalk. "I've heard a motorcycle around here lately. No one in the vicinity owns one. I wonder . . . I mean, I hope whoever killed that guy doesn't think we know anything important."

Her mouth dropped open. "You're scared he'll come after you?" She laughed mirthlessly. "And I thought you had something to hide."

"What are you talking about?"

"You had a grudge against Goat. His sister told me all about it."

His brown eyes widened incredulously. "She knew?"

"She told me how you'd blamed Goat for the ants invading your yard because he wouldn't use pesticides. So you put granules out and one of his cats died as a result. He responded by dropping tarantulas into your window."

Hector's mustache quivered. "You're right, senorita. He had no right to refuse the exterminators. It's part of our homeowners' agreement."

"Normally, they just spray inside." She reined in the dog's leash. Spooks tugged at the other end. "I assume you got rid of the spiders."

"I'm surprised you didn't hear my wife shriek. I decided right then, that lunatic was a menace to our community. He kept snakes, noisy parrots, and farm animals which you could smell from our backyard. I reported him."

She had no idea this feud had been going on

right under her nose. So much for her powers of observation. "What happened?"

"He got cited for a code violation. I was so mad, I wanted to run him out of town."

Looks like you've succeeded, pal. Or someone else did it for you. Giving a resigned sigh, Marla asked a loaded question. "Were you acquainted with Yani Verkovich, the dead man found in Goat's house?"

"No. Why? Should I be?"

"Well, if a person wanted to get rid of Goat, framing him for murder would do the trick."

"You . . . you think I would stoop to something so low?"

His furious expression made her take a step back. "I didn't say I suspected you," she hedged. "It's just as likely Yani wasn't the actual target. Maybe the killer made a mistake."

"You are as loco as your friend. I merely tried to do my civic duty."

"Sorry, but we have to consider all the possibilities." *No, we don't. That's Vail's job, remember?*

Bless my bones, I've done it again.

"Forgive me, Hector. I've had threatening things happen to me lately, and I don't really know why. I'm concerned about that motorcycle you've heard. Ever seen its license plate?"

He shook his head, anger fading into anxiety. "I'm sorry, too. It's unfortunate when bad things happen in the neighborhood. It turns people against each other."

"How about I watch your back, and you watch mine?"

"Deal."

They shook hands, then Marla headed home.

As she opened her front door, the phone rang. She raced into the kitchen to pick up the receiver. Spooks pranced at her feet. "Hello?" she called, cradling the phone on one shoulder while she untied his leash.

"Hi," Dalton Vail's voice said. "I haven't spoken to you all week. How's it going?"

"Great. You?" Despite her reluctance to resume their relationship, her heart soared at the sound of his voice.

"Things are progressing. I thought if you didn't have any plans, you might want to come over for dinner. I'm doing salmon fillets on the grill."

"Oh. Will Brianna be there?"

"She's working on her homework. I've been tied up in my office, but I needed a break. I'd hoped you and I could, you know, review the facts on the Verkovich case."

"Heck, Lieutenant, I thought you weren't allowed to divulge details."

"You already know most of them," he said with a hint of amusement.

"Don't you usually use Brianna for a sounding board?"

"She suggested we call you since you always come up with fresh insights."

Thanks, honey. "Okay, what time do you want me and what should I bring?"

His voice deepened. "I want you all the time, and you can just bring that luscious body."

She ignored his innuendo. "I'll get ready, and then I'll come over."

"Actually, how about if you bring back Brie's chess set? It doesn't matter that you haven't found a matching game board. We can use one from another set. I'd like to get started teaching her how to play."

Marla's throat tightened. "Sure, I'll go get it right now so I don't forget."

Hanging up she wondered, while changing into a long skirt and sweater, how to explain the missing piece. Vail was already sensitive about his late wife. He wouldn't be pleased to learn she'd ruined part of his gift.

"Spooks, it's all your fault," she said to the dog, who followed her like a shadow. Guilt assailed her for having left the chess set lying around where he could get it. This would only serve as another wedge between her and the detective.

After fixing her makeup and hair, she made a quick phone call to Tally to confirm their dinner date for Tuesday night, checked in with her mother, and guiltily phoned her brother at Anita's urging. She'd just switched handbags when the sound of the telephone jarred her senses.

"Now what?" She grabbed for the receiver in her bedroom. "Hello?"

Silence.

"Who's there?" Her tone sharpened.

"Marla . . ." a raspy voice grated.

"What? Who is this?"

"It's me. I'm calling to warn you."

Her sweaty fingers gripped the receiver. "Goat! I don't believe it. Where are you?" She barely recognized his voice.

Static sounded. Her Caller ID said PRIVATE CALL. No way to trace it. "Stay away from . . ." His next words were garbled.

"What? Stay away from the white home?" Whose white house? "I can't hear you; the reception is bad. Can I call you back?" *Click.* "Hello?"

Darn, he'd hung up, or else they had been disconnected. Either way, his message puzzled her. He'd said he was calling to warn her. But against whom, or what? The only white house that came to mind was the one in the nation's capitol . . . or the residence on Evan's ranch. She wasn't fool enough to venture there by herself again, so why did he feel it necessary to contact her?

Her body trembling, she waited by the phone in case Goat decided to call again. Was he all right? Or had he been detained by his enemies and interrupted in his effort to warn her? Biting her lower lip, she counted the minutes until she realized the wait was useless. Might as well go to Vail's and tell him about it. Besides, he might have something new to share with her.

Brianna opened the door, looking every inch the teenager with her midriff exposed under a busty top, tight jeans, and shoes from Nine West. She'd pulled her dark hair back into a ponytail and applied a subtle touch of makeup that Vail probably hadn't noticed. Greeting Marla, she grinned broadly.

"I'm glad you could come," Brianna said, flinging herself into Marla's arms.

Stunned, Marla hugged the girl. This was the first time Brianna had made any show of affection toward her. Marla's paranoia kicked in again, and she wondered if the girl had an ulterior motive for inviting her over.

"Daddy is in the kitchen. He's making a mess."

Clutching her purse and a shopping bag, Marla followed Brianna through a short hallway and into the kitchen. As always, the room produced immediate claustrophobia in Marla. Its single window over the double porcelain sink was too small, not letting in enough light. The dropped ceiling with plastic panels and fluorescent lighting increased illumination, but it hailed from the seventies, as did the speckled linoleum floor. Patterned fruit wallpaper, tacky prints of wine and cheese, a grandfather clock, and antique furniture pieces made her cringe. So did the collection of angel figurines and painted plates in a wooden cabinet. No way could she ever live in a kitchen like this. Admittedly, it had a comfortable, cozy feeling, but one more in tune with another woman's personality.

Marla swallowed her disquiet and smiled at Vail, who stood by the sink preparing a salad. "Hi," she said, admiring his physique. He wore a polo shirt tucked into a pair of tan Dockers. Her breath caught when he swung his penetrating gaze in her direction. Smoky gray eyes slammed into her senses with sensual force. Somehow, being in a kitchen with him put their relationship on a different keel. It almost felt . . . right.

"Hi," he said, his glance traveling her length.

"I brought a bottle of chardonnay, and here's your chess set." She withdrew the items from her bag and put them on a counter. "Uh, about your game . . ." Might as well get it off her chest. "I had a little accident. Spooks got hold of one of the pieces and thought it was a chew toy. I'll get a replacement."

His mouth tightened. "I see."

"I can always buy you a new set," she offered.

"That's not the point. This one is special. Or at least it was." He dried his hands on a towel and stepped over to pry open the lid. "It's missing a knight." He said it matter-of-factly, but she caught the hard edge in his tone.

"I'm sorry. I know how much this means to you. I promise I'll get a close match."

He must have noticed her contrite expression, because his face softened. "Accidents happen."

All that worry, and he was actually being nice about it. She glided over and kissed him. "I would have told you earlier, but I was afraid you'd be angry."

"Don't worry about it," Brianna called out. She sat at the maple dining table, schoolbooks spread in front of her. "Daddy's more eager to play that stupid game than I am."

"Your mother and I bought this set on our trip to Europe," Vail explained.

"So? You bought a lot of things together. That doesn't mean I have to like them. Right, Marla?"

She exchanged a glance with Vail. "You have the right to your own opinions," she told his daughter. "I'm sure you treasure some of your mother's things."

"I have her needlepoint pictures in my room, and I like her angel collection and her crystal bells. Some of the other stuff is okay, but it makes the house too dark. You should see my friend's place. Andrea lives in this huge house in Weston. It has vaulted ceilings, a really modern kitchen, and not nearly as much junk as we have scattered around. Her parents' bathroom is bigger than my bedroom. It's awesome."

"Pam wouldn't have cared to live in a house like that," Vail said quietly. "Too impersonal."

"Mom wants us to be happy. I don't really think it matters to her if we fix the house up or not. It's embarrassing to bring my friends here. You tell him, Marla."

Been there, done that. "I think we should get on with the meal. Do you want help?" she asked Vail. "Or shall I tell you about the phone call I got just before I came here?"

"Go ahead."

"Goat phoned me. At least I think it was him. The reception was bad. He warned me not to go near someone's white home."

Vail stepped toward her, then stopped. "How did he sound? Did he say where he was calling from?"

"Unfortunately, no. He just got a few words out; then we were disconnected."

"Freakin' phone company. What about your Caller ID?"

She shook her head. "I guess he was warning me against going near Evan's ranch. It's a white building. Goat must have learned about my previous visit there."

"That means either he's been keeping watch on things, or he's been in contact with someone. Damn, if only he'd turned himself in."

"He may do that when you catch Yani's killer. Any leads?" Her attention shifted. "Brianna, honey, you should get yourself a sapphire file. It's much better for your nails than that metal one."

"Is that right? Can I get a manicure at your salon?"

"Brianna, you're supposed to be doing your

homework, not your nails." Vail selected a knife and began slicing tomatoes. "I have a chablis open in the refrigerator. Want some?"

"I'd love it. Where do you keep your wineglasses?"

"Left top cabinet, second shelf, unless you want to use the crystal ones in the dining room."

She reached inside the cupboard. "These are fine." Feeling as though she were invading another woman's space, she checked the dinnerware. "Shall I set the table?"

"Yep. The salmon won't take long to cook. It's already marinated. I made rice, but it doesn't look right."

"He used the wrong kind," Brianna piped in. "Daddy never listens to me, except when he's discussing his cases. That's the only time my opinion counts."

At the stove, Marla lifted the lid off a saucepan. "This rice isn't fully cooked."

"I don't know why," Vail said, pouring them each a glass of wine. "All the water got absorbed."

"Were you using Minute Rice?"

"I don't know. The box is in the pantry."

A few moments later, Marla chuckled. "No wonder. This is arborio rice. You have to cook it slowly and keep adding water. It isn't prepared the same as Minute Rice."

"What do I know? Usually the housekeeper prepares our meals."

Their gazes locked. "You need a woman around full-time who knows what she's doing. Or next time, listen to your daughter."

"How about if I tried both? Where do you think

I could get the woman?" he asked in a teasing banter.

"Get to the point, Daddy." Brianna gave an exasperated sigh. "He keeps talking about asking you to move in. It wouldn't bother me." She studied her fingernails. "We could, like, go to the mall. They do ear-piercing at Claire's."

"I thought I told you not to bring up that subject again," Vail said sternly.

Now we get to the real reason Brianna wanted me over. She felt like a pawn in their familial chess game, caught between two opposing armies. Was this what would happen if she became part of their enclave? She'd end up fighting battles? No thanks. Domestic bliss wasn't all it was cracked up to be. She'd fought enough skirmishes with Stan to have learned that lesson.

"I'm hungry," she stated firmly. "Let's eat and review your case. That's why you asked me for dinner."

"It's not only my case. It's yours, too. I don't like Goat's warning, and I also don't like the fact that another stylist was involved in an accident." Vail carried the salad bowl to the table.

Marla found a box of instant mashed potatoes in the pantry and set about preparing it. "You heard about Lori?"

"Did you know her?"

"She was in my class. Only Kenya and I are left from the gang who played that trick on Wyeth Holmes. His name isn't listed on the roster I had printed out from our beauty school. Maybe you should track him down."

"I'd like a copy of that list."

"I'll fax it to your office in the morning."

"It might be safer for you to stay here tonight."

She paused, spoon in hand while she assessed his impassive features. Was the man genuinely concerned for her safety, or was this another ploy to land her in his bed? Couldn't be the latter, not while Brianna was afoot.

"I'll be all right. My alarm system works now, remember?"

"Your alarm system doesn't go with you when you walk Spooks."

"So I'll let him out into the backyard until things quiet down. I'm not actively seeking trouble."

"Ha! Trouble has a way of finding you. Now listen to what I've found out."

Chapter Fifteen

"Animal Farm pet store is owned by a man named Wake Hollander," Vail said. Leaving Marla with her mouth hanging open, he picked up the dish of salmon fillets and strode out to the screened patio.

After setting a lid on the pot of mashed potatoes and removing it from the heat, Marla trailed after him. She brought her glass of wine, needing a big gulp. "That's where Goat gets his supplies."

"I checked on the owner. Hollander has a lot of receipts from a guy called Lujan Chang. Chang just happens to be Yani Verkovich's Chinese associate at Stockhart Industries."

He set the fillets on a gas grill, while Marla admired his masculine form. She could get used to having him around, but she didn't know how she'd feel about having Brianna around all the time. Fond feelings aside, teenagers presented a burden Marla wasn't sure she wanted.

Or was it one she feared she couldn't handle?

"What kind of receipts did you find?" she asked, taking another drink. Focusing on his case was a lot easier than addressing personal issues.

He gave her a flippant grin that turned her heart upside down. "Chang buys birds. You know how that's a popular thing in Hong Kong. Birdcages are everywhere. Except I think some of the specimens he buys aren't available through normal channels."

Marla sat on one of the patio chairs. "Remember how I heard Evan and Wake talking about a shipment? Something Wake expected wasn't coming in on time, and he said Tiger would be upset. Do you suspect Tiger and this Chang are one and the same?"

"It's highly likely. There are other peculiarities."

"Such as?"

"I've been looking into Chang's background. He likes to go to the local pound and collect animals doomed to be put to sleep. He says he finds homes for the dogs and cats but has never documented his claim. It seems as if they disappear."

"Bless my bones, you don't think he—" Her throat closed.

Vail nodded grimly. "It would account for a few things."

She sipped her wine while mulling over the possibilities. "I can't believe he'd be involved in the pet-fur business in addition to smuggling illegal birds into the country."

"I presume Chang is either a collector or he resells the birds to fellow countrymen. Either way, he's the purchaser, not the smuggler. That honor goes to Evan Fargutt. We have a couple of other agencies interested in his operation."

"Have you checked out his ranch?"

"Yeah, I got a search warrant. He has over eight hundred birds in metal and wood cages alone, plus the aviary and the birds-of-prey section. Just the caged birds are worth about five hundred thousand dollars. I didn't see any signs of the laboratory you'd mentioned. There are three larger buildings: his house, a guest house for the ranch hands, and a quarantine station for imported birds. Assorted pieces of equipment lying around: aquariums, incubators, cages, and such."

"If he makes so much money being an aviculturist, why would he bother with smugglers?"

"You want the simple answer? It's a lucrative trade worth several billion dollars a year. Since the Wild Bird Conservation Act restricted exotic bird imports, up to one hundred thousand are smuggled into this country every year. That's just birds. Who knows? Maybe Evan brings in other stuff. Thousands of illegal animals enter the United States, and they're often hidden in legal shipments. South Florida, in particular, is a magnet for smugglers, since we're so close to Central and South America. Birds, reptiles, primates, snakes, tropical fish, you name it. Asian remedies use bones and other body parts from endangered animals. Animals are wanted, dead and alive."

Hadn't she heard about bird's-nest soup, a Chinese delicacy? Marla shivered at the images conjured in her mind.

Regarding Vail, she narrowed her eyes. "Like certain gourmet dishes, secret formulas may require exotic ingredients. Perfume, cosmetic, and skin-care product companies claim to add special factors to their compounds. What if Cutter and his pals were developing a hair-growth tonic that needed rare elements, like ground boar's teeth or something? Yani could have obtained them from either Chang or Evan. Did he threaten to expose Chang's larger operation? Or did he get greedy and turn the tables on them to keep the formula for himself?"

"That doesn't explain the bag of money left at Goat's place, or how Goat got involved with the bad eggs in the first place," Vail replied, his gaze pensive.

"Daddy said your friend Goat worked at Evan's ranch," Brianna said, trundling out to the patio. "What if he asked Wake Hollander, one day when he was buying supplies, if any extra work was available? Pet stores have to keep their animals groomed. Maybe Wake didn't need help, but he referred Goat to Evan. That could be how Goat got the job at the ranch."

"Very good, honey. Have a seat. The fillets should be ready any minute. Shall we set the table outside?" Marla asked Vail. "It's quite pleasant out here. Your backyard looks so tropical."

"I had a landscaper come in after my citrus trees were chopped down."

They transferred all the accoutrements for the meal to the patio. Vail cut some slices from a long loaf of Cuban bread, and Marla helped herself. Her head was beginning to float from the wine, and she needed something solid in her stomach. She slathered margarine on her bread while Vail dished out the salad. He brought the mashed potatoes and added some freshly microwaved asparagus.

"Let's say Goat got his job through Wake

Hollander," Marla continued once the fillets were on the table. Vail had used a teriyaki sauce. Its delicious aroma made her mouth water. "Do you think he knew what was going on between Evan and Chang? From what you're saying, I gather Wake is essentially a middleman."

"It's possible Goat learned about their trade in birds. I'm wondering how Verkovich got involved. My guess is, Chang introduced his colleague to Evan Fargutt."

"I thought Yani's relationship with Cutter led him to Evan."

"Boy, is this confusing," Brianna stated. "Marla, can I taste your wine?"

"Certainly not!"

"Lots of my friends drink. You should see what they do when their parents aren't home."

Marla smiled indulgently, not believing a word of what she said. "Tell me about it, honey."

"Brianna, you're not doing anything against my rules, are you?" Vail snapped. "I'll have to call your friends' parents."

"Better not." Brie's dark eyes twinkled mischievously. "Maybe I was exaggerating."

Or maybe you just want more attention. Marla curbed her impatience to discuss Goat and instead queried Brianna about her schoolwork. While she listened, part of her mind continued to stew regarding Vail's revelations. She presented her mental arguments after they'd cleaned away the dinner dishes.

"Lujan Chang is likely mixed up in operations that have nothing to do with Goat," Marla concluded while slicing a lemon meringue pie Vail had defrosted for dessert. "If Chang has a connection to Evan through Wake Hollander, where does Cutter fit in? Or Yani, for that matter? They're all linked in some manner that led to one man's death and another's disappearance. Not to mention the other stylists from my class. What do I and my classmates have to do with any of it?"

"You tell me," Vail prompted.

"Goat collected articles on Martha Matilda Harper. That has to be the key. Maybe I'm on target with my theories about secret hair-growth formulas. Talk about a lucrative business! Whoever invents a way to stimulate new hair growth will be very rich."

"I'd need more evidence to go with you on that one," Vail said. "Anyway, I didn't invite you here to monopolize our conversation with details about my case. Want to go out on Saturday?"

Marla was just as happy to change the subject. Her brain grew too befuddled by all the possibilities, and the wine added to the effect. She was finding it increasingly difficult to think straight. "Passover starts on Wednesday night. I don't like to dine out during the holiday."

"Why not?" Brianna demanded, helping herself to a second portion of pie.

At least the girl had a healthy appetite, Marla thought, glad that Brie didn't starve herself for a slim figure. "We're not supposed to eat products made from flour. That leaves out a lot of things in restaurants. I'm just more comfortable eating at home."

"Okay, I'll come to your place," Vail announced. "Besides," he added with a wink, "it's your turn to cook dinner next. Brianna is invited to a party, so she'll be sleeping over at a friend's house."

They locked gazes, and she understood his unspoken promise. Her face heated with the awareness that the teen was watching them. "I'll let you know. Let's see what develops this week."

Monday brought a new opportunity when Marla realized she was nearly out of dog food. "I'm sorry," she told Spooks, who hovered at her heels. "I haven't been paying much attention to you lately, have I? I have a few other errands to run. I'll stop and get you a new bag of Science Diet."

Bingo! A light bulb popped on in her head. She needed food for her pet. What better place to go than Animal Farm, where Goat went for his supplies? It couldn't be considered snooping if she was going in there for a legitimate reason. A single visit wouldn't put her in any danger, and she might learn something new.

Various smells and sounds assailed her as soon as she pushed open the door to the pet shop. She grimaced at the unhappy sight of dogs confined to cages. She'd bought Spooks at a poodle-breeding parlor, and he'd come complete with pedigree papers and photos of his parents. Pet stores were so distressing. She wanted to take home each of the pathetic creatures. Her eyes bulged when she noticed a birdcage holding a scarlet macaw with a price tag of fifteen hundred dollars. And she'd thought the five hundred dollars she'd paid for Spooks was a lot.

The owner fit right into the jungle motif with his safari clothes, squashed fisherman's hat covering self-shorn hair, and his short, wiry figure. He'd been tabulating some figures by the cash register and glanced up at her entrance.

"May I help you?" he asked in a gravelly tone.

She sidled up to his counter. "Do you carry Science Diet?" Although the front of the store displayed an array of pets, she noticed rows of shelves holding supplies toward the back.

"Sure do." His blue eyes squinted. "What kind?"

"Canine light-maintenance. I have a miniature poodle. He started getting these milky white spots on his eyes. The dog eye specialist said they're cholesterol plaques because he doesn't metabolize fat properly." She grunted. "Talk about expensive doctor visits. I should've claimed Spooks as a dependent on my income tax."

The man laughed. "I know what you mean. I get a pretty hefty vet bill keeping these guys healthy." He waved at the cages. "What size bag do you want?"

"Twenty pounds. I'm glad you carry Science Diet. You can't get it in Publix, and I thought pet stores dealt mostly in animals. I've always gone to the big chains for supplies. My dog groomer suggested I come here."

"I sell wholesale to folks in the business. It earns me my overhead, you know? People come in to buy pets sporadically, plus there's a lot of competition. So I earn my bread-and-butter with the supplies. Wait here; I'll get your stuff."

"Is this your card?" Marla asked, holding up a business card from a holder on the counter. "You must be Wake Hollander."

"That's right." He retrieved her order and dumped the bag by the cash register. "Anything else?"

She withdrew her credit card and handed it to him. "Just some information. My groomer's name is Kyle Stanislaw. You might know him as Goat. He's been missing for several weeks, and I'm concerned. Have you heard from him at all?"

His gaze narrowed as he studied her credit card. "Your name sounds mighty familiar."

Her heartbeat picked up speed. "A man's body was found in Goat's town house. Yani Verkovich. Ring a bell?" She signed a credit slip after he completed the transaction.

"Are you a cop?" His voice lost all traces of warmth.

"No, I'm just worried about a friend. But I have heard your name mentioned in certain circles." She tucked her card back in her wallet.

"How's that?"

She detected a flicker of fear behind his expression. "Cutter Corrigan was my teacher in beauty school. He has . . . had a relationship with Yani. I understand you're acquainted with one of Yani's colleagues, along with Cutter's cousin, Evan Fargutt."

His gaze darting nervously to the door, Hollander moistened his lips. "I don't know nothin' about what happened to Verkovich. He was up to something with Fargutt, but I never stuck my nose into their business. As long as Fargutt came through on my orders, that is."

"Oh, yes. You buy your birds from Evan's stock, or else he ships in what you require. Or rather, what Mr. Chang requests."

A moment of silence passed between them. "What is it you want, Miss Shore?"

"My friend's safe return. That will happen only when Verkovich's killer is found. Do you think Yani discovered too much about his Chinese colleague?"

Hollander leaned forward. "Mr. Chang ain't involved in this fellow's death. If you ask me, look to Fargutt's ranch. There's more than one rotten apple in that bunch."

"Meaning?"

"I've said my piece. You can't fool me, missy. I know you must be working for the cops. That detective asked me about those people who lived up in Loxahatchee."

"Pardon me?"

He swished something in his mouth and then spit into a trash container. "Back in ninety-five, a couple of bird breeders disappeared from a ranch in Palm Beach County. I used to deliver their feed, but that was my only contact. The two of them vanished, leaving their ranch untended. All I did was notify the police that no one had picked up their seed from the front gate when I drove by later that week. The place had a stench that told me something was wrong."

"So what happened to them?"

"No one knows. Could be they crossed someone or owed money and decided to skip town. Ranch hands weren't much help. Jimmy Laredo . . . Jimbo had quit his job two weeks before, and the other guy was picked up in Georgia for driving with a suspended license."

"Jimbo? Is he the same man who works at Evan's ranch?"

"Yup. Breeders know each other, see? Doesn't mean nothing for workers to change locations. Could be Fargutt made him a better offer, or else Jimbo applied for a new job without letting on about his history. As for the cops, tell them I had nothin' to do with no murder. I got my scruples, and they don't let me go that far."

Oh yeah? Your scruples allow you to engage in illegal animal traffic. How about those poor creatures who don't survive transit? Or become captives for life? I don't see you showing any compassion there, pal.

Gritting her teeth, she lifted the heavy bag of dog food. "Well, thanks for your help. At least I know where to come for supplies from now on. Here's my business card. Next time you're ready for a haircut, stop by my salon. I guarantee you'll be satisfied with the results."

Always the promoter, she thought, *even when interviewing suspects.* You never knew where your next client would come from.

She laughingly told Nicole about it the next day at work. "Boy, would I be shocked if he walked in here."

The sleek stylist peered at her before swiping her countertop with a clean towel. "So you don't believe this pet-store guy had anything to do with the murder?"

Marla sorted foils for her next highlights job. "No, and despite the illegal goings-on with Yani's colleague, Wake implied Chang wasn't involved, either."

"Hey, Marla." Giorgio breezed into the salon, just a few minutes earlier than his first appointment of the day.

"Since when do you wear driving gloves?" Marla asked, noticing the black gloves he casually tossed into a drawer.

"They protect my hands." Grinning, he wiggled his fingers at her. "They are, after all, a valuable asset." He sauntered closer, giving Marla a playful once-over. "You would like a demonstration?" White teeth gleamed under a trim mustache. Waiting for her reply, he ruffled his curly black hair as though to offer further enticement.

Marla stared at him. Dark-haired, Latin good looks, possessing a cosmetology license.

"What's the matter? You eat lemons for breakfast? Oh dear, you must have heard the news."

"News? From your expression, it can't be good."

Giorgio and Nicole exchanged furtive glances. "You tell her," Giorgio said.

Nicole, putting aside her towel, pursed her lips. "There's no easy way to say this. Carolyn Sutton is opening her salon this week."

"Shit. I've been so busy that I forgot all about it."

"She'll be two doors down, on the other side of Arnie's bagel place," Giorgio said, his voice oozing sympathy.

"That woman hates me. She'll do everything she can to steal business from us."

"I thought she was already enticing customers away with free offers," Nicole said.

"That's true. Some people have returned to my chair, saying they don't like how she conducts operations. But that was when her salon was still across town. Now we'll be in direct competition with each other."

"If you ask me, she'll be the one at a disadvantage, not you," Nicole said reassuringly.

"Just what I need, another headache."

"Marla, you got a headache? I have some Advil if you want it," Jennifer called from across the room.

"I was talking about something else," Marla said,

annoyed by how easily voices carried in a salon. "How was your dentist appointment yesterday?"

The blond stylist continued cutting her customer's hair. "Would you believe it cost me two hundred fifty dollars to get a cavity filled? Man, we could have used that money toward a new dishwasher. Our old model broke last week."

"Tell me about it," Marla said. "Prices have gone up everywhere."

"What's that?" Giorgio asked, indicating the sheet of paper lying faceup on her counter.

"It's a list of people who were in my class at cosmetology school. I promised Detective Vail I'd fax it to him."

His dark eyes gleamed brightly. "Planning a reunion?"

"Something like that. One member is missing. I asked Dalton to try to track him."

"Is that the fellow you told me about?" Nicole interrupted. "The one you made go bald?"

"Ouch," Marla said, grimacing.

Giorgio tapped her arm. "What's this?"

"Another shameful incident from my past, that's all." She turned away to make sure all her plugs were firmly in the sockets. Thankfully, the rest of her employees were busy with clients, because gossip spread quickly. She kept in mind that people liked to listen in to other folks' conversations in salons. Hearing the buzz around town was part of the attraction in being there.

Giorgio planted his hands on his hips in an effeminate gesture. "Let's have it, Marla."

"I don't have time. My highlights will be here any minute."

"Give me the shortened version, then. I'm all ears."

She rolled her eyes, knowing he wouldn't stop haranguing her until she spilled the beans. "I'm not a total schnook. A gang of us in school experimented with a formula I'd discovered while doing research for a history paper. We thought it would promote new hair growth. As a joke, we applied it to our classmate Wyeth's hair, pretending it was a coloring solution. Wyeth went bald. A short fuzz grew back, but then we graduated, so I don't know if his hair ever regained its former thickness or not."

"You mean the guy might have stayed bald? That's pretty drastic. Why would you pull such a nasty trick?"

"Wyeth was a conceited jerk. I suppose we wanted to prick his bubble."

"You might have ruined his life. Did you ever consider the consequences?"

Her face reddened. "Not at the time. Believe me, I'm considering them now, since several of my classmates have met with unfortunate accidents."

Giorgio leaned closer. "I told you to be careful. The past has a way of coming back to haunt you."

Chapter
Sixteen

"I don't know, Marla," Tally said, Tuesday evening when they met for dinner. They'd already been served their minestrone soup at Jacaranda Italia restaurant. "Your theory seems pretty far out. I mean, Rogaine is already on the market. What else could be gained by another hair-growth formula?"

Marla regarded her friend, who'd come straight from work at Dressed To Kill boutique. Tally's blond hair and azure eyes were set off by a metallic blue silk blouse tucked into a pair of black faux-leather pants. She had a figure to die for, although she constantly complained about fighting an expanding waistline.

"Male-pattern baldness is a sensitive topic," Marla replied. "Women have it too, but we don't talk about it as much. Most products on the market today merely prevent further hair loss, so a formula that stimulates new hair growth could be extremely valuable. That's what I think Yani was working on." Marla shoved a spoonful of steaming liquid into her mouth. Its spicy edge kicked her tongue. She chewed a piece of garlic bread to chase it down.

Tally raised her glass of merlot. "How did you come to that conclusion?"

"Cutter met Yani at a citrus canker workshop. They were opponents to the cause, but they must have found something in common. Yani started coming to Cutter's shop as a customer. Cutter learned Yani worked at Stockhart Industries in the biochemical department." Putting her spoon down, she leaned forward. "I think Cutter had my notes on the hair-tonic formula developed by that chemist who used to work for Martha Matilda Harper. He believed it had merit, and he brought Yani into the fold to develop it. They needed a place to work, so Cutter approached his cousin Evan."

Tally nodded without ruffling a hair on her French braid. "Sounds logical so far, according to what you've learned. But even if this is true, how would a new formula be different from something like Rogaine?"

Marla waited while the waitress delivered their entrées of eggplant parmesan. "You have to understand what causes hair to grow. We're born with all the hair follicles we are ever going to have. Hair grows in three stages. First, it develops in the follicles under your skin. At the base of the hair root is a network of blood vessels that feed the hair. Rapidly dividing cells push forward and up through the follicles until they reach the surface where they die. In other words, what you see on your head is dead hair cells."

Marla paused to swallow a forkful of eggplant covered in rich marinara sauce. "How long your hair grows is genetically predetermined. That's why some women come in for cuts every month, while other people I don't see for ages."

Tally grimaced. "It took forever for my hair to grow long. I still looked like a boy when I was five years old."

"No one would make that mistake now!" Marla said, chuckling. "Anyway, a lot of scams claim to make your hair grow thicker and longer. Look at this ad I just pulled out of a magazine." She withdrew a folded paper from her purse. "See this? It offers to send you a bottle of some rapid-growth formula. The ad uses faulty rationale by saying your scalp lacks the proper nutrition for your hair roots to grow normally. This formula will free clogged roots and provide a miraculous growth molecule to nourish them. As a result, your hair may grow to your waist! Nowhere do you see a list of ingredients. It also claims to contain protein which will make your hair silkier and fuller. That's a lot of baloney. Proteins are too large to penetrate to the hair's inner medulla. Conditioners can make your hair silky and fuller, but nothing is going to make your hair grow real long if it isn't in your genetic makeup."

Tally smiled. "Sounds like those medicinal concoctions that claim cures for every ailment."

"You still get a lot of schmucks who believe this stuff."

"What's the second stage of growth after the hair pushes through the scalp?"

Marla swallowed another bite. "In the transition stage, your hair is dormant while the root moves up to the surface. Finally, the root separates from the base of the follicle. A new hair starts growing and pushes the old one out of the way. This is why you find loose hairs in your hairbrush. You shed about twenty-five to one hundred hairs a day."

"What do the true growth formulas do? Retard this process?"

Marla held up a hand while she took a drink of water. "You can't grow new follicles, but you can affect hair growth in other ways. Improving blood flow through the follicles is a valid point. As you age, the blood vessels feeding your follicles deteriorate. Weakened follicles produce hair that is fine and thin. The growth cycle shortens, so when your hair sheds, there is diminishing regrowth to replace it. Theoretically, preventing the blood vessels from breaking down should rejuvenate the failing hair follicles."

Tally glanced at her thoughtfully. "How did you learn all this? Was it included in your curriculum at beauty school?"

She shook her head. "It was part of my research for the history paper on Martha Matilda Harper. What was the scientific basis for her nourishing hair tonic? How could an errant scientist transmute that into a revitalizing formula? Increasing circulation to the follicles is one possibility."

"Huh. You'd think a scalp massage would do the same trick."

"Right. Here's another idea: a hormonal by-product of testosterone is called DHT. As we get older, more DHT is found in our blood. Because of their rich blood supply, hair follicles have a higher concentration. So maybe it's the higher

DHT content that inhibits hair growth and causes your hair follicles to shrink. The only problem here is that hair on the rest of your body increases as you get older."

Tally tilted her head. "How does this relate to women?"

Marla didn't intend to bore her friend, but the topic fascinated her. She'd done enough studying and still wasn't clear on how a truly effective formula might work.

"Testosterone is a type of androgen," she went on. "After menopause, our estrogen levels no longer counteract the androgens in our bodies. So we'll have a similar hair-loss pattern to men. Aside from estrogen replacement therapy, reducing the amount of DHT may help retain hair. There is a product on the market, Propecia, that prevents testosterone from making DHT. So far, it appears to be effective."

"Is that how Rogaine works?"

"No one is sure. It may convert tiny follicles into larger ones so you get more regular-size hairs. You have to start treatment early to get the best results, and keep using it indefinitely."

"Terrific." Anxiety clouded her friend's eyes, as though she was daunted by visions of aging.

"Who's to say how Yani Verkovich modified my original formula?" Marla said. "Why would testing the solution on dogs or cats have any relevance to human hair?"

Tally gave her a curious glance. "How does this relate to those stylists in your class having accidents?"

Marla hung her head. "I have no idea. I meant

to visit Kenya today, but I had no time. I'll have to see her tomorrow. She's the only one of my gang left, other than Wyeth Holmes, and he's vanished off the face of the earth."

"How does Dalton feel about your ideas?"

Food caught in her throat, and she choked. After a coughing fit in which her eyes watered, she regained control. "He's willing to listen," she spit out between ragged breaths, "b-but I think he believes Goat stumbled into a smuggling ring. That may be true, but it doesn't explain Goat's notes on Martha Matilda Harper or how my former classmates and I are involved. Dalton is worried about me. He wants me to move into his house."

Tally raised an arched eyebrow. "For safety reasons?"

She took a deep, settling intake of air. "We've talked about it in terms of getting closer. You know what I mean."

"Holy smokes, Marla. That's a serious step."

"Ma wouldn't be thrilled. She respects Dalton, but she's still hoping I'll hook up with Roger's son. I'm not sure if I want to accept responsibility for Brianna, either. On the other hand, I feel for the girl. She's at the prime age for needing a mother."

"Do I see a sign around your neck advertising maternal abilities? The last thing you ever wanted was to be burdened with kids."

Marla examined a speck on the table. "It's not so much the burden. It's the caring. So many bad things can happen. I don't want to suffer the pain and anguish."

"What about the good side?"

She returned Tally's frank gaze. "You and Ken

aren't rushing to raise a family. You always wanted to keep your independence along with your figure."

"Touché. But my reasons are different than yours. You've been through a tragedy and saw how it affects a child's parents. It's a risk you decide to take when you have children. You're risking the same thing if you get more involved with Detective Vail. He could get shot chasing after suspects."

"That scares the hell out of me."

"Well, you should go into a relationship with your eyes wide open."

"I'm not a total schlemiel, you know."

"So what are you planning to do? Take him up on his offer?"

"I haven't decided. Right now, my main concern is bringing Goat home and finding out who's threatening me and my friends."

True to her words, Marla phoned Kenya when she got home that night. She only had a phone number for Kenya's salon, so she left a message on the answering machine. Then she didn't think anymore about it while she prepared the sweet potatoes for the next night's dinner at Arnie's house and got ready for bed. She was watching the news on TV, cuddling Spooks, when the phone rang. Her Caller ID read PRIVATE CALL. Marla's heart lurched. Maybe it was Goat calling her back.

"Hello?" she said, clutching the receiver to her ear.

Heavy breathing sounded at the other end.

"Who is this?"

No answer.

Rattled, Marla hung up. Her hand hovered over the cradle while she debated whether or not to call

Vail. *Am I getting in the habit of calling him every time I get scared?* Compressing her lips, she grabbed for Spook's warm, comforting body and held him close.

Marla found time to run over to Kenya's salon on Wednesday. She needn't have wasted the effort.

"Kenya isn't here," said the receptionist, a perky middle-aged woman who wore her auburn hair in a blunt cut.

Have you looked in a mirror lately? Your white roots are a mile long. "It's urgent that I speak to her. Can you phone her at home? My name is Marla Shore."

"I'm sorry; we've tried calling her, but she hasn't shown up. I can give her a message when she comes in."

Marla hunched her shoulders. "What do you mean, Kenya hasn't shown up? Did she have clients scheduled for today?"

"She was supposed to come in yesterday. I don't know what happened. I've had to cancel her appointments, and Angie is real mad that we're losing business."

"Is it possible for you to give me her home address? Maybe she's ill. I'd like to check on her." Alarm frissoned down her spine. This couldn't be happening, although there still might be a logical explanation. A sick family member, or a simple misunderstanding about her schedule. Or an accident . . .

"I can't give out that information." The receptionist's voice was firm.

"I'm really worried. Is she usually reliable about

being here? Won't Angie send someone to her place to see if she's all right?"

The receptionist signaled her boss. "Hey, Angie, this lady wants to know about Kenya."

Marla strode over to a woman straightening supplies on a display shelf. "I'm Marla Shore from Cut 'N Dye Salon. Kenya and I went to school together. It's urgent that I see her. I think she may be in danger, and I'm concerned about her absence."

"Really?" The attractive dark-skinned woman regarded her with the same enthusiasm she would have shown for a fungus infection under a fingernail.

Marla realized she sounded dramatic, but how to convince the manager she was for real? "Some of our classmates have met with fatal accidents recently. It's being investigated by the police. I'll have to notify Detective Vail that Kenya is missing unless you cooperate."

Angie's nut brown eyes widened. "I don't see any harm in giving you her address. You let me know if she's okay, hear?"

Fear gripping her heart, Marla raced to Kenya's street, which thankfully was only five minutes away. Her gaze drifted to the clock before she shut off the ignition on her Camry. Only ten more minutes before her next customer arrived. She'd have to make this quick.

Kenya lived in a rental complex by the Palm Haven post office. No one answered at her apartment number, so Marla rapped at several of the neighbors' doors. "Excuse me," she said to a mother who opened the door while holding a squirming toddler under her arm. "I'm trying to locate Kenya

Dobson. She didn't come into work today, and I'm worried about her."

"Your guess is as good as mine, honey. I haven't seen her car in its space since Saturday. Maybe she went on vacation."

"Is there anyone here who is close to her? You know, a friend she might confide in?"

The mom struggled with her unruly child. "I haven't a clue. Sorry I can't be more helpful."

Marla turned away after having the door shut in her face. She sniffed around Kenya's doorway but didn't smell anything bad to arouse suspicions. Might the landlord have a key? She tried the apartment building office, but they refused to invade the privacy of Kenya's apartment on Marla's word alone. That left her with only one option: Dalton Vail.

She used her cell phone to call him at the station on her way back to the salon. After she explained her mission, she got the desired response. He promised to check it out.

"I'll get a warrant," he said in his deep, commanding tone. "It shouldn't be a problem, considering what happened to the other gals in your group. I've assigned one of my detectives to reexamine those accidents. Meanwhile, I'm following leads on that Chang fellow."

Marla kept her hands on the wheel, speaking to the telephone on its cradle. "Did you figure out what Goat meant by warning me away from the white house? Maybe we should revisit Evan's ranch. If we go when they're not expecting us, we might find the lab. Showing them your warrant the last time got you the official tour. I'll bet we could snoop out the real goods."

Vail laughed, a low, rumbling chuckle that stirred her feminine nerve endings into heightened awareness. "Working in the salon isn't enough for you, is it? Don't you have customers waiting?"

"Yeah, I do." She pulled into the parking lot at the shopping strip where her salon was located. "I have to get back to work. Heck, that's where Carolyn Sutton just opened. She's calling her place Hairstyle Heaven." A thoughtful frown creased her brow. Cutter's establishment was Heavenly Hair Salon. Hadn't he mentioned developing a franchise out west? Could this be where Carolyn got her financial backing? The similarity in names struck her as being a little too coincidental. But maybe she was making a connection where none existed.

"It's unfortunate that she moved into the same location," Vail said. "I hope it doesn't make things more difficult for you."

"Tell me about it. If you think I'm bad, that woman is trouble with a capital *T.*"

"You have enough to worry about right now— I'll call you later to discuss making another visit to the ranch."

"Tonight is Passover. I won't be home. Arnie invited me for the first night at his house."

A pause. "I'll miss you."

"If I know you, you'll be buried in paperwork."

"Don't forget to reserve Saturday night for me. I get too restless when we're apart. Know what I mean?" His suggestive tone told her clearly what he meant.

Sitting in her parked car, she felt her body stir. "Me too," she replied in a husky tone. *Get over this*

*hormonal surge every time you speak to him. It distracts
you from thinking rationally.* "Please notify me when
Kenya turns up," she added. "Until later, then.
Bye." First Goat vanished, now her classmate. At
least Goat was still alive. Grasping her purse, she
detached the cell phone and lifted it from its cradle. Time to fulfill her other obligations.

"Marla, where have you been? You shouldn't
run out on us like that." Giorgio's voice assaulted
her as soon as she entered the salon. "Out to lunch
with your handsome detective?"

"No, I had an errand to run," she said with a pre-
occupied air. "Hi, Mrs. Fagelson. I hope you weren't
waiting long," she told her gray-haired client. "You
can go back and get washed."

She was midway through the blow-out when
power cut off. No juice playing the background
music, no noise from the dryers, no heat to the curling irons. *Nada.* Stunned silence swept through
the salon, but it didn't last long.

"Flicker, Power, and Light," Nicole sneered
from the next station where she was applying highlights. "What now? Some car hit a pole? It isn't
storm season yet."

Marla plunked her hair dryer on the counter.
"I'll go next door and see who else is affected."

A few minutes later, she returned. "We're it,
guys. The lights work on either side of us. I'll
check the circuits." They were turned to the ON
position. She switched off the air-conditioning, in
case of a power surge when the electricity came
back online.

"I'll call FPL," she told her waiting staff. "I can't
imagine what's happened. Sorry, Mrs. Fagelson. I

hope we can fix this fast, or we're dead in the water."

Where had she put the electric company's phone number? Marla couldn't find it anywhere, not on the front desk, in her Rolodex, or in her files. She'd have to look it up in the Yellow Pages.

Crouching down behind the reception desk, she slid open a cupboard. As she reached for the thick directory, a black object scurried away from the natural light into darker recesses.

"Ahh!" Marla shrieked, jerking backward and banging her hip on the opposite counter. Springing to her feet, she lurched into Giorgio's outstretched arms.

"What is it?"

"A palmetto bug."

"Pah! You're afraid of the little creature?"

"It's not little. The thing is bigger than my thumb. You get it. I'll give you a bonus."

"No kidding. How much?"

"Giorgio!"

He grinned wickedly. "I have you at my mercy, no? I like this very much."

While she knew he was teasing, for a moment something odd flashed behind his expression. "Go on. You're just ribbing me."

His face eased into a smile. "Don't worry, your hero will get the big bad bug."

"Excuse me," said an unfamiliar male voice. A silver-haired man stood by the reception counter, looking slightly bewildered.

Marla searched for the receptionist, but the girl hadn't yet returned from the bank where Marla had sent her. "Yes?" She edged out of Giorgio's way, hoping the man wouldn't think their actions peculiar.

"I was wondering if anyone had time to give me a haircut this afternoon."

She opened the appointment book. Everyone else was fully occupied. Marla had the only available slot, having purposefully not filled it in so she could leave early. "I can take you after I finish Mrs. Fagelson, but we're having a problem with the power right now."

The man gave a shy smile. "You can come get me when you're ready. I'm Sam Levy. I work down at the hardware store."

She knew the place. It was a privately owned store, one of a rare breed left in these days of chain stores that outgunned the independents. "I'm Marla Shore, and this is my salon. You're only a few doors down. I'll let you know when I'm finished."

His eyes crinkled. "You're mighty kind, miss. I should be retired, you know, but after my wife passed on, I couldn't stay home alone. I used to be in the building business, so the hardware store is the perfect place for me."

Marla grinned. "My neighbor Moss is supposedly retired, too. He still does carpentry work." A loud whack from behind made her jump.

"Got it," Giorgio exclaimed. "Here are your Yellow Pages."

Marla waved at Sam as he left the salon, and signaled to her customer that she'd be right back. She dialed the number for FPL and got connected to the service department.

"Well, Miss Shore," the lady on the other end

said after she'd explained her problem, "we have here a request you made earlier. You told us to shut off the electricity and to cancel your account."

Chapter
Seventeen

Marla told Arnie and Jill about the power loss later that evening when she went to Arnie's house for the Passover seder. "Someone did it on purpose to cause me trouble," she said, helping Jill carry plates of gefilte fish into the dining room.

"Like who?" Jill, a buxom blonde, dressed tastefully in a pink satiny suit with mother-of-pearl buttons, smiled at her. She wore her hair in soft waves reaching her shoulders.

"I can think of a number of people who hold a grudge against me," Marla said wryly. "By the way, the table looks beautiful." Settings for twelve glistened with silver, bone china, and crystal on a white damask cloth.

"Thanks. These were mostly wedding gifts for Arnie and his wife. He hasn't used them in a while." She lowered her voice, glancing into the kitchen where Arnie was carving up the turkey. "I could see he was thinking about Susan when he brought them out. This must bring back painful memories, poor man."

"Susan's car accident happened five years ago. It's about time for him to reestablish family traditions, especially for his kids. Where are Josh and Lisa?"

"In their rooms with friends. I'm so excited. This is my first seder, and I've always wanted to go to one."

"Do they cover it in your conversion classes?"

Jill glanced at her engagement ring. "We're just getting into the holidays. I've been reading about it, though. I hope I don't make any mistakes."

Marla touched her arm. "You'll do fine."

Arnie strode into the living room where the other guests had congregated. "Let's get started," he said, rubbing his hands together. "Kids, come on." He signaled to them before claiming his place at the head of the table. "Please turn to page nine in your Haggadah," he said once everyone took their seats. Settling his yarmulke on his head, he began the service.

"Since this is Jill's first Passover celebration, we'll explain things as we go along. Here is the seder plate." As tradition warranted, he held up each item as he spoke about it. "The roasted bone stands for the lamb our ancestors sacrificed for the holiday, and the roasted egg reminds us of the destruction of the holy temple. These bitter herbs stand for the bitter life our ancestors suffered as slaves in Egypt. Haroset represents the mortar they used to build bricks for the Pharaoh."

Marla remembered she had to bring the Haroset tomorrow night for the second seder. Thankfully, it was an easy dish, and she had in stock the chopped walnuts, apples, cinnamon, and kosher wine. She watched dutifully while Arnie explained about the Karpas, holding up a sprig of parsley, symbol of regrowth. Matzos, the bread of affliction, came next, in their three-tiered holder. Then began the blessings. Candles were lighted and the Kiddush was said while everyone drank the first of four cups of wine for the evening. The children giggled, this being the one time they were allowed to sip a sample from the grown-ups' glasses, although their own glasses held grape juice.

Marla's stomach rumbled with hunger as Arnie alternated between Hebrew and English in reading how their ancestors were delivered from bondage in Egypt. It was an ageless story celebrating freedom and decrying the oppression of people everywhere. They sang "Go Down Moses" and "Dayenu" and dipped their little fingers into wine for each of the ten plagues brought upon the Pharaoh. Marla visualized the movie version with Charlton Heston as Moses. Ma had made her and Michael watch *The Ten Commandments* every year. She'd never admit to anyone it was one of her favorite films.

These traditions were important to her, she realized with a flash of insight. She could no more give them up than sacrifice her other rituals of existence. Her thoughts drifted to Dalton, who clung to the past with similar tenacity. Perhaps his focus differed from hers, but this might be a common ground from which the well of a lasting relationship might spring.

Sustenance tonight came not from her inner

flow of self-realization but from the main meal that followed the second cup of wine. Marla dipped her piece of boiled potato in salt water, representing the tears of oppression. She ate her hard-boiled egg, appreciating the fact that it stood for eternal life. Everything had a meaning, but soon she became more interested in the food than in the meanings. She chased down a course of gefilte fish with a bowl of matzoh ball soup. By the time she got to the turkey and brisket, she was almost full and barely had room to scarf down a macaroon for dessert. No wonder their ancestors ate in a reclining position. They were stuffed!

After dinner, the kids opened the door to welcome Elijah the prophet. She used to believe his spirit actually drank from the full cup of wine on the table. *If he visited every Jewish household, he'd be mighty drunk by the night's end. Sort of like me.* She felt tipsy after singing more songs and downing more wine.

Forcing herself to remain sober, she accosted Jill as they carried dirty dishes into the kitchen. "I meant to ask you about Yani Verkovich's colleague," she said, admiring the glossy sheen of her friend's hair. "Did you identify him to Detective Vail?"

"The man's name is Lujan Chang." Jill put a couple of delicate crystal goblets near the sink.

"Did he mention what Yani was doing with Cutter?"

"I couldn't ask direct questions, or he'd become suspicious. I pretended I was interviewing him as part of my public relations job. I told him I was looking for employees with interesting hobbies that we could use to improve our image."

Marla grabbed a dish towel while Jill began washing the crystal by hand. "Did he mention he collects birds, or anything about a connection with Wake Hollander, the pet-store owner I told you about?"

Jill gave her a frank stare. "Tell me about that again."

"Presumably Evan Fargutt imports the birds or breeds them on his ranch. Evan sells them to Chang through Hollander. The man's obsession with birds does not explain why he goes to the local pound and collects dogs and cats destined for death row."

"He did ask me if I wanted to buy a fur coat for a cheap price." The blonde resumed washing dishes.

"Maybe he was responsible for the skinned dog I found in Goat's backyard. Goat could have found out what he was doing and tried to save the animals."

"I thought you said Goat worked part-time on Evan's ranch. How would he meet Chang, unless the guy ran into him on the property?"

Marla gripped the dish towel, excitement coursing through her. "They might have met at the pet store. Goat bought his supplies there."

"Yani may not have known about Chang's little side businesses. Maybe Goat clued him in, and Yani got upset. Chang killed Yani to keep him quiet, and meant to get Goat, but your neighbor got away."

"So what was Yani doing at Goat's house, and who brought the cash? Was Chang a passenger in the Corolla, or was he the motorcycle rider my other neighbor heard?"

Jill's face scrunched. "Chang seemed glad Yani wasn't his lab partner anymore. Apparently, Yani's sexual preferences bothered him. He didn't mention Cutter by name, but he said Yani had been bamboozled by a friend into believing he could perform miracles."

"Did you ask what he meant?"

Jill nodded. "I tried to appear disinterested. With my acting background, it's easy to pretend I'm a brainless twit. 'Why, sugar,' I said to him, 'if I'd known Verkovich could make miracles, I'd have asked him to do my boobs instead of paying the surgeon. He could have saved me a fortune.' " She laughed, propping up her golden globes.

"How did Chang respond?"

"He leered at me with his ugly face. Yani preferred men, he said. Verkovich had been working on a formula to restore hair on bald guys."

"All right!"

"Wait, there's more. Chang said Yani should know house pets could only be used as test subjects in certain kinds of experiments. They do animal testing at Stockhart Industries, but I believe they use smaller species."

Marla gazed at her thoughtfully. "Do you think Chang could've been supplying Yani with dogs and cats for their makeshift lab?"

"Only if there was something in it for him. That's where he might have worked a deal with Evan regarding shipments of birds."

Marla's brain clouded. "This is too confusing."

"Is there anything else you want me to find out?"

"Ask Chang if he's ever heard of Wyeth Holmes."

Thursday, Marla repeated their conversation for

Vail's benefit. "At least Jill confirmed what I've believed about the hair formula," she told him on the telephone, sparing a few moments in the salon.

"You may be right, but a few links remain that don't connect. How about if we go early Sunday to check out Evan's ranch?"

"What about Saturday night? I thought you wanted to come for dinner."

"I can still make it. Brianna is going to a bat mitzvah on a charter yacht and staying at a friend's house overnight. I'll go broke at this rate. She has to give each kid a gift, and Brie won't wear the same dress twice. She found this Teen Angel place with expensive clothes, and now she insists on getting all her outfits there. Did you have this kind of affair when you turned thirteen?"

Marla smiled. "I had a bat mitzvah, but it wasn't as fancy as the parties today, especially in South Florida. It's a good thing she's one of the oldest in her class and already had her birthday. Now she doesn't have to worry about outdoing anyone else. How about bringing her to the salon Saturday so I can fix her hair?"

"Brie already suggested I make an appointment and said something about a French manicure. What am I going to do?"

Marla laughed. "Live with it, Daddy. You don't need an appointment. Just bring Brie and I'll fit her into my schedule." *You can make time for the teen, but not for your mother?* Marla refused to contemplate her motives. "Give me a chance to get my act together after work. Come around seven-thirty for dinner."

"You're on. Just be careful until then, you hear?"

"I'll be at Cynthia's house tonight, and I'm working late tomorrow. No chance for me to get into mischief. How do you plan to sneak into Evan's ranch?"

"We'll park at Flamingo Gardens and walk over."

"And if we get caught? I don't want you to get into trouble with your superiors."

"I can always say I saw Goat. It's acceptable to go after a known suspect. If we get caught, we'll have other problems than what to say to my chief."

Giorgio strolled into the storeroom, scratching his head of curly hair. "Watch out, beautiful, I have to use the sink." He withdrew a tube of color from a shelf, got a clean bowl and bottle of developer, and proceeded to mix his solution.

"I gotta go," Marla said into the receiver. "See ya soon."

"You working late tonight?" Giorgio asked, flashing her a grin. A row of even teeth gleamed white in his tanned face.

"No, I'm going to a Passover seder at my cousin's house. I'm working late tomorrow night instead."

"This seder is like a feast, no?"

"Yes, and we have a service that goes along with it." A few steps away, she threw a pile of dirty towels into the washing machine and set the controls.

"It sounds like a late night." Grabbing a stiff brush, he stirred the coloring compound.

Stretching, Marla yawned. "I didn't get home last evening until after eleven. Arnie went through the service very slowly so he could explain everything to Jill."

"You must be tired." He shot her a sympathetic glance.

"Actually, I came in here for a cup of coffee and then remembered I needed to call Vail." Reaching around him, she rinsed out her coffee mug and poured herself a fresh cup from the staff's private coffeemaker.

"Anything new with your neighbor?"

Nicole peeked around the corner before Marla could answer. "Your two o'clock is here. Shall I tell her to get washed?"

Marla shook her head. "I'll go get her. Time for work, Giorgio." She left to greet her regular client, Babs Winrow.

"How is Babs?" Cynthia asked that evening when they were schmoozing in the kitchen at her seaside estate. "I haven't seen her since I resigned from Ocean Guard's board of directors. It's enough that Bruce has to deal with those lunatics as trustee, but I'd had enough after our little fiasco. I always liked Babs."

"She's planning to visit her daughter. I see your Annie has a new boyfriend."

Cynthia gave a cynical smile. "We'll see how long this one lasts. I wasn't going to let her invite him, since we usually don't have outsiders, but the kid has a single mom, and she had to work tonight. I feel bad for them."

"We'll certainly have enough food." Marla gestured at the dishes piled high in the kitchen.

"He's not the only new face you'll see here tonight. I should warn you—"

"Marla, *bubula*, come say hello to your *tanteh*," a shrill voice cried.

"Hi, Aunt Polly," Marla said dutifully, kissing her mother's older sister on a wrinkled cheek.

Polly's filmy eyes peered at her through spectacles held together by adhesive tape. "Where's your brother? I want to tell him about this place that recycles old computers."

Marla hid a grin at the sight of Polly standing next to Cynthia. A great chasm separated Polly's style of clothing from Cynthia's. Polly wore a sickly yellow blouse with chipped buttons, a shamrock green skirt, and a scarf to cover her ragged gray hair. Cynthia's smart linen ensemble suited her sophisticated lifestyle. Same for their habits: Polly rarely turned on her air conditioner, so as to save money, while Cynthia didn't think twice about writing checks for anything.

"Michael and Charlene haven't arrived yet," Marla said, "but here are Julia and Alan. *Someone should teach Julia how to put her lipstick on straight.* She greeted the newcomers with a false warmth that matched their own less than enthusiastic response.

"Marla, how good to see you," Julia crooned. "Cynthia. Hello, dear," she said, air-kissing her cousins while Alan handed their dinner contribution to one of the hired maids. Turning to Marla, Julia winked. "I hear we're going to meet someone important tonight."

Alan glanced at his watch. "Where is everyone? If you set the time for seven, we should get started."

Marla blinked. Was there a message she'd missed? She had already greeted her other relatives out on the patio. Michael and his family were the only ones yet to arrive. He was supposed to pick up her mother on the way down. Her confusion deepened when Michael and Charlene breezed in with their two young children but no sign of Anita.

"Where is Ma?" Marla asked her brother after kissing them all. Delicious smells wafted to her nostrils: rich chicken soup, tangy horseradish, roasted meat and potatoes. Saliva welled up from under her tongue. It would be a while before they ate. Leaning against the counter, she sneaked a couple of black olives into her mouth.

"Don't you know?" He gazed at her incredulously, dark eyebrows raised in a masculine face with similar features to her own: firm jaw below cupid's lips, a slightly upturned nose, and toffee eyes against an olive complexion.

"Everyone else seems to know what's going on except me."

A commotion at the door drew their attention. "See for yourself; here they are."

Marla whirled in astonishment at the sound of a booming, familiar tone. *Oh no, what's Roger doing here at our private seder? And Barry, too?* She felt her face go scarlet as Barry rushed over to grasp her in a possessive hug.

"Marla, isn't it delightful that your cousin invited us to join you?" he said, thrusting her away to gaze at her with warm blue eyes.

With her relatives' glances fixed on them, she could only manage a polite reply. "I'm so happy you could be here. I see Ma is already showing off your father." *Too bad he didn't absorb any of your fashion sense.* Roger looked like a peacock strutting about in his lime leisure suit. She winced at Julia's condescending smile. *I may not like Roger, but don't offend my mother, or you'll answer to me,* she silently warned her cousin. She took a few protective steps toward Anita, then changed tactics.

"Barry, please don't get insulted, but have you ever gone shopping with your dad?"

Surprisingly, his face eased into a chagrined smile. "I know what you're saying. I've tried, but he won't listen to me. He wore dark suits for so much of his life, that now he doesn't care. When my mother was alive, she kept him in line. I was kinda hoping Anita would influence him."

"Ma is so awestruck, I doubt she even notices what he wears. My cousins notice, though, and it reflects on her."

"Dad works hard to please your mom. Maybe I should give her some money to buy him a gift."

Or maybe I should fix her up with someone else, like that nice Mr. Levy from the hardware store. "Don't bother. I'll talk to Ma." And so she found herself in the unusual position of conspiring with Barry for their parents' sake.

"Damn inspectors came out to my yard again this week," Roger said after the seder service had concluded. "This time they said my trees were questionable, whatever that means."

Marla glanced at him seated across the table from her diagonally. Barry sat to her right. "They should send a plant pathologist out to examine your trees next. I've been reading up on the procedures."

"Don't tell me about their so-called procedures. They barge onto your property and remove your trees without any regard to your rights." Roger draped his arm possessively across Anita's shoulders.

Marla leaned forward. "Have you gone to any of the workshops?"

His heavy brows drew together. "I've done better, doll. I joined REACT. You know what that is?"

Alan pitched in. "It's a citizens' organization, isn't it?"

"Right. We filed suit when the bill passed permitting countywide search warrants. It was a *shandah* when that happened."

"Have you ever met Cutter Corrigan at those meetings?" Marla asked. "He used to be my teacher in beauty school, and now he runs a salon on Las Olas Boulevard. I understand he actively opposes the citrus canker eradication program."

Roger's hazel eyes brightened. "Of course I know Cutter; he's one of the founders of the group."

Marla's pulse accelerated. "He became friends with Yani Verkovich. Yani, a scientist, defended the government's viewpoint. Did you ever notice them together?"

"They held some heated verbal sparring matches. Are you saying they were friends outside of this business? That's hard to believe. They stood on opposite sides of the fence." He belched, patting his large belly. Marla hadn't missed how he'd made two more trips to the buffet table. His nose had reddened, veins protruding.

"Verkovich is the guy who was killed in Goat's house," Marla remarked, watching his reaction.

"Yeah, I remember you telling us."

"Has Cutter seemed upset lately at the meetings? I mean, since Yani was no longer on the scene?"

"Nah, he brought his other friend with him. That guy stuck close to his heels, if you get my drift."

"What friend?"

Roger gave her a broad smile. "Why, the bald fellow who drives a motorcycle. He showed up a few times before. If anyone didn't like Verkovich, it was him."

Chapter Eighteen

Marla drove into her garage, her mind on the conversation with Roger. The rest of the evening had passed in a blur. She'd been too focused on figuring out what his words meant. The bald guy who drove a motorcycle. A stranger who'd accompanied Cutter, and who didn't like Yani. Possibilities scrolled through her brain. She couldn't wait to tell Vail this latest tidbit.

Shouldering her purse, she emerged from her car, hearing Spooks's frantic barking from the kitchen. Before letting herself inside, she hit the control to lower the garage door. She'd just reached for her house key when a rustling noise from behind alerted her. She swirled around but wasn't fast enough. A stiff blow cracked her shoulder. Crying out, she crumbled against the wall as white-hot pain streaked down her arm.

"Bitch. Now it's your turn," hissed a voice near her ear. His muffled tone sounded vaguely familiar, and he smelled like something she should recognize.

Hauled upright, she fought futilely while her masked assailant opened the driver's door to her Toyota and shoved her inside. She gashed his arm with her fingernail, trying to free herself. With a cry of rage, he swatted her on the jaw as though she were an insect. She tumbled backward across the seat.

Looming closer, he grabbed her purse and stuck her keys in the ignition. While he occupied himself twisting the key to start the engine, Marla scampered away, reaching for the passenger door.

"You're not going anywhere." Grabbing her ankle, he tugged her in his direction. Marla screamed, fury and fear fueling her voice. Hands circled her throat, squeezing. Her lungs dragged for air, but she couldn't expand her chest. Lights danced before her eyes. She felt her body go slack as consciousness ebbed.

The pressure on her neck eased. Her ears picked up the sound of a door slamming, footsteps stomping away. A loud snap, followed by a rumbling noise. She didn't move. Her breath coming in short gasps, she concentrated on breathing. More rumbling, then just a steady vibration.

She blinked, focusing her vision. A deep, long breath rattled through her constricted throat. She still lay on the front seat in her car, and the doors were all closed. The ignition was running, she realized slowly.

Oh no. Her assailant's intent became evident. Leaning upward, she bit back a cry of pain as her left shoulder folded. That was the side she'd hit against the wall. Carefully pushing herself upright, she turned off the engine while wondering if her light-headedness was due to the blows she'd received or car fumes. Her gaze caught on the automatic garage-door opener. She pressed the button. Nothing happened, although she heard the motor. *This isn't right.* She tried again. The door remained shut.

She saw her purse lying on the ground; the intruder was gone. While able to think clearly, she popped the door locks open. Drinking four glasses of wine at dinner had contributed to wobbly knees. At least she was awake, and agile enough to stumble from the car.

If she hadn't turned when her attacker first struck, his blow might have cracked her skull. Or maybe not, if he intended this to appear as an accident. Choking her unconscious would leave marks though, wouldn't it? *Another hairstylist bites the dust. Not this time.*

Holding her breath to avoid taking in any more exhaust fumes, she let herself into the kitchen, where recessed lights burned brightly overhead. Slamming the door, she locked it while the security alarm shrilled. Spooks barked wildly, charging her ankles. Should she leave the alarm on until the cops came? Letting it ring, she considered why the garage-door opener hadn't responded. Air had to be let in to disperse the fumes in the garage, but she would wait on that—her attacker might still be watching the house. He would return if he realized she'd escaped.

Her fingers shaking, she withdrew her cell phone from her handbag and dialed Vail's number. He didn't answer, so she left a voice message.

The doorbell's insistent ringing and Spooks's

loud response brought her to the front door, where she peered out the viewport. A uniformed officer faced her. She asked to see his badge before letting him inside.

The policeman found out what was wrong with her garage door right away. "It's on manual," he said, after he'd fixed it and then raised the door to ventilate the space. "See this spring? You have to snap it back into place on the track. The guy who attacked you must have raised it manually from the inside and closed it the same way. If you hadn't seen him do it, you wouldn't know why the automatic opener wasn't working. He must've planned for you to be unconscious long enough to absorb a toxic level of carbon monoxide."

By the time the officer finished getting her statement and conducting an inspection of the premises, it was after midnight. Marla didn't want to stay home alone for the rest of the night. She could let herself into Anita's house with her key, but what if the killer followed her there? Would it be safer to stay with Vail? Chewing her bottom lip, she quaked with indecision while the responding officer spoke to his supervisor.

Another car pulled up, one that Marla recognized. Relief swept through her as Dalton strode in her direction, his face grim.

"Are you all right?" He scrutinized her from head to foot. His mouth tightened as he noticed her rumpled appearance and the darkening bruises on her arm and cheek.

She allowed herself a weak smile. "I'm fine. How did you know?"

"Officer Gallagher called me. The guys know we

... I have an interest in your safety," he ended lamely.

"I left you a voice message. You didn't answer your phones."

"I'd retired early for the night for a change."

She noticed the shadows of exhaustion under his eyes. "I'm sorry to have disturbed you and for making you leave Brianna."

"She has Lucky to protect her. Where's Spooks? Didn't he warn you?"

"The man who attacked me must have been hiding around the corner of my house. I assume he slipped inside the garage when I drove in." Briefly, she related her ordeal. "I locked Spooks in my study so he wouldn't interfere in the investigation."

"You can't stay here. Get your dog and come to my house." He gripped her by the shoulders, eliciting a grimace of pain. "You've been hurt," he said gruffly. "How bad is it?"

"I'll live. That's what counts."

Gently, he prodded her left side. "Let me know if you want to see a doctor."

"Thanks, but I'd rather see a bed right now so I can collapse."

Ten minutes later, she held a hastily packed overnight bag in one arm and Spooks in the other. The poodle yipped excitedly when she placed him into the backseat of Vail's car. Vail's face settled into an impassive mask as they drove away. Lost in her own thoughts, Marla barely noticed when they turned into his driveway fifteen minutes later. He parked the car, then sat unmoving while he regarded her with a strange expression.

"What is it?" she said, wondering what he wasn't revealing.

"I have some bad news."

Her heart lurched. "Oh, no. It's not about Goat?"

"This doesn't relate to the case at all. I just had to tell you, although I know this isn't the best time. Carmen is quitting."

"What happened?" She could tell by his taut voice that he was upset.

He waved a hand. "She's moving up north to be near her sister. Guess I'll have to start advertising for another housekeeper."

"That's a shame." *Too bad, you have your* tsuris, *and I have mine with Carolyn's salon. Why can't things ever run smoothly?*

"It'll be tough on Brie for a while, coming home to an empty house."

"She's a resourceful girl. I'm sure she'll manage." *This is what partners in a successful relationship do,* she thought wistfully. *They share problems. It's easier to face things when you're not alone.*

"Don't be surprised if she calls you more often," Vail added, studying her reaction. "She holds you in high regard."

"Ha. That's a switch from when we first met."

"Since you're ending up here so often lately, I should give you a house key."

Warning bells rang in her mind. *No way, bubula.* "Why do I get the feeling that would lead to chauffeuring jobs, helping with homework, and cooking meals several times a week?"

He tickled her arm, making her notice his hair, and how his silver streaks gleamed in the moonlight. "I'd like you to be here when I come home, too."

She swallowed. "I have a salon to run. I can't play housewife and mom."

"I'm not asking you to cook and clean. I'll still hire a housekeeper. That's not why we need you."

We need you. Her eyes moistened, and she blinked furiously. Stan had never needed her. It had been the other way around with their relationship, and he'd taken advantage of her vulnerability to control their lives. Now she stood firmly rooted with her feet on the ground, and she wouldn't let another man dislodge her.

"I was nearly killed tonight, and you're pressuring me to move in? I don't want to deal with this right now."

His smoky gaze captured hers. "That's why I'm talking about it. I want to protect you." She opened her mouth, but he touched his fingers to her lips. "I know you can handle most things on your own, and I respect your ability. But in this, I'm well trained. I let you do your job. Why won't you let me do mine?"

Feeling herself falling under his spell, she brushed his hand away. "This is more than your job. It's personal."

"Damn right." He leaned over and kissed her.

The press of his mouth on hers made her fears melt away. As she yielded to his tender exploration, she realized he hadn't offered anything beyond her moving into his house.

Springing back, she opened her car door. "There'll be a better time for this discussion. Let's go inside."

She was too exhausted to do anything but settle Spooks, change into a nightshirt, and retire to the guest room. Sleep didn't come easily. She tossed and turned, feeling the assailant's breath on her face and wishing she could figure out why he smelled so familiar.

Friday presented a busy day at work, distracting her from nightmares. She went about her business with a remote feeling, hoping Vail would conclude his case so she could get on with her life. Little things that wouldn't ordinarily bother her were making her jittery.

"Hey, Giorgio," she called to the stylist during a lag between customers. "Did you reorder those supplies like I asked?" She strode over to where he was cleaning his shaver and tapped him on the arm. When he winced, she frowned at him. "What's the matter?"

His eyes were intent on his task. "It's nothing."

No? Her gaze narrowed. She'd scratched her assailant last night, and now Giorgio's arm hurt. And, as she'd noticed before, he fit the description of Cutter's friend: dark hair with Latin good looks, plus he had a hairdresser's license. He could easily have been the man Virginia saw with Cutter at the hair show. But how or why would Giorgio be involved? Could he be related to Wyeth? Nah, they looked nothing alike. If memory served her correctly, Wyeth had a narrow face with blue eyes. Giorgio was just as tall but stockier, and his eyes were brown. Not that she remembered Wyeth all that clearly. Fourteen years had distorted the memory cells.

He turned his gaze on her. "Are you all right? You seem out of sorts today."

"I'm fine," she said, a bit too harshly.

"Don't worry about the suppliers. I called them earlier. Did you know they sent us the jasmine volumizing fixident instead of pure liquid hair gel? I corrected the order."

"Thanks. Nicole, when you're finished drying your hair, can you run over to the bank for me? I have another deposit."

"Sure thing, girlfriend." Nicole paused, blow-dryer whirring. "I didn't see your car in the parking lot this morning."

Marla's cheeks warmed. "Dalton gave me a ride. I had a problem last night and had to leave my car at home."

"Uh-huh."

"Don't give me that look."

"Take my advice. You're not going to find a better man."

"Oh yeah? What about Barry?"

Nicole shrugged. "He's okay, but I don't see you getting all hot and bothered over him."

"I'm not hot and bothered over anyone." She rolled her shoulders, biting back a curse when a gripping pain caught her unaware. "Ouch, that hurt." She'd had trouble putting on her pullover sweater this morning. Just what she needed, a disabling injury. All right, so she was in a bad mood.

She addressed the issue bothering her when Vail arrived at eight o'clock to take her home. "I don't think we should wait until Sunday to check out Evan's ranch," she told him during the drive home. "This has to end now, before anyone else gets hurt. Have you found any trace of Kenya?"

"I put one of my detectives on her trail." He gave Marla a sly glance. "Anyone at work been unusually inquisitive lately?"

She shot him an irritated look. "Why?"

"Just wondering how someone knew you would be out Thursday evening."

"My attacker probably watched the house, just like he did when he stole Goat's envelope." Maybe that's why the man had smelled familiar. She'd grappled with him before.

"Mmm."

Vail's noncommittal reply raised the hairs on her nape. "Do you know something I don't? If a staff member of mine is involved, you'd better tell me."

"I have a theory, that's all. But you're right. We need to do a more thorough search of Evan's property. I think I know where that secret lab may be situated."

"Let's go tomorrow night. I'll be finished working for the weekend," Marla suggested. If it were up to her, they'd go now, but Vail had to pick up Brianna from the bowling alley.

"Sunday morning is better. That way we won't stumble around the woods in the dark," he said, his gaze focused on traffic.

"No, dark is good. It'll cover our tracks. It was just a full moon recently, so there should be enough light."

He glanced at her. "You won't do anything stupid and go by yourself tonight while I'm gone, will you?"

"I'm not that dumb. I'll stay home with the alarm on, but only if we go tomorrow night. I don't want to wait any longer."

"We can't go tomorrow—not if you still want to park my car at Flamingo Gardens, that is. The place will be closed at night, and for all we know, the parking lot may be secured by a gate. Even if it wasn't, our car would be too conspicuous there by itself." He paused. "Besides, it's supposed to drop into the fifties later. I know how much you like cold weather."

Marla hadn't thought about sneaking around after dark while shivering from cold. The idea didn't hold much appeal. "It'll be trickier dodging the workers on the ranch in daylight. I still think we should go tomorrow night. We'll find a place off the road to hide your car." She deepened her voice to a sultry tone. "Agree with me and I'll fix you a special dinner next time we're alone."

"You owe me a meal Saturday anyway."

"That doesn't count. We'll be rushed if we're going to the ranch. I'm talking about the next time we have no obligations and Brianna is otherwise occupied." She tilted her head. "I'll make it a feast worth waiting for."

"Tell me more."

"It could be a memorable evening."

"Memorable, huh?" His heavy-lidded gaze seared her. "All right, you're on."

They crossed the boundary on foot to Evan's property late Saturday night. Clouds partially blocked the moon, making their trek more difficult. Marla's black leather jacket didn't provide much warmth as the chill air penetrated. She stood by a strangler fig tree while they got oriented.

"Brr. I should have worn my fur coat."

Vail, hands in his jean pockets, regarded her with bemusement. "I thought you were against animal abuse."

"I may not condone cruelty to animals, but I see no objection to wearing fur coats. Cavemen wore furs for survival. There's no reason why we should give up the practice. Not that I'd go out and buy one. I inherited a mink coat from my mother, and I'm proud to wear it."

"Well, this isn't the appropriate occasion for mink. Your turtleneck sweater should be warm enough."

"Nothing is warm enough for me in this weather." A chill wind bit her face, and she thrust her hair over her ears for protection. "I'm freezing my *toches* off."

His eyes gleamed. "I'll tell you what. When this case is over, I'll take you to a fancy restaurant, and you can wear your fur coat. Deal?"

"You got it. Where do you think the lab is hidden?" she asked, fidgeting. She shouldn't have drunk so much coffee. Finding a bathroom was not one of their priorities.

"The quarantine shed."

"Didn't you look there on your tour?"

"I just glanced inside. They probably figured sick animals would drive off any troopers."

"Rightfully so." She smirked in the darkness. "Let's move. Standing in place makes me colder."

The sounds of rustling leaves and a dry, earthy scent gave way to a squawking of birds and the smell of dung as they neared the compound. Shrouded, knotty trees surrounded them, rising like wraiths in the night. Marla crunched a twig underfoot and cringed as the noise seemed to reverberate throughout the hammock. She skirted a laurel oak, skipping over a clump of roots on the ground and drawing to a halt beside a cluster of ferns when something brushed her face. Imagining a cobweb with a monstrous spider, she bit back a cry. Nearby, a stand of bamboo creaked in the cool breeze. An owl hooted, but Marla's attention was snagged by a sound much more human.

Footsteps plodded ahead on a gravel trail. She could hear the rhythmic scrunch of shoes on pebbles. Speech died in her throat. Beside her, Vail stood motionless like a hunter stalking prey. A rabbit dashed past, a patch of fur missing on its rump.

While they waited, Marla got her bearings. To the right was the aviary. Somewhere in the distance was Evan's house. Then there were the work buildings, storage areas, and the quarantine shed which she had not seen during her last visit. Did Vail know which way to go? She held her hands out and shrugged, hoping he understood the message.

He pointed in the direction of the footsteps. Taking the lead, he selected a course parallel to the gravel path. As Marla made her way carefully through the undergrowth, a spicy scent tickled her nostrils, but she pinched her nose so she wouldn't sneeze. Her gaze flickered between Vail's broad back and the ground littered with fallen branches, pine needles, rocks, and dried coconuts.

Voices drifted their way. Vail swung his arm out, bringing her to a stop. She barely made out the outline of a building beyond a pair of cabbage palms.

"Never mind about the freakin' birds. There's nothing wrong with them," Evan Fargutt's voice grated in a low tone. "We just keep this quarantine post because of regulations."

"I don't like it," Cutter said. "We should clean out the lab. Soon as we get the sample back from Goat, we can figure out what variable Yani used on the formula. In the meantime, I'll hide the stuff at my place."

"Bad idea. We'll move everything to one of the storage sheds. Come on."

They slipped into the building, and Marla wondered how she and Vail could observe without being spotted. Moreover, how could they get the evidence Vail needed? She turned to him to ask, but closed her mouth when she noticed a shadowy figure emerging from the trees on the other side of the building. Tapping Vail's arm, she pointed.

Catching on, he nodded, the whites of his eyes visible in the moonlight. Without her being aware of it, he'd somehow slipped his gun into his hand.

The hulking figure bent over, holding something at a tilt as he strode purposefully around the structure's edge in a slowly moving circle. Marla sniffed the air. Gasoline fumes, or something similar.

The man stopped, dropping his burden. A moment later, a flame erupted from a device in his hand.

Realizing Cutter and Evan might be trapped inside the shed, Marla screamed a warning. It didn't matter that they were conspirators; no one should die in a burning building. Startled, the arsonist tossed his lighter and fled.

Vail charged after him, shouting.

Fargutt raced from the building, hollering for his ranch hands. Cutter thumped after him, spotted Marla, and snarled in rage. Men erupted from the shadows, closing in on her position.

Chapter
Nineteen

"How can they believe it was Goat?" Marla asked Vail. "He wouldn't set fire to a place, especially not if he believed there might be animals inside."

"Fargutt and his friends think Goat tried to destroy their lab. Laredo is out searching for him right now."

Vail squirmed uncomfortably, an action that produced a wrench to Marla's sore shoulder. They were trussed back-to-back together inside the quarantine building, a stuffy, enclosed space with a musty smell. Her shout had brought Evan's ranch hands upon them, and the detective had been disarmed before he could switch his aim. Evan and Cutter held a huddled conference in a corner, while workers stood guard outside. Birds of prey mingled with exotic cockatoos and macaws in cages on tables around the room. They didn't like their space invaded. The resultant noise made overhearing Marla and Vail's captors' conversation impossible.

"If we can get a few minutes to ourselves," Vail hissed, half-twisting his head, "I can free us."

"They took my purse, but I still have my cell phone in a pants pocket. They frisked you, but they didn't think to search me." Her smug tone hid the fear behind her words. She'd seen the lecherous look Jimmy Laredo had given her as he hauled her inside the shed. She remembered all too clearly her last encounter with Jimbo. He would have been none too pleased about her escape. She just hoped he didn't take his revenge right away. Her breath hitched when the ranch hand strutted through the doorway to consult with his boss. Three pairs of eyes glanced in their direction. What next?

"Keep them talking. It will buy us time," Vail advised as the men stalked toward them.

"We have a few questions for you," Evan snapped, his gaze stone-cold. "If you're wise, you'll cooperate."

"I'm a police officer. Harm us, and you're in for it. If *you're* wise, you'll let us go," Vail replied. Marla's neck jolted as he squared his shoulders.

Evan gave a harsh laugh. "Excuse me? You two are intruders I caught trespassing on my property."

"You took my wallet. Inside is my badge. I've interviewed you before. No one will believe you didn't know who I am."

"Sorry, but with all the confusion, I couldn't tell who was running around outside in the dark. All I know is someone tried to destroy my property. I couldn't help it if you were caught in the crossfire when we chased the arsonist."

So that's their plan, Marla thought with a hard

swallow. *Kill us, and claim it was a mistake.* "Did you catch him?"

"Unfortunately, no. But you'll help us find him."

"Let me have her," Jimbo sneered, his filmy gaze fixed on her body. "I'll find out what you want to know."

Behind her, Vail growled. He twisted his head so he could see the man. "You touch her and you're dead."

"Dalton." She issued a warning in her tone. He was a law officer. Of all people, he had to uphold the justice system.

"Get rid of him," Cutter intervened in his effeminate lilt. "Marla will tell us where Goat's sister lives."

"Why do you care about Jenny?" Marla said. "She can't help you find her brother."

"If we hold her hostage, Goat will come to us." Cutter gestured to his cousin. "Throw Vail in the pond. The alligators will finish him off."

Evan aimed a gun. "Separate them," he instructed Jimbo. "I'll take care of this."

"No, wait," Marla cried in panic as the rancher leaned forward to loosen her bonds.

Vail struggled to knock the man over, earning himself a blow to the head that sent him to the floor.

Freed from her bindings, Marla rubbed her wrists while frantically wondering what she could do to help Vail. "Aren't you going to show us the laboratory?" she asked in desperation. "We know it's hidden in here. I'd like to see where you've been working on the hair formula."

Jimbo thrust his ugly face in front of hers. His onion breath made her cringe. "I'll show it to you," he offered with a malicious grin. He grasped her arm, stroking the swell of her breast so she understood his intent.

She lurched away, but his grip held tight. "Have you succeeded in refining the formula?" she asked Cutter, hoping to snare his attention. Meanwhile, his cousin had prodded Vail to his feet. The detective stood with his hands secured behind his back, his expression glum. Marla wondered whether he'd make a move if she weren't in the way.

"I don't see any harm in giving them a tour of our facilities," Cutter said, ruffling his wheat hair as though nothing mattered but how he looked. He'd even dressed for his clandestine operation in sharply pressed khakis and a new-looking knit top—a far cry from Evan, who wore work clothes, or Jimbo, whose baggy trousers smelled like animal droppings.

Evan's gun hand wavered. "I think we should sink them both. We're wasting time. Whoever tried to torch us might come back."

Cutter faced the ranch owner. "This is my project. I promised I wouldn't expose your little sideshow with Hollander if you let me set up operations here, but that guarantee is off if you don't follow my orders. *I* want to show them the lab." His nasal voice had taken on a whiny note.

"You goddamned faggot. Your ego always was larger than your dick. If this formula ever works, maybe you should use it to grow hair on your chest."

"Shut up." Cutter signaled for Marla and Vail to follow him. "We're just missing one element in the formula," he said. "I know it will work with the right combination. Then I'll be rich."

Vail glowered when Evan pushed him ahead of

Marla. "Don't you make enough money from your salon?" Vail asked.

"Not for what I need. My reputation is growing. People demand my services, my expertise. I have to open more salons so my empire can expand." He puffed out his chest. "Marla, tell him. I asked you about your location, didn't I? Western Broward is ripe for development."

"Did you finance Carolyn Sutton's move to Palm Haven?" Marla asked in a flat tone. "I didn't think she had enough business to carry her weight."

"What do you mean?"

"Virginia at the beauty academy told me Carolyn brings in girls from abroad and pays for their training, then she hires them. Carolyn can't afford that herself. Her last place was rundown and situated in a crummy neighborhood. Now she's moved into the same shopping strip where my salon is located."

"Sucks for you."

"Are you edging into my territory?"

Cutter glanced at her, his gaze shrewd. "It's not me. Someone else must be supporting her."

"Like who?"

"How should I know?" Cutter halted by the far wall, which hosted a display of tools. Marla eyed the implements with interest. If she could grab that rake . . . Cutter twisted a hook, and the wall swung aside.

The ranch hand's grip tightened painfully on her arm as he thrust her ahead. She wondered how much of a stake Jimbo would get if their scheme succeeded. He had to be in it for less than Evan and Cutter. He also had to know about Evan's arrangement with Wake Hollander and the Chinese scientist. Maybe there was some way she could convince the other two that Jimbo was a liability, much the same as Goat was. Nor had any of them yet revealed who'd killed Yani Verkovich.

Ushered inside the makeshift laboratory, Marla glanced around in amazement at the assortment of test tubes, Bunsen burners, and other paraphernalia. Small mammals scurried in stacked cages as the group entered.

Cutter sneered at her. "Think how famous I'll be when I present a cure for baldness. Why, I'll have clients coming out of the woodwork. Companies will ask me to showcase their products. My designs will be all the rage. I'll be far more well known than Martha Matilda Harper. The general public has never heard of her, but they'll know me."

"You kept all my notes, didn't you?" She shook off Jimbo and straightened her shoulders. "Goat must have found some of them while he was working here. He'd asked his sister to research Harper. Was it you who stole his mail when I collected it?"

His pale blue eyes cooled. "I don't know what you're talking about. I did further research myself. You were wrong when you believed the formula to be defective. Wyeth's hair fell out after your stupid prank, but a short fuzz grew back. I figured we could improve on the formula by altering the ratio of ingredients."

"You couldn't do it on your own," Vail said, his expression neutral. "When you met Yani Verkovich at a citrus canker workshop, you saw your opportunity."

"After I learned Yani worked at a chemical plant, I told Evan about my plans to develop the formula. We needed a lab where Yani could conduct experiments. I'd been waiting for years. Finally, I'd met a scientist who could help me reformulate the stuff."

"Yani started coming to your salon as a customer," Marla stated. "But you soon developed a closer relationship, didn't you? Is that why he agreed to help you, or were you paying him for his work?"

Cutter stared at her. "Yani and I had a lot in common, other than the citrus canker business. We never agreed on that topic."

"Did Goat come between you? Maybe you meant to kill him that night, and you got your lover instead?" Vail persisted.

"Don't be ridiculous. Goat is straight, even though he wants you to think he's not. He's shy around the ladies, and that's his way of making sure they don't approach him."

Marla raised her eyebrows. She'd never asked Jenny about her brother's sexual preferences. Could this be why Goat acted so strange? He was just shy?

"We're wasting time," Evan griped.

Cutter rounded on his cousin. "I'll handle this. I won't risk my reputation over any more of your blunders."

"Was killing Verkovich one of your cousin's blunders?" Vail said in a deceptively mild tone.

Evan's eyes flashed angrily. "Yani went to Goat's place on my orders. Goat had stolen our newest sample of the formula. We offered him cash in exchange for its safe return. I don't know what happened that night, but obviously Goat double-crossed us. He's the one you want."

"Then let us go," Vail urged, still in his calm tone.

"Don't listen to him, boss," Jimbo rasped, spittle on his stubbled jaw. "They know too much, and you promised me the girl if we caught her again."

"How did Goat get involved?" Marla asked, eager to clear her neighbor. "Was he in it for the money?" If he had a big cash inflow, Goat could afford to buy a farm up north. But she couldn't believe he was so greedy.

"Goat worked part-time on the ranch," Cutter drawled. "He got the job through Hollander, who referred him to Evan. Goat saw Yani conducting skin tests on some of the animals. He snooped around and discovered my notes on the formula. At first I thought he'd stolen the prototype to stop our tests, but then he got smart and demanded money."

"Did you put a skinned dog in his backyard?"

Cutter wrinkled his nose in disgust. "Certainly not. I wasn't involved in the actual testing. That was Yani's domain."

"What about the other stylists?" Marla asked. "Did you kill them? Or were their deaths truly accidents?"

"You'd like to know, wouldn't you? Tell me where Jenny Stanislaw lives, or you'll be the next one to meet an untimely end." He tried to give her a menacing leer, but with his effeminate mannerisms, it didn't quite work.

As he leaned closer, she caught a whiff of a familiar scent. The same scent her attacker in the garage had worn. It struck her as a combination of holding spray and pungent chemicals from a salon. Was he lying about the other stylists?

"Those dead girls were all in my class, Cutter. You were our teacher. We were the only ones who knew about the formula. Are you killing us so no one else can stake a claim? Was it you who attacked me in my garage Thursday night?"

"I haven't been near your place. Why should I invite more trouble?"

"Maybe you killed Yani to double-cross your cousin, and now you're knocking off everyone else associated with our gang. You want it all for yourself."

"I haven't killed anyone. And you're forgetting, there's still—" His face paled, and he clamped his lips shut.

"Who did you bring to the hair show when you ran into Virginia? Was it Wyeth Holmes, whose name is mysteriously missing from our class roster? Or did you bump him off, too?"

"Nonsense. You're just jealous of my success. You don't want me opening salons out west, do you? You're afraid I'll pull clients away from you."

Marla's hands curled into fists. "Carolyn's already done that, thanks."

Vail cleared his throat. "Where does Lujan Chang enter the picture? He wouldn't be bald, would he?"

"What do you know about Chang?" Evan snapped, raising the gun in his hand.

Marla's eyes widened when she realized it was Vail's weapon. She gave the detective a surreptitious glance. While they'd been talking, she noticed him wrestling with his bonds. Had he managed to free himself? He stood against a counter, where no one could see his wrists. His casual posture might fool their captors, but she knew better.

"Lujan Chang, whom you also know as Tiger, is involved in a shady dog- and cat-fur operation," Vail stated. "He collects animals from the local pound, and I suspect skins them on your property where you can dispose of the bodies. That's a major call for an animal-abuse citation."

A corner of Evan's lip rose. "Like I have to worry?"

"I'm not the only one in my department who's interested in your activities. Chang also finances certain illicit shipments of birds on the endangered species list through your middleman, Wake Hollander. Chang doesn't like it when your shipments are late, does he? Maybe he killed Verkovich to teach you a lesson."

Evan's brows collided in a scowl. "That's absurd."

"You don't like that theory? Then how about this one: if you had nothing to do with Verkovich's murder, maybe your henchman here did." He tilted his head toward Jimmy Laredo. "Were you aware Laredo worked for those two bird breeders who disappeared in central Florida?"

"You mean Mole and Molly? Everyone heard about them. They owned five acres and had a stock worth about five hundred thousand dollars. Some say they owed delinquent import fees and staged their own vanishing act. Others say it was competitors who iced them. Beats me what happened." He glanced at his ranch hand. "You didn't tell me you used to work there."

Jimbo grinned, showing his crooked yellow teeth. "I'd quit before Mole and Molly went missing, boss."

"Did Laredo tell you he'd stolen thirty thousand dollars from Mole?" Vail said. "He returned it, less five thousand, when Mole chased him down. I think Mole's mistake was to accept him back on the ranch, especially since I heard smugglers were involved in the owners' disappearance."

Evan swung his gun toward his employee. "You lying sonovabitch. Are you working for Chang behind my back? I'll bet Yani found out, and you killed him."

Jimbo's face reddened. "I didn't kill no one. I was helping with some of those skin tests that night. Yani needed readings. He was mad you'd picked him to make the exchange with Goat."

"You still lied to me. You're fired. Go tell Tiger our deal is off. Was Wake in on this?"

Jimbo, eyes fixed on the gun, backed toward the doorway. "He didn't know nothin'." Whirling on his heel, he dashed out into the night.

Marla shrieked as Vail took advantage of the distraction to hurl himself at Evan. When his gun toppled to the floor during their fight, she shoved Cutter out of the way and dove for the weapon. It weighed heavily in her hand as she jumped to her feet and swung it toward her former teacher.

Vail subdued the hairdresser's cousin, then herded the two miscreants into a corner.

"Marla, use your cell phone to call for backup," he ordered, telling her what number to dial. While she complied, he confronted their adversaries and began reciting their rights.

Chapter
Twenty

"**I** don't understand," Marla said to Vail on her front doorstep. Although her watch read midnight, she was too wired from the evening's events to be fatigued. "If none of them admitted to killing Yani, who did? I can't believe it was Goat."

"A few other possibilities come to mind," Vail said in a weary tone.

"Such as?"

"Let's discuss it tomorrow. This has been a long night, and it's not over for me yet. I have to file a report. Are you sure you'll be all right here by yourself?"

"Now that Cutter and his cousin are put away, I'll be fine."

Spooks greeted them when she opened the door and deactivated the alarm.

"I'll just make sure there aren't any surprises waiting for you," Vail said in a gruff tone. He did a thorough search, then gave her a perfunctory kiss and left abruptly.

She wondered at his hasty departure. It was almost as though he wanted to follow up on something that he clearly didn't mean to share with her. No matter. She figured that by the time she got ready for bed, her brain would have settled into relax mode.

She'd just finished brushing her teeth when the phone rang. Who would be calling this late? Almost afraid to pick up the receiver, she answered hesitantly. "Hello?"

"Marla, I'm so sorry to disturb you." It was Giorgio's voice. "You must have just gotten home. I tried to call you a few minutes ago. I'm on my way to the salon. I got a call that a fire alarm went off."

Her skin prickled. "It's probably a false alarm, but I'll go check it out. You can save yourself a trip."

"I'll feel better if I meet you there. I didn't want to tell you this, but you know when the electricity went off? I was talking to some people in Carolyn's salon. They said she'd called the electric company and pretended to be you to cancel our account. This alarm might be another one of her pranks. Unless she's turned arsonist."

Like the fellow who had tried to set fire to the lab at Evan's Wild Bird Ranch? Good thing his lighter hadn't hit the fuel spilled on the ground. What if the same person had torched her salon?

She cursed under her breath as she grabbed her purse and keys. Remembering what happened the last time she went into her garage, she opened the garage door from inside her kitchen, but then exited her house through the front door. After inspecting the lit garage for intruders and making sure her car was untouched, she proceeded on her way.

What had Giorgio been doing in Carolyn's salon, anyway? Her brow furrowed as she contemplated his motives. Had he been snooping on her behalf? If so, she'd have to speak to him about his behavior. Carolyn might resort to underhanded stunts, but Marla followed certain standards and expected her staff to do the same.

When she arrived at the shopping center where her salon was located, she scoured the dimly lit area for Giorgio's car. Several unfamiliar vehicles and a motorcycle were the lonely occupants on the asphalt. She pulled into an empty space, listening for the jarring bleat of a fire alarm but hearing nothing. Her storefront appeared as she'd left it, interior lights on and stations empty.

Locking her purse in the car, she clipped her cell phone to her pants pocket before striding toward the salon. *Giorgio must've run into a delay in getting here. Looks like he was right about a false alarm.*

Marla wouldn't feel satisfied until she'd checked the place herself. A chill crept down her spine while she acknowledged an uneasy silence. It seemed as though the night air sweated expectantly.

She unlocked the salon door and pressed inside to punch out the alarm code. It didn't appear as though anyone else had been there. Only the hum of the air-conditioning system broke the stillness. Marla wheeled around to study the equipment. No disturbances. That left the laundry room, lavatory, storeroom, and the private area reserved for facials and waxing.

"Looking for someone?" Giorgio asked, emerging from the darkened rear of the salon.

"Where did you come from? I didn't see your

car in the parking lot." Her gaze dropped from his smug expression to the black gun in his hand.

He flashed her a grin, his even white teeth gleaming against his swarthy complexion. "Yes, that's right," he said in response to the look of dawning comprehension on her face. "This is the weapon I used to kill Verkovich. The cops never found it, even though Detective Vail questioned me a couple of times."

Marla, rendered speechless with surprise, recovered her voice. "You . . . you killed Yani? Why?"

"He came between me and my lover. Using Goat as a scapegoat, pardon the pun, seemed logical."

Giorgio approached, making Marla back up against the counter by her station. Her heart hammered so fast she felt light-headed. A quick glance at her implements told her the power was still shut off for the work areas. It was one of her safety measures to turn the power off when they closed for the day, just in case someone left a hot curling iron on. While Giorgio spoke, she calculated what she might use as a defensive weapon.

"I don't get it," she said, hoping to keep him talking. "What lover? I thought Yani had a relationship with Cutter Corrigan." Her lips parted. "You mean, you and Cutter were together? How is it I knew nothing about this? You've been working for me for eight years, since I opened the salon."

"You knew I was gay. I never let you find out much else about me on purpose." He raised his gun arm. "I've been planning this for years, ever since you made me go bald."

"No." Her mind refused to acknowledge the implications.

"You get it now, don't you? I'm Wyeth Holmes."

Watch out for the white home. She hadn't heard Goat's warning correctly. He'd said Wyeth Holmes, and she'd thought he meant Evan's white ranch house. Her gaze drifted to Giorgio—no, Wyeth's—head of curly black hair. "Didn't your hair grow back?"

"For a short while. Then it fell out again and never grew in." He yanked a toupee off his head, revealing a bald pate. His expression darkened. "You ruined my life. I'd planned to be an actor, so I worked part-time as a model in order to meet influential people. I lost those jobs after my hair fell out. Bald wasn't beautiful in the old days."

"Why attend beauty school? Was being a hairdresser just a means to earn money while you pursued an acting career?"

"I'd hoped to connect with rich benefactors by working in upscale salons. Women were attracted to me, especially wealthy ones. But not anymore, after you poisoned me."

She saw his gaze harden with resolve. Her fingers were inches from a can of holding spray. If she could just slide a bit more to the left . . . "We believed the tonic would work. We never intended any real harm."

"What if I'd been allergic to the stuff? You didn't even do a patch test. The original formula had promise, but you knew it wasn't right. I wondered if you would try to develop it."

"That was never my aim."

"I've sacrificed for it. The patent should be mine. I altered my appearance and name to get a job in your salon. You never recognized me since I gained weight, changed my eye color with contact lenses, and showed up with a full head of curly hair. I've been watching, waiting to see if you would figure out a way to improve the formula. I kept tabs on your gang, in case someone else developed it."

"You could have stolen my notes and worked on it yourself. That's what Cutter did."

"Cutter had the idea to refine it when he met Yani." His lip curled in a snarl. "Ever since beauty school, Cutter and I had an intimate relationship. I respected his knowledge, and he liked having a younger man look up to him. It was a perfect arrangement, until Yani came along. I don't know what Cutter saw in him."

Using her body as a shield so he wouldn't notice, she snagged a pair of shears on the counter behind her. "What made you think they were working on the formula? It had been years since we'd been together in school."

He sneered. "Cutter became secretive. We'd shared everything before. Besides, your pal Goat confirmed they'd set up a lab on the ranch."

"Oh?"

"Yani figured out the variable that had been missing. I tested the new sample on myself. Look." He turned around to show her the back of his head, where hair sprouted in an irregular patch.

Now. Sticking the shears into her pants pocket, Marla grabbed the can of spray. She squirted it at Wyeth's eyes when he turned in her direction. Howling with rage, he fired, but his aim flew wild. Marla sprinted for the entrance, expecting a bullet in her back at any moment. Wyeth cursed, and something crashed to the floor. Footsteps pounded behind her. She cried out when Wyeth tripped her with his foot. She tumbled forward, breaking the fall with her hands before her face hit the floor. A shooting pain paralyzed her injured shoulder.

"Bitch." Wyeth hauled her to her feet and dragged her toward the shampoo area. "Damn gun jammed. We'll try something else." She kicked and scratched, but his strength overpowered her. Facing the row of sinks, he squashed her onto a seat opposite from the way her clients normally sat. Whipping her wrists behind her back, he secured them with an extension cord left on the counter. The awkward position wrenched her painful shoulder.

A moment's respite came when Wyeth disappeared. Her ears picked up a creaking noise followed by the sounds of switches being flipped. He must be turning on the circuits. Bringing one leg up and over the other, she rotated in her seat. Now if only she could boost herself from the chair, but the chair's slope made it difficult to achieve leverage.

"Where do you think you're going?" Rushing back, Wyeth pushed her down and turned on the faucet. While water spilled into the shampoo bowl, he used additional cords from curling irons to bind her to the chair facing the sink. Humming, he plugged a blow-dryer into a receptacle on a nearby wall.

Panic flared in her breast as she realized what he intended. She said the first thing that came to mind to delay him. "How did you obtain a sample of the formula for your head if you didn't have access to Evan's lab?"

"I paid Goat to be my spy. He was eager to earn extra money. You didn't realize I knew him, did you? He'd groomed my dog once, and we got to talking. I'd visited Evan's ranch before with Cutter.

When Goat said he worked there, I hired him to keep me informed about what Yani and Cutter were doing."

"How did you know they were making progress? No one else could make the formula work."

His expression lit. "Goat told me Yani got real excited one day. I assumed the experiments had been successful. That tonic belonged to me. Once it was developed, I wouldn't let anyone else interfere. That left me with some unfinished business: to get rid of you and your classmates who knew about it."

Oh God, he'd murdered how many people? And she was next! "What about Yani?"

"He took Cutter away from me. I knew I could get Cutter back if Yani was out of the picture."

"Didn't Cutter suspect you?" she croaked, her throat dry.

"He thinks Goat murdered Yani. Cutter promised to come back to me and share the formula. I told him I'd known about it all along."

"So you killed my friends. What happened to Kenya?" Hope blossomed as she wriggled her hands. The more she moved, the looser her bindings became. She realized the surface of the cords was slick because they were coated wires.

"Beats me. Kenya disappeared before I could get to her. I thought I'd dispose of you on the highway, but your car didn't get too smashed."

"No, just my head. So you're the one who cut into my lane. I suppose you put the news clipping on my salon chair. Were you responsible for stealing Goat's envelope, and for attacking me in my garage?"

He smirked, nodding his agreement. Noting

the water level, he shut off the faucet. "Know what else I did? I sold Carolyn Sutton your customer list."

"You vermin!" She squirmed in her seat, realizing she could slip her wrists out from the loose knots. "What about the skinned dog in Goat's backyard?"

"I put it there as a warning. Goat realized the prototype was valuable, and that's when he decided to sell it. I sent him the warning as a message that he'd better give the sample to me, or else. I'd ordered him to steal it in the first place."

"Did you . . . ?" She couldn't say the words.

"Evan's Chinese friend did the dirty work. You don't need to know any more." Grabbing a chunk of her hair, he bent her head toward the sink until her nose touched the water.

"Vail arrested Cutter and Evan," she cried, working herself free of the knots. If Wyeth plunged her face underwater, she might not regain control. Sweat slid off her icy fingers, making the wires even more slippery. "He knows everything. You're wasting time when you could be getting away." Her voice burst out in labored breaths.

"Sorry, this comes first."

She twisted her head as he dunked her face underwater. The whir of a blow-dryer hit her ears. Another few seconds, and he'd . . . "No!" she yelled, breaking free. Even as she scrambled from the chair, her fingers ripped the shears from her pocket.

"Marla!" shouted a familiar voice as the front door crashed open. Running footsteps. More cries, men hollering.

Wyeth tore around the counter, hands reaching toward her with murder in his eyes. She leapt upward at the same time as he launched himself at her. Then everything seemed to happen in slow motion. Frozen, his eyes widened. Marla glanced down to where her hand gripped the open shears, now imbedded in Wyeth's chest. Blood seeped down his shirt. His mouth opened. He worked his jaw, as though trying to speak while Marla stared at him in horror.

"Let him go," Vail said, appearing miraculously at her side. Gently, he pried her hand away while signaling for his team.

Over. It was over.

Vail brought in his crime-scene technicians but left someone else in charge. "I would've been here sooner, but I encountered an old friend of yours on the way," he told her when they had finally broken free to exit to the parking lot. "I'd figured Wyeth would make his move tonight, and I was watching your place to see what happened."

"You knew about him?"

"I checked into your story about your classmates. The only one unaccounted for was Wyeth Holmes. I tracked him down, and it all made sense. He'd been working for you under a different name. Someone else was watching you, too. That's why I got held up in the parking lot. Goat was ready to rush in to defend you."

"Goat!" It came to mind that Vail had been using her as bait. She didn't mind, now that the threat was gone. Wyeth hadn't survived his stab wound. She wouldn't think about that now. "Where is that rascal? And why did he wait until tonight to make his reappearance?"

"He was afraid of Wyeth and of being framed for Yani's murder. I guess he decided his future was less important than protecting you."

"What a sweetheart. I can't wait to see him." She felt a tug on her heartstrings. "Is he all right? You didn't arrest him, did you?"

"Nah. He cooperated willingly, told us everything we needed to know. The shmuck just wanted to protect animals but got carried away by the scent of money. He was responsible for the anonymous tip I received about the dead man in his house. Your neighbor wanted someone to find the body."

"What about Kenya? Did you locate her, too?"

"She ran off to stay with her sister. Your phone message scared her enough to make her wary."

"Good for her." She paused, reflecting on his revelations. "When can I reopen my salon?"

"The techs will be finished by Tuesday," Vail reassured her. His craggy face relaxed into a smile as he placed a hand on her good shoulder. "I'll follow you home."

"I'm going to visit Goat," Marla announced the next morning when Vail stopped by to check on her. She felt refreshed after eight hours of sleep. "Wait here, I'll get Spooks." Marla left the detective standing on her front stoop while she attached the dog's leash.

Goat strolled out of his house as they neared. Her assessing glance took in his straw-colored hair, moussed into spikes, with no remaining traces of his temporary black dye; his beard that had grown thicker, making her wonder if he'd applied some of the formula to his jaw; and his knobby knees that showed below baggy shorts worn with a Hawaiian shirt.

Marla hugged him tightly, surprised when he patted her on the back in return and said, "I was so worried about you. I'm glad you're safe."

"No, I'm glad *you're* safe," she responded. Goat drew back abruptly, his face reddening.

Vail beamed at both of them.

"Uh, want to come in? I cleaned up the place," Goat said with a hopeful expression.

Spooks tugged on the leash as though anxious to enter. Curious, Marla strode inside. Goat had opened the windows, she noticed, inhaling the strong smell of Clorox. Barking came from behind the closed door to the spare bedroom. Spooks pulled in that direction.

"I have a new friend," Goat said. "Ugamaka, ugamaka, chugga, chugga, ush," he chanted, dancing a jig. "Colors mix and match, black and white in flight. Guess who I mean, or she'll take a bite."

Marla laughed. "I give up."

Vail jabbed her. "*I* know," he said with a wink.

Goat pranced ahead and opened the side door. Out bounced a black poodle with short, curly hair, long ears, and soulful dark eyes. Spooks trotted up to the other poodle. The two evenly sized dogs sniffed each other eagerly. "Her name is Rita," Goat said proudly.

"Oh, no. Spooks is in love!" Marla moaned.

"They wouldn't let me keep Gertrude."

"I doubt owning a goat is in our homeowner's agreement. Now tell me how things went so wrong for you."

Goat wrung his hands. "I took the formula so

Evan and his cousin couldn't torture any more animals," he said in a more somber tone than Marla had ever heard him use. "But then I felt—and this is bad, I know—they might be willing to pay to get it back. I set up a meeting with Evan to make the exchange. Yani showed up, but so did Wyeth after I stupidly informed him of my plan. I felt an obligation to him, you see."

"Did Wyeth mean to kill both of you?"

"Yep. I threw an iguana on him and took off in Yani's car. Wyeth followed on his cycle but lost me on Nob Hill Road when I turned onto I-595."

"That's the motorcycle Hector said he'd heard. Giorgio, I mean Wyeth, never drove it to work."

"He tracked me to Siesta Key. That day I saw you at our beach house, I followed you to the restaurant. I'd hoped to warn you about him. But he spotted me, and I had to take off. I left Jenny's car behind and took a bus to Fort Lauderdale. A friend loaned me a car and a place to hide. Then I decided to set fire to the lab," Goat continued, confessing as though she and Vail were priests. "I meant to destroy Yani's notes."

"But you still have the sample, right?" she asked, amazed at how well Spooks was getting on with the other miniature poodle.

Goat gave a sheepish grin. "Well, Junior happened to get thirsty one day and slurped the stuff. Want to see?" He retrieved his snake. "Look at this patch of hair. Colder temperatures activate the formula. It must contain some kind of genetic resequencer for hair follicles. Yani's sample was the only prototype. Detective Vail said his notes were encoded. No one can figure them out. So it's the end of the hair tonic."

"Oh, my." If men were willing to kill for such a thing, wasn't it best left to history?

"Did you tell Moss and the others that you were back? Everyone has been concerned about you." Marla gave him an admonishing glare.

"I will. Thanks for coming by."

She realized by his expression that he was embarrassed. She'd have to work on his shyness.

"Maybe there's someone I can fix him up with," Marla muttered to Vail on their walk home. "He needs a good woman to straighten him out."

"So do I." Vail reached into his pocket, halting on the sidewalk. "Here's the house key I promised you."

Marla held tightly to the dog's leash, realizing Vail offered more than just a key. "I'll take it on one condition."

"What's that?"

She gave him a coy glance. "You let me teach Brianna about makeup, and she's allowed to shave her legs."

"Sweetcakes, you drive a hard bargain." His gray eyes danced with merriment.

"Oh, I finally found a chess set that's a close match to yours, and it comes with a board. I've ordered it from a gift catalog."

"Good. Now make your decision. You're only delaying the inevitable."

"Oh, all right." She snatched the key and stuck it in her pocket. "Someone has to look after the two of you. But don't think I'm moving in yet. I intend to keep my own place."

"Naturally." His grin broadened.

She hated his self-satisfied smile. At the same

time, the feeling of the key in her pocket warmed her heart.

"Don't expect me to cook meals. Or to play chauffeur. Or to attend school functions." She shuddered. *What am I getting into?*

"I know. You're a busy woman. You have your career."

"That's right."

"So tell me,"—he paused to give her a fierce kiss—"what's for dinner tonight?"

At her change of expression, he laughed. "Just kidding. If you didn't make other plans, how about taking the day off to visit South Beach? We can have lunch and then hit the shops. They have some neat stuff down there."

Was he offering to take her shopping? Asking her, rather than telling her, about their plans for the day? That was a switch from her prior experiences with men.

A slow smile spread across her face. If he was willing to cross the bridge in her direction, she should make the same gesture. It was time to put the past to rest while recognizing what remained important to bring with them into the future.

"Sounds like a great idea," she agreed, taking his hand in hers.

AUTHOR'S NOTE

Probably the most interesting research for this book involved the citrus canker issue. As I wrap up the story, articles are still appearing in the newspaper every day reflecting the controversy between homeowners and the state agricultural department. Citrus canker disease continues to spread while individual residents protest the invasion to their property and block implementation of the eradication program. Where it will end is anybody's guess, but at least I still have the four citrus trees in my yard.

I love to hear from readers. Write to me at: P.O. Box 17756, Plantation, FL 33318. Please enclose a self-addressed stamped #10 business-size envelope for a personal reply. You can send an e-mail to nancy.j.cohen@comcast.net or go to my Web site: www.nancyjcohen.com.

Here is a bonus recipe:

HAROSET

½ cup ground walnuts
1 apple, peeled, cored, and chopped
3 tablespoons sweet kosher wine
¼ teaspoon cinnamon

Mix together all ingredients and serve as an appetizer with matzoh (or crackers).

Grab These
Kensington Mysteries

Available Wherever Books Are Sold!

Visit our website at **www.kensingtonbooks.com**

Mischief, Murder &
Mayhem – Grab These
Kensington Mysteries

__**Endangered Species** by Barbara Block	1-57566-671-5	**$5.99US/$7.99CAN**
__**Dying to See You** by Margaret Chittenden	1-57566-669-3	**$5.99US/$7.99CAN**
__**High Seas Murder** by Shelley Freydont	1-57566-676-6	**$5.99US/$7.99CAN**
__**Going Out in Style** by Chloe Green	1-57566-668-5	**$5.99US/$7.99CAN**
__**Sour Grapes** by G. A. McKevett	1-57566-726-6	**$6.50US/$8.50CAN**
__**A Light in the Window** by Mary R. Rinehart	1-57566-689-8	**$5.99US/$7.99CAN**

Available Wherever Books Are Sold!

Visit our website at **www.kensingtonbooks.com**

More Mischief, Murder
& Mayhem in These
Kensington Mysteries

More Mysteries from
Laurien Berenson

Available Wherever Books Are Sold!

Visit our website at **www.kensingtonbooks.com**